The Moon God's Wife
A Novel of Enheduanna

by Shauna Roberts

Nicobar Press
Weaverville, NC

ISBN-13: 978-1-948077-00-2 (paperback)
ISBN-13: 978-1-948077-01-9 (ebook)

Cover image: Anthony/stock.adobe.com

To my Clarion classmates and teachers

CHARACTER LIST

Boldface indicates people who actually lived.

City of Akkad

Bashtum	music teacher
Esh-tar-da-ri, "Esh"	birth name of Enheduanna
Gal-dingir	a guard of the women's quarters
Ibarum	Enheduanna's youngest brother
Ilaba'is-takal	Enheduanna's second-youngest brother
Kalki	Ubil-Eshtar's scribe
Manishtushu, "Mani"	Enheduanna's oldest brother, twin of Rimush
Nin-sha-su-gu, "Ninsha"	hostage from Ur, Enheduanna's best friend
Rimush	Enheduanna's second-oldest brother, twin of Manishtushu
Sargon	father of Enheduanna
Tashlultum	mother of Enheduanna
Ubil-Eshtar	uncle of Enheduanna
Za-mu-ba-ni-mah, "Za-mu"	hostage from Kutallu

City of Mari

Asqudum	palace guard
Azzu-eli	Hidar's mother
Bad-su-bad	palace guard
Bel-i-a-mi	cook in the pay of Akkad
Belizunu	Azzu-Eli's servant
Gigbe	head scribe

Shauna Roberts

Hidar	king of Mari, Enheduanna's husband
Ishqi-Mari	Hidar's son
Paila	high priestess of Dagan
Satpa	Enheduanna and Ninsha's servant
Tamma	Hidar's daughter
Tu-ru-Dagan	councilor to the king

Cities of Ur and Uruk

Adda	Enheduanna's shaperum
Ba-u-ta-lu, "Ba-u"	priestess of the goddess Ningal
Buru	priestess of the goddess Ningal
Dan-i-li	ensi of Ur After Kaku
Enheduanna	Sargon's daughter, wife of Hidar, high priestess of the gods Suen and Anu
Ilum-pal	Enheduanna's hairdresser
Kaku	ensi of Ur
Lu-Ab-u	husband of Ninsha
Lugalanne	ensi of Uruk
Me-zi-da	priest of the god Suen
Mul-la	caravan leader
Naram-Sin	son of Manishtushu and king of Akkad and Sumer after Manishtushu
Ningbanda	priestess of the goddess Ningal
Sim-tur	priestess of the goddess Ningal
Ur-dumu-zi	senior priest of the god Anu in Uruk

Marsh

Hab-ba	a man of the marshes; Tila's gambling buddy
Dingir-sukkal	a man of the marshes; Gan-Utu's husband
Gan-Utu	a woman of the marshes; Dingir-Sukkal's wife
Gu-gu-la	former priest of the god Suen who lives in the marshes
Silim-Utu, "Silim"	son of Dingir-Sukka and Gan-Utu
Tila	a thief who lives in the marshes

TEMPLES AND RELATED BUILDINGS

Temple name	God (Sumerian name)	God (Akkadian name)	City	Comment
Akitu House	Nanna	Suen, Sin	Ur	used only during Akitu festivals
Gipar House	Ningal	—	Ur	also Enheduanna's residence
House of Heaven	Inanna	Ishtar	Uruk	
House of Plenty			Ur	storage building for the gods Suen and Ningal
House of the Mountain	Enlil	Enlil	Nippur	
House Sending Light to the Earth	Nanna	Suen, Sin	Ur	
House That Is a Ziggurat	Enki	Ea	Eridu	
Tummul House	Ninlil	Mulliltu	Nippur	
Ulmash House	Inanna	Ishtar	Akkad	

MAP

Outline map: MysticaLink/stock.adobe.com

Section I

City of Akkad

Age 6

CHAPTER ONE

Stomach fluttering, I leaned forward to hear better, careful not to show myself. In the courtyard, the sharp dawn light flashed off Father's rings and armbands as he sat on a stool on a daïs. More men than I could count waited to see him, milling about the courtyard and overflowing into the vestibule.

My older brother Manishtushu and I peeked out from behind the curtained doorway in our father's office as we watched Father impress his cylinder seal into documents on clay tablets, listen to petitions, and dispense advice and orders. He gave some men silver rings and others, hard looks. Beside him stood a scribe who took notes on the decisions Father made.

I stood tall and puffed my chest out. Everyone respected my father and relied on his wisdom. I would stand behind the curtain all morning if I could, but I knew Nurse would find me sooner or later.

The scribe drew my attention. He poked the clay with his reed, and later, someone else would know what my father had said and done. Writing was magic.

A magic I somehow needed to learn. I tugged on Mani's skirt. "One day I'll write hymns to Inanna," I whispered before returning my attention to Father.

"You've said that before." Mani tousled my hair. "I have to go to class now. Do you want me to take you back to the women's quarters?"

I clutched the curtain, my attention still on the courtyard. "I'm going to stay and watch Father."

"The longer you stay, the more likely Mother will discover you're missing," he warned.

3

I shrugged. "She went to see the women in the weaving building."

"Come by this afternoon. I have a gift for you."

Attention caught at last, I turned and clutched his hand. I was so excited, I could barely keep my voice down. "A new doll? A necklace?"

He smiled. "Something I think you'll like even better." He patted my head and left.

Smiling, I turned back to the courtyard. My father was the most handsome man there. His long, brown hair, streaked with white, had been braided and wound into a ball at the back of his head. A wide band of gold encircled his head. Several rings of bright stones set in gold sparkled on his fingers. He had a muscular warrior's shape, unlike some of the merchants in the crowd, whose ample paunches proceeded them.

"Esh-tar-da-ri!" Nurse hissed from behind me. "Child, come away!"

To my chagrin, she picked me up and swooped me across the office, my face in her white hair.

"I don't want to leave."

"What if your mother the queen knew you were here by yourself, with all those strange men just outside!"

"No one saw me. Besides, Mani was here with me."

"It's not your own head you put at risk if your mother finds out, but mine," Nurse chided, panting. "You should be more thoughtful."

My cheeks flamed in shame, and I hugged her. "I don't want to get you in trouble. But the women's quarters are dull, and Mother wants me to be quiet and sit still."

With a groan, Nurse set me down and took my hand to pull me through the maze of rooms and courtyards. She had been Mother's Nurse, too, so she was ancient. "One day you'll be a great lady. You need to prepare so that you will do your husband honor. You won't have to work as I do."

I dropped my head. Servants' work, as far as I could tell from watching Nurse, the cooks, and the musicians, allowed time to laugh and joke with friends. "I won't marry. I'm going to be a priestess of Inanna."

Nurse's voice softened. "I know being still and quiet isn't easy. But if you and Ninsha will sit nicely and talk in soft voices, I'll let you hold the babies."

4

"I'll try to be good." I liked my tiny brothers with their soft skin and pudgy hands, and my servant Ninsha adored them with a passion. "I can't wait for the babies to be big enough to play with."

"Ilaba'is-takal will soon be following you and Ninsha around, just you wait and see. Ibarum will be a baby for a long time yet."

We greeted the guards at the women's quarters, and went past them, through the vestibule, and into the courtyard. Already the shade was sliding away, and the courtyard was bright. The singers were practicing a hymn to Ilaba. Nurse whispered, "Now go find Ninsha and play quietly. Your mother will be back soon."

ॠ

Ninsha and I were quiet enough while sewing that Mother didn't object when Nurse gave us each a baby to hold. Ninsha nestled Ibarum into her arms and rocked him, crooning.

Ilaba-is was too squirmy to rock, so I held him under his armpits and bounced him up and down.

The two-year-old loved it. He giggled and shouted, "More! More!"

I was happy to oblige. I bounced him higher, and he shrieked with joy.

"That's enough!" Mother said sharply. "Why can't you be more like Ninsha?"

My stomach turned over, and I let Ilaba'is slide through my arms to the floor, where he stood up and toddled off.

The cooks entered the room with a crock of beer with several straws poking out, bread, and a pot smelling of herbs and venison, but I was no longer hungry. Another servant carried in bowls. Nurse took back the babies and laid them on a pile of fabric. Then the others ate in quiet, all except Ibarum, who still ate only milk but reached for our food anyway. I played with my food and nibbled on a piece of bread.

That afternoon, after the adults fell asleep in the heat of the day, and Ninsha was curled up on the floor next to the babies, her shiny black hair fanned out, drowsily examining their hands, I decided to go see my brother Mani. I stuffed Dolly under my elbow and slipped through the courtyard and the vestibule.

5

Outside the women's quarters stood two guards. Each had a sword and a spear, and their chests glistened in the partial light. Both smiled to see me. "Little one," Gal-dingir said, "where are you going with your doll?"

"To see my brother Manishtushu in the main palace."

"Very good. Do you need an official royal escort, princess?"

"No. I know the way."

"Have fun."

The guards and I were friends. I didn't tell on them if I found one leaning against the wall, and they didn't tell on me for going into the main palace alone, as long as they knew where I'd be.

Sometimes I got lost in the palace. Doing so could be fun...as long as I didn't stray into Father's office when men were with him, or profane the family shrine with its sacred statues of Ilaba and Inanna, or, worse yet, come across my other older brother, Rimush, who was Mani's twin.

Even though Mani and Rimush looked so much alike, with their identical wavy brown hair, arched eyebrows, and long noses, that some people couldn't tell them apart, I secretly thought different gods must have blessed them at their births. One god gave Mani intelligence and kindness, and the other gave Rimush...well, I wasn't sure what good traits Rimush had. He never showed any around me. He was Mother's favorite, though.

I kept to the sides of the passages to avoid getting in the way of the scribes and court officials who rushed busily about, waving tablets and talking in loud voices that echoed against the brick. I kept my eyes on my feet to avoid stepping near any scorpion that hid in a dark corner. I had feared scorpions ever since one of the cooks was stung and died of it.

I found Mani in a small courtyard sitting on a rattan bench in the shade. Several palms in pots cooled the air and provided extra shade. In one palm a bulbul chirped, its white cheek flashing. A cat crouched motionless behind a pot, staring at the bird.

When he saw me, Mani put down the tablet he had been studying.

"Mani!" I held my doll tighter and climbed up on his lap. "I brought Dolly to see my present."

"Hello, Dolly." Mani put an arm around me. "Have you had fun today?"

"I got to hold Ilaba'is."

"He must be getting big. Is he walking yet?"

"Yes, but he wobbles a lot."

"Are you ready for your surprise?"

"Yes!" I clapped my hands.

Mani lifted me off his lap and onto the bench. He lifted the cloth on the other side of the bench to reveal a clay tablet and a stylus cut from a reed.

I reached across him to touch the shiny clay. Its smooth, damp surface was blank. "A tablet for me? Thank you, Brother!"

"For you to use here with me. I'll teach you to write a few words."

I clapped my hands. "I want to learn to write. I'm going to write 'Inanna.'" I dropped Dolly on the floor and reached for the stylus.

Mani laughed and pulled it back. "Not so fast. Watch me first." The tablet lay in his palm, and he pressed the stylus against it. The line it left was straight up and down, with a triangular wedge at the top. "There are five characters in 'Inanna.' This is the first. Now you try it. Lightly."

He held the tablet in front of me, and I took the stylus. It was awkward to hold and so long it poked me in the cheek when I leaned over the tablet. I pushed the reed down into the clay below the mark Mani had made.

My skin tightened into goosebumps. I had made a mark! I was writing! The wedge mark was at the top, just as it was supposed to be. Now I possessed the magic of the scribes. I ran around the courtyard. "Inanna! I wrote Inanna!"

Mani chuckled. "Not yet. Four more marks before it means the Queen of Heaven. Now sit and watch. The second sign leans against the first." I came back to the bench, he demonstrated, and then I got to copy.

The third sign leaned away from the first and second ones, and the fourth sign was straight up and down like the first. Mani demonstrated each, and I copied below.

"The last sign is lazy. It lies on its side." He pressed the stylus in the clay across the first four, with the wedge on top of the first character. "Now it says 'Inanna.'" 7

Awestricken, I made the final mark and stared at the tablet, mouth hanging open. I wrapped my arms around my torso. "I'm doing magic," I whispered.

"Is that enough writing for today?"

I clutched the stylus. "No. I want to learn all the words now."

Mani chuckled. "Let's stick with 'Inanna' for today." He smudged out my characters from the tablet, leaving only his own. "I have to make a translation for tomorrow. While I'm working on it, you can practice on the front and back sides of this tablet. Be careful not to let the clay touch your tunic. It might leave a stain."

"I'll be very careful." I held the tablet in my hand and wrote the set of characters that made up the word "Inanna" over and over again until both sides of the tablet looked as if birds had tromped all over it.

Mani took the tablet, smoothed away all the writing, and wrapped it carefully in damp linen. "You were very patient today. I'll teach you another sign some other day if you like."

"Yes! But Mani, how will I practice if you keep the tablet and stylus here?"

"You want to practice?" His eyebrows rose.

"Just as you do."

"Hmm." He rubbed his chin. "Take this stylus." He leaned down close. "Here's a secret: It's easy to pry up the bricks in the courtyard floor with a stylus. You can write in the dirt underneath."

CHAPTER TWO

The next morning, before we could go to our music teacher, Bashtum, for a lesson, Nurse corralled Ninsha and me to hem sheets. As Nurse fussed with the babies, and three musicians plucked their harps and lyres, Mother and her body servants sewed and talked, discussing chores, the previous night's supper, and the king's next campaign, drowning out the music. Several times, Ninsha and I looked up from our needles and over the piles of woolen fabric in our laps to roll our eyes at each other.

Lunch could not come fast enough. The cooks brought in stewed small birds and rolls, and we all grew drowsy from the beer. When everyone was asleep in the shadowy, cool room, even the babies, and Ninsha had gone to the washing chamber to give Dolly a bath, I yawned and went into the courtyard. I needed to practice writing.

Fierce sunlight scorched the space, and the potted flowers sent out a heavy perfume. The plaster walls so glared with light that the fresco of date palms could barely be seen. All was unusually quiet. I knelt at the edge of the courtyard, where a slice of shade protected me from the searing Mesopotamian sun, and I prodded a floor brick with the stylus. Once I loosened it, I pried it out and set it aside, revealing the underlying dirt.

Holding the stylus tightly in my fist, I pressed it into the dirt to form characters. I was delighted when I finished all five parts of "Inanna." I jumped up and ran in a circle. Then I squatted again, rubbed out the word with my fist, and wrote the goddess's name several more times.

9

My hand ached from clenching the stylus. I dropped the tool and rested my elbows on my knees. How odd that a drawing of five sticks could stand for a god. Inanna was the beautiful goddess of the sky, Who helped people and animals make babies and Who had stolen the elements of civilization and given them to humans. The goddess rode a lion and appeared in the sky as the morning and evening stars. She loved me even though my mother didn't. Yet I saw none of these attributes in the shape created by the five sticks. Perhaps the two upright sticks were like the tall reed bundles that were one of Inanna's symbols, but then what were the other three sticks?

A brilliant light pulsed on my right, and I smelled something sweet. My skin tingled. A glowing fleecy skirt, whiter than any sheep, brushed against my knee. Inanna! The goddess had come to visit me again. Breathless, I shaded my eyes and looked up at Her.

Light sparked from Inanna's holy headdress of cow horns and from the arrows in the quiver on her back. Her skirt was split nearly to her waist.

I half-closed my eyes against the Her light and brought my hand to my nose in greeting. I couldn't wait to tell her what I was doing.

Inanna smiled and laid a hand on my head. "Why are you playing in the dirt, child?"

"I'm writing Your name, great lady." Fingers tingling and hand shaking, I touched the finished sign. "My brother Mani showed me how."

Where's your dolly?"

"Ninsha is giving her a bath. Ninsha likes to do things like that."

I wrapped my arms around the holy knees, and She stroked my hair. "And you'd rather write my name?"

"I need to learn it. One day when I'm Your priestess, I'm going to write hymns about You."

"Keep learning, little one. Don't let anyone keep you from learning the signs."

"Esh?" Ninsha walked into the courtyard, squinting and blinking. She shaded her eyes from the sun with her hand. "Esh? Dolly wants you to help put her to bed," she said in Sumerian. Ninsha was Sumerian, one of the black-headed people, and Father had chosen her as my servant and companion so that I would learn to speak Sumerian in addition to the Akkadian spoken by my family and the court.

I stood. I turned to say goodbye to the goddess, but She was gone. I smiled anyway, I was so happy to have seen Her. More than that, She had stroked my hair and said to keep learning the signs. Now I had a path to follow to become Her priestess. "You interrupted me, Ninsha."

The older girl ran across the courtyard and stood next to me in the shade. "Oh, look at you, Esh. You're all dirty. I better clean you up before the queen sees you."

Ninsha led me to the washing room, shocking in its sudden coolness and darkness, and positioned me next to the drain. She grabbed a square of linen and dunked it in the large jar of water. "Hold up your tunic," she instructed.

I did as she asked. As Ninsha scrubbed my legs, we sang a song about a foolish man and his donkey. Neither of us knew all the words, and we laughed louder and louder as we took turns singing. When we ran out of lyrics, we made up our own words.

The room went dark. Mother stood in the doorway, sighing and blocking the light from the courtyard.

I braced myself.

"Esh-tar-da-ri, what evil are you up to now?" Mother was wrapped in a fine fringed linen robe, and her thick dark hair was threaded with bands of gold. Even so, the angry twist of her mouth was what I always saw first. "Nin-sha-su-gu! I've told you before, girl, don't encourage my daughter in her bad ways. She must learn to be a lady."

Ninsha knelt, trembling. "Lady queen, I apologize."

Stomach quivering, I stepped in front of my servant and lowered my gaze. "It's not Ninsha's fault. She was taking care of Dolly and didn't know what I was doing."

"And what were you doing?" Mother's hand tapped against her leg in a rapid tattoo.

My chest tightened. "I was playing in the courtyard—all by myself—and my knees got a little dirty."

Another long sigh; faster tapping. "You'd better show me."

I led her to the shaded part of the courtyard. "Over here."

She grabbed my ear and pulled me to the hole that I had forgotten to cover back up with the tile. "You were digging in the dirt, weren't

11

you? No." She paused, and I knew she had seen the stylus. "You had a boy in here!"

"No, Mother. It was just me," I squeaked. My stomach started hurting, even though I didn't know what I had done wrong.

Mother squinted, and her mouth twisted. "You were pretending to write like a scribe. That's not your destiny. Why can't you stay with the women and learn a lady's duties?"

I didn't want to end up like Mother. She thought my lot in life would be like hers, but she was wrong. Writing was my destiny. My hymns would move people to worship Inanna and love her as I did.

Mother dragged me back to the washing chamber. "Ninsha, don't let her out of your sight. I know she's slippery as an eel, but you must work harder to keep her out of trouble. She needs to learn the limits of her proper place."

She looked down at me. "As for you," she said in a threatening voice, "you're not too young to spend your days spinning with the slaves, if you keep disobeying."

ॐ

The next afternoon was another hot one, and Ninsha and I sheltered inside our bedchamber while the adults rested elsewhere. Mother had been gone all day, checking on her properties outside the city walls.

"Let's go visit Mani!" I slid off the bed and pirouetted about the room.

Ninsha's face lit up and then fell. She crossed her arms. "Only yesterday your mother told you to sit around and be bored," she complained. "And I'm supposed to watch you, which is even more boring."

"You can watch me visit my brother. You can make sure I don't get dirty."

Ninsha exhaled. "If I take care of you, then you have to take care of Dolly." Ninsha handed the doll over.

"I will." I took the doll and walked it across the bed, then wedged it under my elbow. "Let's go now before the adults wake up."

We found Mani in the same small courtyard as the day before, sitting on the rattan bench.

"Mani!" I climbed up on the bench. "I brought Dolly and Ninsha today. Ninsha's supposed to keep me from being naughty."

"Hello, Ninsha." He smiled at her. "You have your work cut out for you." Mani put an arm around me. "Isn't skipping your sewing naughty by itself?"

"Mother thinks everything I do is naughty." I shrugged. "So I might as well be here with you."

"I'll watch her and make sure she doesn't get dirty," Ninsha said.

"Good idea," Mani said. "Esh, my assignment for tomorrow for school is to copy this tablet. You and Ninsha can watch. Then you can learn another sign if you want."

"Yes! Yes!" I gave Dolly to Ninsha so I could focus my entire attention on the two clay tablets. Mani, his face squeezed with effort that made the few hairs on his face seem to stand up, slowly said aloud the words on the tablet as he used the stylus to create each character of each word.

"If you're going to be the king one day, why do you learn to be a scribe?" Ninsha asked timidly.

"Father thinks it a bad idea to have to rely on the scribes in every matter," Mani said. "Sometimes a king needs to read for himself." When he finished his work, he set it aside and uncovered a fresh damp tablet. "Today, Esh, you'll learn to write the name of the god Anu. It has only four characters." He demonstrated writing the characters. "All the characters have their wedges on the top or left. See?"

I leaned over the tablet. "It looks like a star."

"Yes. This sign means not only 'Anu' but also 'sky' and 'god.' Practice writing this word." He looked over at Ninsha. "Do you want to learn to write too?"

"Not at all. Mommies don't need to write."

"Esh, keep working while I read over my translation."

I drew the star sign several times, repeating "Anu, Sky, God," under my breath.

Raucous laughter came from the corridor. My brother Rimush and Za-mu-ba-ni-mah came into the courtyard. Za-mu was the son of the ensi, the governor, of the small Sumerian city of Kutallu. He lived and studied with Mani and Rimush, a hostage for his father's good behavior.

A handsome boy, he wore his black hair long in the Akkadian style. Ninsha and I usually tried to avoid him because he spent his time with Rimush. Today, both Rimush and Za-mu wore sheepskin kilts and carried stabbing spears and shields, tall, rectangular constructions of hardened hide stretched over a reed frame that covered each from ankle to neck.

Rimush looked around imperiously. "We have room to practice here. Just watch out for the girls." He looked at Mani and sneered.

"The girls should watch out for themselves." Za-mu lunged toward Rimush.

The older, more experienced boy danced aside, swung his stabbing spear, and struck Za-mu on the head.

Ninsha whimpered and clung to Mani, while I couldn't keep my eyes off the fight.

Za-mu's face reddened. "Take this, you barbarian!" Looking at Rimush's head, he stepped abruptly to the left and jabbed around Rimush's shield at the prince's calf.

Rimush saved himself from a vicious leg wound by leaping in the air. Coming down, he swung his spear.

Za-mu didn't move fast enough to dodge it. It hit his arm, and he jumped backward, clutching his injury.

Rimush took firm hold of his shield and charged Za-mu. Shields collided. The hostage stumbled backwards and landed on his backside on the brick floor.

"Oww!" Za-mu cried.

"You're doing better," Rimush said, panting. "That was an almost credible feint."

Mani set down his tablet and stood up. "Our homework for today was to copy a tablet and to practice archery. Which one are you doing?"

"Shut up, Mani." Rimush wiped his forehead with his arm. "What are you doing here, Esh? Shouldn't you be carding or spinning or doing some other tedious activity involving wool?"

I drew back from his scorn, then gathered my courage and looked straight at him, modesty flown to the winds. "I'm learning cuneiform," I said proudly.

"You shouldn't have told him," Mani said.

"Why?" Rimush sneered. "Because I'll tell Mother?"

My chest tightened. "Please, Rimush," I begged. "Don't tell on me. Or on Ninsha."

"Maybe I won't tell Mother—" Rimush inspected his fingernails "— if you do something for me."

"She could polish your weapons." Za-mu got up from the floor. "Or oil your shield."

Mani crossed his arms. "Both of you, stop it. You're frightening the girls."

I remained afraid of Rimush. He liked to pinch and poke me and call me names. When Mother saw him, she just laughed. So today I wanted to placate him. "Yes, I promise to do you a favor," I said. "Just don't tell Mother."

"I'll keep quiet for now," Rimush said with a cruel grin, "but one day I'll ask you for something, Esh, and you'd better do it."

CHAPTER THREE

The next several days passed quietly and excruciatingly slowly, except for the mornings we spent with the musician Bashtum, learning to play the lyre and to sing hymns. In the afternoons, I tried hard to be the quiet, still girl in the sewing room my mother wished I were. If only the adults would be quiet so I could hear the musicians play! Ninsha, the women, and I finished hemming the sheets and started on door hangings of heavy wool. My lap was always sweaty from the pile of fabric.

One day, a servant came from the main palace. "Esh-tar-da-ri, your father, King Sargon, the great king, king of Akkad, overseer of Inanna, king of Kish, anointed of Anu, king of the land, governor of Enlil, has asked that I escort you to him."

I clapped my hands and leapt up, stumbling out of the fabric that tangled about my legs, and followed the servant, leaving the fabric snarled on the floor.

"What am I going to do with that girl?" Mother muttered.

With the servant leading, I could walk in the middle of the passages and rooms, and the scribes and officials made way for us. I was led to the king's office, and the servant announced, "Your daughter, the princess Esh-tar-da-ri." He saluted and left.

I brought my hand to my nose in a salute of greeting. The room smelled of soldiers and beer.

"Welcome, little bird. Come, give me a hug, and tell me what you've been doing."

I ran to him and hugged him. When I stepped back, I looked at him. Although he looked tired, he still looked like a king, from the lapis lazuli cylinder seal pinned to his robe to the fine linen of his clothes to his leather sandals decorated with punched holes. I was always a little in awe of him when he gazed at me so solemnly. Then he smiled and took my hand.

"Is your sewing improving?"

"Yes, Father. We made sheets this week, and I helped hem them."

"What about your Sumerian? It's important to know the language of poetry."

"When we're alone, Ninsha and I speak only in Sumerian, just as you told us to." I paused. "But Father, Ninsha doesn't know the Sumerian words for some of the things adults talk about."

Father leaned back. "I hadn't thought that problem would come up for a while. I'll give some thought to it. In the meantime, are you having enough time to play?"

I grinned. It was a private joke between us. "There's never enough time to play. You taught me that people must always be learning new skills and practicing them."

"I wanted to talk to you about learning new skills. I never intended that you should learn cuneiform."

My chest constricted. I dropped my head. "You know?"

"It would be hard not to know. I've been informed of your studies by several people. Some want me to whip you. Some think I should give you time to learn."

"I think I should have time to learn," I whispered.

"You need to learn skills useful to your future as a queen."

"But Father, I'm going to be a priestess of Inanna. That's why I work really hard at my music lessons. That's why I need to learn to write."

"Whether you're priestess or queen, you'll have scribes to write things down for you."

I stubbornly set my jaw. "But what if the gods send me a poem while I'm bathing?"

Father slapped his leg and laughed. "Oh, my little one." He stroked my hair. "You are like a cool drink after the hot, blasting wind of my generals' arguments. You almost make me want to give you permission."

"Why won't you let me learn?"

17

"Your mother says you've been disobeying and leaving the women's quarters when you should be working. I can't reward you for being bad. What lesson would you learn from that, eh?"

"I'd learn that you love me." My eyes burned as unwanted tears began to spill down my cheeks. My future was in jeopardy.

"I do love you. That's why I plan for your future." Father wrapped me in his arms and pulled me toward him. "I'll always love you, no matter what, Esh. Never doubt that. You're my favorite daughter, you know."

I smiled through my tears. "I'm your only daughter."

"Then you can't doubt my sincerity. Listen now. I'm about to go on campaign to the north. When I return, I want to hear a good report from your mother that you've been working hard and learning to be a great lady. If so, I'll allow Mani to teach you. But only in the evenings after both of you have finished what you need to do."

I gave a little hop as happiness swelled in my chest. "Thank you, Father! Thank you!"

"Only if you're good for the months I'm gone. Can you do it?"

"To learn to write, I will."

The first month of his campaign dragged by. Father had taken both Mani and Rimush, along with Za-mu, on campaign—not that Za-mu or Rimush would have deigned to play with me anyway, but I was used to spending time with Mani.

Mother was more short-tempered than usual, and the babies cried more. The adults dismissed the musicians and talked only of the battles while we sewed. Once messengers started arriving from the field, the women were obsessed with how many enemies had been killed, how many ensis had been deposed, how many treasures had arrived by wagon from the ransacked cities. The northerners were weaker than us and would be easy to defeat. My father would be king of the world, they said. It would be glorious when he finally conquered them.

But even I soon understood that the raids were not entirely wonderful. The women also talked of who in the palace and women's quarters had lost husbands, fathers, or sons, and my mother took time away every day from the mounds of sewing to go to the temples of the city gods Ilaba and Ishtar (the Akkadians' name for Inanna) to pray for the Akkadian soldiers.

Early one morning, Ninsha and I were pulling a toy, a baked clay sheep on wheels, around the courtyard under the eye of Nurse. The musicians were gathering in their room to practice, and the cook was accepting a delivery of grain.

"Come, Esh. Put on your jewelry! We're going to the temple. You too, Ninsha." Before we could even stand, Mother was tapping her foot impatiently. She was already fully dressed, with a large gold and lapis brooch holding her robe together at her left shoulder and a necklace of gold and lapis beads hanging around her neck. Gold bands crisscrossed in her hair, and her eyes were heavily kohled.

We girls ran to our room, Nurse lumbering behind. We put on longer tunics and sandals. Nurse found a kohl container and put kohl our upper and lower eyelids to protect our eyes from the sun. Then Nurse draped several strands of pale steatite beads around my neck and pinned my frog-shaped lapis lazuli amulet to my tunic.

Nurse combed our hair. "Now, Esh, obey your mother and don't run or yell. The lives of our soldiers depend on the gods, and you don't want to disrespect Them."

"I'll make sure she's good," Ninsha said, fingering her agate turtle amulet.

"Don't let her lose her hairpins or her amulet," Nurse responded, pinning my curls down flat. I winced with each sharp pinch. "Now, hurry and join your mother."

As soon as we entered the courtyard, Mother swept away toward the vestibule. Mindful of her admonition not to run, we walked like two ducklings as quickly as we could after her. Four guards awaited and surrounded Mother as we walked through the palace. A fifth servant fell in behind us leading two white sacrificial sheep.

Outside, the narrow streets were still shaded by the unbroken blocks of houses and crowded with people chatting and stands selling figs, sesame oil, and goat milk. A cobbler cut leather for sandals, and two women wove in the shade. Ninsha and I held hands tightly to keep from getting separated.

We walked for several blocks uphill until we came to the tall wall of Ilaba's temple enclosure. We went through a small door and up some steps into the bright temple courtyard, full of activity. Some priests carried offerings of milk and meat to the altar while others sang. As our royal entourage passed, the priests brought their thumbs to their noses.

The high priestess walked toward my mother. "My lady, welcome to the house of Ilaba."

Mother acknowledged her with a brisk nod. "I wish to petition the god in His sanctuary."

"Certainly. Follow me. Your servant may take your sacrifice to the kitchen." The high priestess led us through three rooms of the sanctuary, each one deeper inside than the previous one and thus darker and cooler. In the final room, the high priestess bowed and left us.

I could hardly breathe for the holiness around me. Ilaba's statue stood on a daïs. A couple of flickering oil lamps and a smoldering incense jar were all that lit the room. It was too dark to make out the details of His face or costume, but flashes of silver and gold reflected from His clothes, His face, and the edges of the dais. In front of the platform stood rows of clay statuettes of worshippers with big eyes and clasped hands. The god's statue seemed to move in the dancing light.

"Look directly at the god and let Him look at you," Mother whispered. "Stay here." She walked in front of the clay worshippers. She clasped her hands together and stood, looking up at the god.

I heard her whisper but couldn't make out the words. Ninsha and I stared at Ilaba, and Ilaba stared back. The thick incense made me woozy, and my skin tingled. The god's presence was heavy, like wearing a sheepskin, and the god's heartbeat pounded in my ears. Goosebumps broke out on my skin. When Ninsha clutched my arm, I jumped and had to throw my hand over my mouth to avoid disturbing Mother.

At last, Mother was done praying. I hurried to the door ahead of her and made a beeline for the courtyard, not waiting for the high priestess to lead us out.

Blinking in the brightness, I stopped dead at the beauty of the hymn the priests sang.

"God of the fathers, hear our prayer.
"Lord of the wide sky, look upon us with favor.
"Let the scorching sun not burn us,

"Let the biting wind not scour us,
"Let the rolling dust clouds not engulf us,
"Let our enemies not overrun us—"

"Esh, I said, let's go." Mother and the guards were already halfway across the courtyard.

I didn't move. I would be a priestess one day, like the high priestess, shining in her red robe. I noted how still the priests stood as the they sang. Maybe I did need to learn to not fidget. The thought of not fidgeting made my skin itch and I had to move, so I jumped up and down.

"Esh!" Mother hissed and strode toward the gate.

Ninsha tugged on my arm, and we hurried to catch up. *How wonderful it is to praise the gods! One day, I'll write hymns to Inanna, and they'll be like incense smoke rising to the Heavens.*

CHAPTER FOUR

I couldn't wait for Father to come home so I could tell him my sewing skills had improved. I was proud that I had not lost a valuable needle in weeks. Proud, too, that my stitches had become smaller and more even.

One afternoon, after a lunch of grilled barbel and a nap, Ninsha, the women, and I took up our needles yet again.

"Esh, I need you to stay in this room and behave." Mother pursed her lips. "I'm not in the mood for your antics."

I had no idea what she thought I was up to, quietly sitting there weighted down by another heavy door curtain, but my stomach turned over anyway. "Yes, Mother."

Then, as usual, Mother and the women talked of the war and people I didn't know. When no one was looking, Ninsha and I made faces at each other and tried not to giggle.

Halfway through the afternoon, Mother set down her needlework. "We are going to sew an offering to Ishtar so that She will watch over our army and fight on our side."

I clasped my hands together in joy.

"What sort of offering?" Nurse asked.

"A new robe of fine linen." Mother paused, a finger to her lip. "And a cape of beads."

"My lady, will Ishtar be pleased if you don't give Her new jewelry as well?" one of her waiting ladies asked.

Mother sighed. "You're right. I'll commission a shoulder brooch and a necklace of carnelian and gold beads." She turned to Nurse. "Send someone to the market to buy high-quality beads of stone and gold."

"Yes, Lady Tashlultum." Nurse set the babies on some fabric and left the room.

I was so excited to make a gift for Inanna, I kicked my feet.

Mother glared at me. "Esh!" she said warningly.

"I didn't do anything!" The impertinent words were out before I could stop them. My shoulders went rigid with fear.

Mother stood and slapped me across the face. "No one is going to want to marry you with your disobedience and backtalk. I'll be stuck with you forever."

I reeled backward. My face burned with pain and embarrassment. I opened my mouth to protest but this time thought better of it. Who knew what she would do if I provoked her further? Father, at least, would be happy to have me around forever. I glanced over at Ninsha. My friend was cringing and had slunk low as if to hide under the curtain on her lap.

"Mother, would you like to see how much my stitching has improved?" I held up the edge of the curtain I was working on.

Mother fingered it then snorted. "You'll have to do a lot better than that."

I dropped my head, and tears formed in my eyes. I tried hard to be a good child, but nothing I did pleased Mother. Only Inanna loved me as a mother should, and one day I would return that love by being her priestess.

"Look how fast this cat can run," I shouted to Ninsha as I raced past her across the courtyard.

"Esh! Stop!" she cried after me.

I slowed down and walked in a circle around her. "What?"

"I want to play too."

"You'll need to find your own cat." I pointed to the cooking area. "There's usually some over there."

Ninsha went to look among the baskets of food while I picked up the gray-striped cat I had been chasing and sat on the floor with it.

Carrying an orange-striped cat, Ninsha joined me. Both cats squirmed and tried to get away, and my gray cat hissed at the other one. Ninsha held hers tightly with one hand while picking dirt and fleas off its fur with the other.

"I have an idea," I said.

"Will your mother shout at us?"

"I don't care." I scratched the gray cat's chin. "Let's have a cat race!"

Ninsha clapped. "That sounds fun."

"I think my cat will win. It's bigger and meaner."

We both stood and went to the side of the courtyard farthest from the door to the main palace.

I lectured both cats. "When we let you go, run as fast as you can to the door. The first cat through wins." I set the gray cat down on the floor, still holding it. "Are you ready?"

Ninsha set her cat down as well, and the gray cat hissed at it. "Ready."

"Go!" I said. We both released our cats.

They took off running.

Halfway across the courtyard, the gray cat jumped on the orange cat's back, and they rolled in a ball, hissing and spitting. Then the orange cat burst from the knot of cats and sprinted ahead, the gray cat on its tail.

"My cat lost." I stamped my feet. "You're the winner, Ninsha."

"Don't worry. I love you." Ninsha wrapped her arms around me.

Ninsha and I went to the courtyard the next morning to watch the cooks prepare the food for the day. Already the air smelled wonderfully of sautéed onion and garlic. We sat on a bench and watched them bustle about, accepting deliveries, cutting up meat, and putting pots on the fire.

Then something moved at our feet.

I couldn't see anything for a moment, but then a waving tail helped me pick out a yellow-tan creature from the near-matching bricks. Shrieking, I pulled my feet up onto the bench. "Scorpion!" I screamed and kept on screaming.

Ninsha pulled up her feet too and put her arms around me. "You're safe now."

"But it's right there," I sobbed. "We're trapped."

Two of the cooks rushed over to see what the commotion was about. I pointed to the scorpion, which now had flipped its tail high and rigid. Its stinger glistened.

Whap. One of the cooks flattened it with her sandal. It lay oozing liquid. She scraped it up with a tile and flung it into the fire.

I clung to Ninsha, still crying, afraid to put my feet down again. More scorpions could be hiding nearby.

Nurse bustled out of the boys' bedchamber. "What's wrong? Are you hurt?"

"Yes," I blubbered. "A scorpion almost killed me."

She moved faster than I had ever seen her and came to my side, huffing. "Where did it sting you? Show me."

I sat shaking and couldn't answer.

Ninsha let go of me. "She's not hurt, just scared."

Nurse sat down next to me, her body comforting against mine. "There's no need to be frightened now, Esh. I see no more scorpions."

I snuffled, wiped my nose, and peered over the edge of the bench. "Are you sure?"

"I'm sure. Now come along. Your mother is waiting for you in the sewing room." She stood and offered her hand to me. I grabbed it and stayed close as we went to the sewing room. Today, jars and empty bowls sat on the floor.

Mother barely glanced at us. "The robe for Ishtar needs excellent handiwork, so you girls will instead be sorting beads into these bowls." Without further explanation, she picked up the linen and began sewing the edges together.

I put my hand in a jar and pulled out a colorful assortment of beads. The room was too dim to easily tell the small alabaster, steatite, and limestone beads apart, but as I rolled the various beads between my fingers, I realized they differed in smoothness and coldness. As I held them some more, I also noted that beads of the same size but different types didn't weigh the same.

"Watch this!" I said to Ninsha. I lined the bowls up in front of me and put a bead in each one. Then I closed my eyes, caught a handful of beads from the jar, and sorted them.

"Are you peeking? How did you do that?" Ninsha asked.

I opened my eyes and looked at the bowls. Each held a different type of bead, as I had hoped. "Easy. Feel this bead."

Ninsha took it and rubbed it between her fingers.

"Now feel this one."

"They're different!"

"None of the different types of bead feel the same. The differences will help us sort them faster."

Mother rounded on us. "Just look at them and put them in the bowls. There's no need for chatter and playing around. If you can't be quiet, you'll have to sort out in the courtyard."

The jars were large; we could not possibly finish sorting before the heat and sunlight in the courtyard became unbearable. Ninsha and I exchanged a glance. We would be quiet.

We sorted beads until the cooks brought in lunch—stewed kid and bread. I sat up straight, my shoulders aching from hunching over the bowls. I had enjoyed sorting beads. It was a challenge to do them both correctly and quickly, and Ninsha and I silently raced each other to be the fastest to sort a handful. I hoped Mother would let us string them for the goddess. But now, as I shifted from my cramped position, my knee hit a bowl of beads. They sloshed out of the bowl and went rolling in every direction.

Mother's face turned dark. "You're not getting anything to eat until you clean those up."

"I'll help you," Ninsha whispered.

I squeezed her hand. "We'll always be best friends," I whispered back. Together we herded the beads with our hands until we had a flock's worth and could scoop them up. Collecting them took only a brief time with both of us working, but the fun was gone. I ate my lunch without tasting it.

I heard running feet outside in the courtyard, then a servant burst into the room. "My lady, the army's back! The king is home!"

"Praise Ishtar!" My mother threw aside her sewing and stood. "I must go welcome the king."

I popped up. I hadn't seen Mani or Father in three months. "I'm coming too!"

"No, you're staying here to finish your sorting." Mother sounded angry. "If anyone wants to see you, they'll send for you." From Mother's tone, she thought it unlikely.

CHAPTER FIVE

When Mani came to visit us, he had a cloth wound around his left bicep. I called for Ninsha to come to the courtyard and gestured for my brother to sit on a stool.

"What happened to your arm?" I asked.

"I was wounded at Nineveh. My first battle scar," he bragged. "We had routed the soldiers and were searching the streets for booty. As I reached a corner, a soldier in the cross street struck me with his spear. With it still in my arm, I turned and struck him down."

"You were very brave." Ninsha gave him an adoring look. "Now you're a hero."

Mani preened.

"I'm so happy to have you home," I said.

Then it was Ninsha's turn to look proud. "We worked on a gift for Inanna so that She would protect our soldiers."

They continued to talk, but I stared at Mani's arm and thought about his wound. Father had been going on campaigns my whole life. I had never really thought about what he did on them, about the killing and getting injured. If the spear had hit Mani in a different place, he could have died. Father and Rimush too. Instead they killed other people.

But, then, so did Inanna. She strapped on her knife and picked up her battle axe and took joy in spilling blood across the battlefield.

Yet everything Inanna was, She was also its opposite. So did She also cry with the families who lost fathers? Did She bury the dead? Had She stepped in to save Mani from a worse injury? Or was She the soldier who hurt him? Uncle Ubil-Eshtar had been sick, and many of the soldiers too. Was that a god's punishment? Or was Inanna teaching the victorious what suffering was like?

One day when I was a priestess, perhaps I would understand the goddess's mysteries. In the meantime, it was enough to sit here next to Ninsha and know that she would always take care of me.

☙

I hid myself behind a large basket in the courtyard so that Mother couldn't find me. I could still hear the servants talking, but none of them noticed me. Only a cat saw me and came over to have its head rubbed.

"Esh!" Mother called. "Come here!"

I froze in place.

"Esh! Where are you?" My mother sounded irritated, and I compressed myself smaller. "Nurse, have you seen that disobedient daughter of mine?"

Now that I wasn't petting it, the cat wandered away.

"She was here just a moment ago."

"That cat! What was a cat doing behind the basket?" Mother's angry footsteps came close. Then she was peering behind the basket at me. She grabbed my arm and yanked me up. "You're going to the wool shed today. We'll see whether several hours of spinning convinces you to behave. Now go, change your clothes!"

As I was lifting the lid on my clothes chest, I heard Nurse talking softly to Mother. I must not have been meant to hear it, so I got up and stood beside the doorway.

"Maybe you're too hard on the child, my lady."

"Only you can get away saying that," Mother replied harshly. "She needs to be prepared. The world is a hard place for women."

"She's only a little girl."

"One day she'll be a queen. A queen is a bird in a cage. Esh needs to learn self-discipline so that she can pretend to be an ideal princess. She can't be as willful as I was."

"Don't you think there's room for Esh to retain something of herself? Or you, some part of the sweet girl you were?"

"No," Mother said emphatically. "No, there's not. I had to be broken, and now she has to be. The earlier we do it, the less painful it will be. She must become docile and obedient and skilled in women's work. If she doesn't, she won't have a future, and I will have failed as a mother."

My chest tight, I scurried back to the clothes chest and fumbled through the layers, trying to find a stained tunic suitable for the weaving room despite my blurred vision. I didn't understand much of what Nurse and Mother had said, but I got the gist: Mother wanted to make me into another person. I wasn't good enough for her as I was.

I sniffed back my tears. I was good enough for Inanna, and She was a goddess. Her love would have to sustain me.

ت

"Come to the workroom!" Mother ordered. "Some of the women have come down sick, and I need your small hands to string beads for the cape." She looked flustered and angry, and it was still early morning.

"The men are already home," I said. Wasn't that the purpose of the offering?

"Now that Ishtar knows of the offering, She'll be angry if we don't give it to Her. She is not a god to cross."

Nurse walked into my room. "Excuse me, my lady. There's a messenger here. The king wants to see Esh."

Mother rounded on me. "As soon as you're done, come back and work."

I felt as if I could float. At last I would find out Father's answer to whether I could learn to read and write. And I thought I knew what it would be, given how good I had been.

Nurse tried to hold my hand, but I cried out and pulled it away. It was still blistered and sore from spending the previous day at the weaving shed. We headed to Father's office. The palace was more crowded than usual. It seemed as if all five thousand four hundred soldiers who ate with Father walked through the palace at once. All had browned in the sun; some bore wounds or bandages. The scents of oil and sweat surrounded them. Leather creaked; weapons clanked. I stayed close to Nurse's side.

When we got to Father's office, Uncle Ubil-Eshtar already waited on the stool, so I sat on the floor, and Nurse stood in the corner. Because she was old, it hurt to get down on the floor.

"Hello, child." My uncle turned on the stool to face me. He didn't look much like my father. Where my father radiated energy and power, Uncle Ubil-Eshtar seemed smaller than his body and sad in a way I didn't understand. "Are you here to see your father?"

"Yes, Uncle. Did you get hurt when you went to the war?"

"Oh, no, I stayed here to run things. A king's duties don't disappear just because he's gone to fight."

"Were you sad to miss the war?"

His gaze drifted away from me. "No, I was glad to stay home. Unlike your father, I've had enough of war. It can become a madness, one that I'm glad to leave in my past. Besides, I'm more use here than with the army." He banged his cane on the floor.

"Oh." I wondered whether his legs had been hurt in a campaign and whether war was a madness for my brothers, for my father, for Inanna. I didn't think I'd want to be consumed by a madness for anything.

I went to the doorway that opened onto the huge courtyard. The old door curtain was gone, and a new one hung there. I wondered whether I had sewn on it.

Few men were left in the courtyard, and two soldiers were before my father now. A woman stood between them, her head down, her body slumped, and her robe dirty and torn. One soldier said that he deserved first pick of the booty from Nineveh's temple of Ishtar because he led the unit that took it. Then the other soldier stepped forward. He deserved the slave, he said, because he had claimed her first. He had taken no other booty. He wanted only the woman.

I took a step back. The woman had been taken at the temple, so she was probably a priestess. Yet she was now a slave, and two men fought over her. I knew that my father had a great destiny to conquer the world. Yet this woman's fate struck me as unfair. One day I would be a priestess, and I didn't want such a fate.

Father decided for the unit commander, saying that rank must be respected. He did not ask the woman's opinion or even look at her.

I went back to my spot on the floor to wait for Father to be done.

Father came in soon afterward and sat down hard in his chair. Nurse and I saluted him.　31

"You may sit beside me, Esh." He stroked his beard, which was long and beautifully oiled and curled, as befitted a king. "I'm pleased to see you looking well."

"Thank you, Father." I sat straight. "I have many things to tell you."

He smiled, and his face lost its tired look. "Go ahead, then."

Everything spilled out of me—how I had behaved very well, sitting quietly and talking softly; how I had sewn and sorted beads the best I could; how my stitching had improved; how Ninsha and I had accompanied my mother to the temple of Ilaba; how the women were finishing an offering for Ishtar. At the end I took a breath. "I've done everything you asked. Now can I learn to write?"

He stroked his beard. "Did you learn to like helping your mother?"

I laughed, sure that he was teasing me again. "Of course not."

He looked at me solemnly. He wasn't joking after all.

"I did like getting better at something. I also liked figuring out a new way to sort the beads."

"I had hoped that if you applied yourself to your tasks, your natural woman's instinct would take over, and you would enjoy them. Your mother says that you were still disruptive. Spilling beads, for example."

I hung my head. "It was an accident." I had done the best I could, but apparently it wasn't enough. "What about my learning to write?"

"I think it's a bad idea for Mani to teach you," Father said softly. "You both have better uses for your time."

"But I'm going to be a priestess."

"A priestess doesn't need to also be a scribe. Mani doesn't need to be a teacher." Father put his hands decisively on his thighs. I recognized the gesture from watching him hold court. He set his hands down like that when he had made up his mind and was ready to move on. "But I have decided something that will please you. Ubil-Eshtar, will you tell her?"

Uncle smiled. "My scribe, Kalki, will be giving you and your servant girl lessons in Sumerian. It's important for a court lady to be fluent in both languages. You don't know where you'll live when you're grown."

"Thank you, Uncle. Thank you, Father," I said dully. Ninsha and I did want to be able to speak about everything in Sumerian and not be held back by only knowing little-child words. But gaining the privilege of those lessons paled beside losing the expected lessons in writing. "I'll work hard. I'm sure Ninsha will too."

CHAPTER SIX

After Nurse took me back to the women's quarters, I stayed in the courtyard and stood with the cats to watch the cooks. A kettle was on the fire, and the wonderful smells of bread baking and lamb simmering in beer soothed me and gave time for my tear-wet eyes to dry before I had to face anyone. I had worked hard at being quiet with the thought that there would be a reward. Now I had no idea how to achieve my destiny.

The center of the courtyard exploded with silvery light, and the scent of incense surrounded me. Skin tingling, I brought my hand to shield my eyes. Inanna had arrived to visit me. She was almost too bright to gaze on.

My stiff shoulders dropped. I snuffled back my tears and saluted the goddess.

"My daughter, your sadness called me. What made your tears roll?"

"Oh, Lady." I began to cry again. "I wanted to learn to write so I could create hymns to praise you. But Father forbids Mani to teach me."

She squatted and drew me to her breast, and I wrapped my arms around her, hungry for motherly love. Although she looked like the shining moon, her flesh was cool. "Your destiny awaits you, and you must be prepared. If Mani is not allowed to teach you, you'll have to find someone else to."

I stopped sniveling and drew back. "I can do that?"

She smiled. "You'll have to. I'm eager for the hymns you'll create."

The light died. I stood for a moment, torn between sadness at my father's edict and joy that Inanna gave me permission to find a way around it. Then I turned around to see what the cooks thought of my special standing with the goddess, but they continued their work. They hadn't noticed anything. I wasn't surprised; Ninsha never saw the goddess when She visited either.

Tremors overtook me, and I sat on the floor. The favor of any god came with great expectations. The favor of Inanna, who raged and ravaged and made reckonings, was a heavy burden. She had always been kind to me, but what would She do if I didn't find a way to learn to write? If I disappointed Her in some other way? She called me "daughter," but I knew how capricious mothers could be. I needed to tread as carefully with Her as with my real mother.

༒

"I have good news," I said as Ninsha and I sprawled on the bed that afternoon.

"What is it?"

"Father has arranged for us to take Sumerian lessons with the scribe Kalki."

"The king is generous!" Ninsha beamed. "When I finally go home, I won't talk like a little child anymore."

I rolled over to look at her. "Do you think my father will let you go?"

"He'll have to, won't he? Once I grow up, I'll be too old to be a hostage."

"Za-mu is still a hostage. He's big."

"He's not as old as Mani and Rimush. Besides, I think he likes it here, with so many warriors."

"Yes, he likes to fight, he and Rimush both." I yawned. "The sewing was even more boring today than usual."

"You're not doing it right."

"Yes, I am," I squealed. "I'm doing it just as Mother showed me."

"I don't mean how you're sewing the thread. I mean how you think about sewing."

"What do you mean?" I got up and poured some water from a pitcher into a clay cup.

"You know how the oracle priest goes into a trance? Sometimes I can do that when we're sewing. Sewing becomes calming and pleasant that way."

35

"How do you do it?" I drank some of the water and took the cup to Ninsha.

She took a drink. "I don't listen to the music or the talking, and I don't look anywhere but at my needle and thread. I think 'in, out, in, out, in, out,' and after a while I start to enjoy the sewing."

"It sounds like magic."

"Or a gift from the gods," she said.

"Maybe I'll try that." Even as a priestess of Inanna, I would need to sew. If there was a way to make the work more agreeable, I would do it.

Ninsha and I had our first Sumerian lesson the next night in the same room the boys learned in during the day. Kalki, our tutor, was a reed stalk of a man with his head shaved and no beard, although he was not a eunuch, merely following the Sumerian fashion. He paced the room like a cheetah. By comparison, I was the still, quiet creature Mother wanted me to be. Nurse snoozed on a stool in the corner.

The first evening set the pattern for the lessons to follow. Kalki chose a topic—six of the twelve months of the year for the first night—and told us the words, and we repeated after him. Then we drilled until he abruptly stopped pacing and told us our time was up.

I had hoped to learn dozens of words, so I was frustrated to come away with only six new words of limited use. "Don't we get to talk about things and events?"

"Once you have words enough, we will. But I'm not interested in talking about dolls. We'll wait until we have the vocabulary to discuss the people, habits, imports and exports, ensis, city gods, and creatures of each region."

We were going to learn a lot more than just Sumerian, I realized. We were going to learn things a priestess should know.

Although Ninsha rarely complained, she did so after Kalki stalked out of the room after the first lesson. "What's wrong with dolls? I'd rather talk about dolls than emports and ixports any day. I don't even know what they are."

"We send barley, cloth, and dates to other cities, and they send back copper, wood, and lapis. That's exactly what I need to know to trade and make investments when I am a priestess."

"I don't need to learn those things."

I hadn't thought about Ninsha's future before. I was going to grow up and be a priestess. As a princess, I could choose my tasks at the temple. In addition to writing songs, I could choose to feed the goddess, manage fields or grain warehouses, or invest in property or merchants' cargos.

Ninsha, on the other hand, took care of me now and was going to grow up and take care of me forever. She had no reason to learn more than adult Sumerian. I felt sorry for her.

"The more we know, the more we have to talk about," was the best consolation I could offer.

A month later, we were on our seventh lesson on occupations, with no end in sight. We were finally speaking in sentences. Very boring sentences. "The herder of free-range pigs goes to the well." "The sluice-gate opener walks by the river." "The chief performer of laments eats bread."

We had gotten a sentence about a goat driver wrong so many times that Kalki banged his fist on the wall. "Teaching these distinctions would be so much easier if you could see the written words and copy them at night. When I teach boys, I teach writing and speaking together."

I saw the chance the goddess Inanna had told me to watch for. "We would like to learn to write. One day I'll write temple hymns."

"A small girl learning to write." Kalki chuckled and then corrected our sentence about the goat driver. We repeated it, and then he gave us a new sentence to memorize: "The funeral wailers enter the house."

As I listened and repeated that sentence and the ones that followed, I looked around the room. The boys' supplies were scattered about. I picked up a stylus and went to a jar at the front of the room while Kalki was facing the other direction. I fished inside for a damp tablet and pulled it out.

When Kalki paused for us to translate, I said, "May I show you something, teacher?" I slowly and carefully wrote a word. "Inanna," I said out loud. I smoothed the word away with my finger and wrote another one. "Anu. God. Or Heaven." I looked up.

His eyebrows rose as he read the tablet. "Child, you're full of surprises. I'll think about your request."

ॐ

The next evening, Kalki walked in and stood in front of us, stock-still and with heightened color.

We were so startled by his calmness that we immediately stopped chattering. Even Nurse noted the change in our teacher and sat up straighter.

"Esh-tar-da-ri, how many words do you know?"

"Only the two I showed you yesterday," I admitted.

Ninsha, can you write anything?"

"Not a word."

"No matter. I'll start from the beginning for both of you.

"Then you'll teach us writing?" I asked, bouncing on the stool.

"I'll try it out. We'll see whether you can learn to write more than a few words and whether it helps you with your memorization as it does the boys."

"Thank you!" I said.

Ninsha put her forehead in her hands.

CHAPTER SEVEN

"You're mean and selfish." Ninsha held tightly to Dolly and wouldn't let me have her.

We were in our bedroom, and it was time to go to sleep, but I couldn't let her accusation stand.

"I'm not selfish. You get to learn to write too. Before, Mani was only teaching me."

"You don't listen. I told you already, I don't want to write. I want to be able to talk and not have the adults understand. That's it. A secret language for the two of us."

"I'm the princess, so we do what I want."

"I'm a princess too!" she shouted.

I jerked back in surprise. One of the cats came in and jumped onto the bed to wash its toes. Elsewhere, my mother chastised a servant. Somewhere a mole cricket rasped a song, and the cat paused, its foot in midair. "What?" I croaked.

"My father is the ensi of Uruk. I'm here as a hostage so my father does what your father wants."

I got hot all over. "But you're a servant! A princess can't be a servant!"

The corner of her mouth tightened. "The gods can decree bad fates for anyone, even a princess. Your father carries out such fates."

"What do you mean?"

"What do you think happens when he conquers a city? He kills the king and sells the queen as a slave. Then he lifts someone up to be the city's ensi."

39

I was silent, my thoughts whirling. The gods favored my father, and he did what the gods wanted.

Didn't he?

Ninsha went on, relentless. "One day, no matter what you want, your father will choose your future, and mine with it."

My ears pounded, and I shook my finger in her face. "Don't say mean things about my father! He'll make me a priestess; I know he will." The cat leapt from the bed and dashed into the courtyard.

Ninsha started crying. "I wish I could decide for myself what to do."

I wrapped my arms around her.

"Hey, hyena." Rimush leaned against the door to our room. "I need that favor you promised me."

My stomach turned over. I wanted to hide. "I don't owe you a favor. You told Father that Mani was teaching me."

"So? I only said I wouldn't tell Mother. So now you owe me."

"Oh." I drooped. He had tricked me, but I had promised him. "What's the favor?"

"Mani brought home better plunder than me. I want some of his."

Ninsha put her hands on her hips. "If you didn't take good plunder, that's your own fault."

Rimush looked surprised. "The mouse roars."

"She's right," I said, thinking I had a way out.

"Doesn't matter," he said. "You promised. Now here's what I want you to take from his room. A knife with a jeweled hilt. A gold tunic pin embedded with agates. A gold statue of Ishtar. Bring them here and put them under your bed. I'll come for them later."

My stomach hurt at the thought of stealing from my favorite brother. "What if I don't?" I challenged him.

Then I'll tell Father you hit Ninsha and made her cry."

I glared at him. "I never did that. It would be a lie."

"But Father would believe me."

My stomach sank. Maybe Father *would* believe him. I could think of nothing to say and wanted to throw up. "I'll do it, but I don't owe you anything more after that."

I barely slept that night. Betraying Mani stuck in my throat, and I was afraid of getting caught stealing, too. The next morning, after our singing and lyre lessons, I told Ninsha, "The boys are in their lessons. Let's go to Mani's room and get it over with." My stomach jittered with nervousness.

She frowned. "Are you really going to steal some of his plunder?"

"I don't see a way out. I promised." I stared at her, hoping she would solve my problem.

"You were tricked into promising."

"I know. Does it matter?"

"It should. Don't you think so?"

"Maybe." I didn't know what to think. "What should I do?" We both sat on the bed and thought.

At last I said, "What if I tell Mani?"

"You'd tattle on Rimush?"

"Mani's not an adult, so it doesn't count as tattling," I said defensively.

"Won't Mani be angry?"

I shrugged. "Not angry at us." My stomach flipflopped anyway.

"Will Rimush do something bad to you when he finds out?"

"Maybe. But he's already done something bad to me by tricking me into this promise."

That afternoon, we slipped away from the sewing room while the women took a break from sewing. We found Mani in the usual courtyard where he did his homework.

Suddenly shy, I asked him if he would like to hear a hymn we learned that morning.

"Yes, of course." He set down his tablet.

We stood in front of him and sang,

Hail, Queen of Heaven.
Hail, bright-faced lady.
Hail, daughter of the moon.
Your great horned crown gleams like the stars;

Your father's light rims You in silver;
You shine in the east at dawn.
All sing Your praises,
All sing Your praises,
Great lady of Heaven.

Mani dipped his head. "Nicely done. You two are working hard on your singing, I can tell."

Ninsha giggled, while I dropped my head and made circles with my toe.

"You came here for something else, too, I think."

I told him about Rimush's visit and my agreement to steal things from his room because of my promise. "What should I do?"

Mani sat and thought. "Rimush doesn't care about plunder. He might want the knife, maybe, but the jeweled pin is something a woman would wear. What Rimush does like is causing trouble."

"But he said he wants the plunder."

"Knowing him, he wants it to cause trouble. I wonder what he's planning?"

"I don't know." I still felt worried.

Ninsha added, "I don't know either."

"Here's what I want you to do, Esh," Mani said slowly. "I'll give you the things he asked for, but don't put them under your bed. Put them in your chest, at the bottom."

I didn't know why he'd want me to do that, but I agreed. It was a relief to have Mani know and tell me what to do.

We followed him to his room, and he wrapped the pretty things in a soft wool cloth. "Now we'll see what he's up to."

CHAPTER EIGHT

The next morning, I was watching the cooks carry in the new deliveries of barley and meat when my mother came out into the courtyard and ordered me to dress.

"We're going to visit one of my estates. Find Ninsha too. You both need to learn to manage property." Before the last word was out, Mother was hurrying away.

I looked in room after room until I found Ninsha with Nurse in the nursery, watching a serious Ilaba'is-takal toddle from one end of the room to the other, carrying a ball of yarn. A cat saw his approach and streaked away.

"Ninsha, we need to go with Mother to one of her farms. She wants us to get ready."

Ninsha stood up, and we went together to dress for outside.

As when we went to the temple, four guards surrounded us as we walked. I had never been farther from the women's quarters than Ulmash House, the temple of Ishtar, so I turned my head from side to side, staring at shops and people until I stumbled like Ilaba'is-takal from not watching my feet. We headed downhill toward the holy river Buranun, Whose slow course we started to hear as we wended our way through different neighborhoods and sometimes along canals. Small temples to other cities' gods mixed in with houses and shops selling everything from leather goods to honey to softshell turtles. A spiny-tailed lizard left its sunning spot and dashed across the street in front of us.

We reached the tall mudbrick city wall at last and went through the gate to the outside. My first glimpse of the river astounded me. Boats

43

like quarter moons plied the Buranun and crowded Its shores. Storks, spoonbills, and egrets lined the edges of the river, all squawking as if they bargained for fish instead of catching them themselves. Swans slid among the boats.

"Esh, don't gawk. Come this way," Mother snapped. She led us to a canal, and we walked on a path on top of the levee for a long time. The brisk wind tangled my hair and nearly blew me over a few times. The sun got hot, and our shadows got short.

I stopped to look at several long, skinny insects with shimmery wings. I squatted and held out my hand, and one landed on it. It was so light I couldn't feel its weight, and its colors changed as it moved. I wished I were small enough to fly away on it. "What are these?" I asked.

"Dragonflies," Ninsha said in Sumerian. "They like water."

"Dragonflies." Such a wonderful name.

Mother looked behind her. "Esh, come on. Ladies don't play with insects."

I stood and walked with my hand as still as possible, but the dragonfly flew away.

At last Mother stopped. "Here's one of my properties. Now that it's fall, the workers are planting barley. Follow me!"

Smaller channels left the canal and cut through the yellowish-tan dirt, which was piled in long hills in-between the channels. Farther away, a haze of green brightened the dirt, but closer to us several men in skirts bent over the hills, poking the ground with sticks and dropping seeds in the holes.

Mother stepped off the path and onto a narrow hill, walking slowly toward the men. Ninsha and I followed, but the guards remained on the levee.

One man stood, saw Mother, and came toward us, hopping from hill to hill, his hand by his nose. "My lady, welcome to the sowing."

Mother frowned. "You're not done yet, I see."

"We're right on schedule." He smiled at us. "Are these beautiful children your daughters?"

"The scrawny one is my daughter. The pretty one is her companion."

"Welcome, little ones. Behold the heart of Akkad! Barley!" He swept his arm in front of him, indicating the field. "Now, my lady, come out of the sun. We can talk over there."

We followed him to a mudbrick building of two rooms. The thick walls made the inside cool and pleasant. Mother grilled the man with questions—Was he protecting the seeds from the birds? Were the workers honest? Why did he have so many? When would they finish planting? Was he keeping the water channels clear? Had he made arrangements with the storehouse for the spring harvest?

The man must have been used to Mother; he didn't cower, and his voice remained steady as he answered her questions.

I envied him his calm. Meanwhile, I considered how different managing an estate was from the other duties of ladies I had learned. I liked everything about it so far—the walk, the birds, the canal, the little green shoots that peeked up through the soil.

When Mother was done, she led us back to the path on the levee. "Well, that's done, thank goodness. I hope you paid attention, Esh. One day you'll have fields and estates to manage."

"Yes, Mother." I didn't contradict her. I knew that priestesses managed estates for their temple. It was something to look forward to.

ʚ

That evening, after our cuneiform lesson with Kalki, Nurse led us back through the shadowy palace. Her oil lamp lit a small bit of floor ahead of her, but otherwise our path was dark. I expected soldiers to jump out of dark doorways. I kept sniffing for oil and sweat until Nurse got annoyed and shushed me.

When we got back to our room in the women's quarters, I turned to Ninsha. "Wasn't that fun? Soon we'll know as much as the boys."

"I still don't want to learn."

"I've been thinking. Since you're a princess too, how about when I'm a priestess, I let you be one too?" I expected her to be excited.

Instead she stomped her foot. "I want to be a mommy."

If she were a mommy, she couldn't take care of me. I frowned. "I don't think that will work. I need you beside me."

"I know," she said, looking away. "You can't take care of yourself."

"But I can help you with our homework. You need me too."

ʚ
45

Ninsha continued to complain about the cuneiform lessons, but less as time went on, as she became intrigued with the idea of making words with symbols. The next week, after a lesson, when we went back to the women's quarters, we found Father, Mother, Mani, and Rimush in the courtyard.

Father wore a stern expression. "Rimush has made a serious accusation against you."

I looked at Rimush. "We thought you would trick me somehow."

"Trick you? No, you're the one who stole something." Rimush spoke faster than usual, and his mouth twitched with a smile.

"Go into your room, Esh," Father said. He and the others followed me. "Now take out what's under your bed."

"There's nothing under the bed, Father." I shook with fear, as I'd seen others shake in front of my him.

"I'll get them," Rimush proclaimed. He knelt and looked under the bed, sneezed, and shot me an angry look.

Father seemed angry now, and Mother was furious.

"Mani, what should I do?" I whispered.

Mani put his hand on my shoulder. "Did you do what I told you to do?"

His touch calmed me. "Yes, Mani."

"Good." He walked over to the chest, reached down into the bottom, and pulled out the cloth-wrapped bundle. He unwrapped the cloth, revealing the knife, tunic pin, and statue of Ishtar. "Are these what you were looking for, Rimush?" His voice was hard.

Rimush's face paled. "She stole something else from you. I swear it."

Father looked from one boy to the other. He hit his palm with his fist. "But these are the very things you said she stole. Mani, what's the meaning of this?"

"Esh is innocent," Mani said. I shrunk into the background as he explained the promise I had made and how Rimush had wanted me to pay it off. "I thought he must be up to something, so I gave Esh the items and told her to hide them in her chest instead," he finished.

Father's nostrils flared, and his face reddened.

46

Mother turned toward Father. "Mani's lying," she said with a shrill voice. "He's covering up for Esh because she's his pet."

"Yet Mani knew exactly where the items were without being told. He's telling the truth," Father thundered. He turned to Rimush. "If you were one of my soldiers I'd have you killed. Because you're my son, I'll let you off with ten lashes."

"No!" Mother gasped.

Father continued as if she hadn't said anything. "You've lost my trust, Rimush, and need to win it back again. Understood?"

Rimush dropped his head. "Yes, Father."

Father walked out of the room.

"This is your fault, Esh, and yours too, Mani." Mother glared at both of us. "Somehow you tricked my Rimush with your wiles. Mani, you're banned from the women's quarters." She rushed out the door after Father.

Rimush glared at Mani.

"Ten lashes," Mani said, wonderingly. "That's a lot."

"It's because of you. Aren't you sorry now you took her side?" Rimush spit the words out.

A vein pulsed in Mani's forehead. "It's your fault for forcing me to take sides. We're brothers, yet you act as if we're enemies."

Rimush's lip curled. "We *are* enemies. I should be king next, not you."

"Why do you think that?"

Rimush stood taller and puffed out his chest. "I'm the one better suited to kingship."

Mani snorted. "Have it your way: We'll be enemies. But today has shown that you're not suited to be king."

Rimush turned to me. "You'd better watch out."

Mani shoved him. "You're the one who better watch out. Now get out of here."

Soldiers met Rimush at the door. They grabbed his arms and pulled him away.

CHAPTER NINE

One day Father sent a eunuch for me. The tall man led me through the palace to Father's office.

Father waved us in, and I greeted him with my hand to my nose.

Father somberly motioned for me to move closer to his desk. "Esh, I've had a report from Kalki that you're exceling in your cuneiform lessons."

I couldn't hold back a smile. "I've been working really hard."

He folded his hands. "I was surprised because I told you that you couldn't have cuneiform lessons."

I stared at him for a few moments in outrage and dread before I could answer. "Only with Mani, Father. You said I couldn't have lessons with Mani anymore. And I haven't. Only with Kalki."

"You're already thinking like a scribe, twisting my words so they mean what I said, not what I meant. I'm very disappointed in you."

I sank to the floor and cried with raw, gulping gasps. I had not meant to disobey or disappoint him. What could I do to win back his respect?

Father let me cry for a while and then said, "Despite myself, I'm proud of you. Kalki says you learn faster than any of the boys. That's remarkable, given how clever Mani is."

I wiped my nose on my arm and sat up. "Father, will you forgive me? I'm sorry I misunderstood you." I rubbed at my eyes. "The Lady Inanna encouraged me, so I thought it was all right."

"Inanna?"

The air shimmered, and goosebumps popped up on my arms. The room became brighter and brighter, and I smelled incense. I turned around and saw the goddess. The arrows in Her quivers clacked, and She held her bow. She put Her foot up on the stool, and Her robe fell open around her leg. "My dear children."

I shivered with awe. Even her toenails glowed.

Father and I both stood and put our hands to our noses in respect. Father blinked. "You can see Her?"

"Yes. I didn't know you could."

The goddess smiled. "Sargon, once I told you to drop your shovel, leave your fields behind, and walk to Kish. You had a destiny to be king of the world, and you couldn't achieve it as a gardener."

Father dropped to his knees. "My lady, I followed your words then and still do."

"Then know that Esh-tar-da-ri also has a destiny, and she can't achieve it without knowing how to write."

Father looked at me. "My daughter?"

Inanna put one hand on my head and one on his. "Her memory will live on through the ages alongside yours."

"What is her destiny?" he asked. "What should I do?"

I blinked, and Inanna was gone. The scent of incense faded. Father and I stared at the spot where she had stood.

"Well, little bird," Father said, "you were right. The goddess wants you to learn to read and write."

"Will you forgive me?"

"Yes, of course. And you may continue your lessons with Kalki."

I threw myself into his arms.

He hugged me tightly. "Little bird. I'm glad that Inanna speaks to you as well." He stroked my hair. "You have to continue working hard. Inanna can be a cruel and harsh goddess."

Section II

Cities of Akkad and Mari

Age 16

CHAPTER TEN

"Come and sit, girls," Bashtum said. She was old now but still had all her teeth, and she still sang with good enunciation. "You two are among the first to hear this hymn I wrote. It's another antiphonal one, so the one who sings second must try to match the style of the one who sings first. Let's try it first without instruments. Listen to me." Bashtum sang the whole hymn through, both parts. It was a song about Inanna's diverse and contradictory traits. "Now I'll sing it again. Nin-sha-su-gu, please sing part one, and Esh-tar-da-ri, the responses."

"Holy Ishtar,	Queen of Heaven,
"You bring forth thorn bushes.	You cause the ewes to bring forth lambs.
"You scream with the thunder.	You whisper in a baby's ear.
"You chug beer in the alehouse.	You are offered pure water in the temple.
"You wash weapons for battle.	You bathe before greeting Your lover.
"All creation is Yours.	All destruction is Yours.
"Powerful One of the gods,	Wise One, protect us."

Although I had the easier part, Ninsha managed to remember more of the words than I did. "Good job, Ninsha!" I said.

"Yes, Nin-sha-su-gu, your intonation was excellent," said Bashtum. "Esh-tar-da-ri, you usually pick up the words faster than that. Are you distracted?"

"A little," I admitted. "I'm to see my father after class."

Bashtum looked beyond me to the door. "Here may be your escort."

I recognized the man as one of my father's scribes. I stood and brushed the dust from my robe. "Ninsha, stay here and continue with the lesson. Later, we can go over the song together." I turned to the scribe. "I'm ready," forestalling him from listing all my father's titles and announcing my invitation.

He led me through the maze of the palace.

"What mood is the king in today?" I asked.

"Cheerful, almost carefree," was the answer. "I think he's looking forward to seeing you, my lady."

"He's been on campaign so much this past year, I've seen little of him. Did you go on campaign with him?"

"No, he took some of the younger scribes and left us old men to, he said, 'warm our bones by the fire.'"

I laughed. "I'm sure my Uncle Ubil-Eshtar kept you just as busy as usual."

The scribe allowed himself a small smile. "I must admit, I was happy to stay here in my usual routine and share my bed with a wife instead of a soldier."

The palace was quiet. The soldiers must have been drilling, because we passed none. We reached my father's office just as he was dismissing Ubil-Eshtar.

"Come in, my little bird." His usually grave face had a smile.

I greeted him with my hand to my nose. "It's wonderful to see you, Father. Are countries volunteering to submit without a war? You look so happy."

"Oh, but that wouldn't make me happy. I enjoy war. But I do have good news." He paused. "I've settled your future, and it's a wonderful one." He picked up an amethyst cylinder seal from his desk and handed it to me.

"For me?" I turned the cylinder seal back and forth, trying to catch some shadows so that I could make out the design in the pale purple stone. "Thank you, Father! Where will I be a priestess of Inanna? Here in Akkad, so I can be close to you? In Uruk?"

Father pushed forward a tablet of fresh clay, and I rolled my seal on it. It showed a banquet scene. A man and woman shared a jar of beer while servants carried pitchers to serve their guests. I started translating the text.

"Esh-tar-da-ri, daughter of Sargon, wife of Hidar." I looked up at him, disquiet unsettling my stomach and head. "Father, the seal cutter made a huge mistake."

Father cleared his throat. "There's no political gain for this family if you become just another priestess of Inanna. I've arranged a marriage for you with Hidar, king of Mari. You will be queen of a large city-state, as you deserve."

Anger rose in me, fast and furious. I ground my teeth so hard, my jaw muscles pulsed. I slapped the cylinder seal down. "Father, I am meant to be a priestess of Inanna."

"A queen can be a lay priestess in-between her other duties, if her husband permits." He cleared his throat again. "I need you to keep King Hidar loyal to me, particularly now that he's conquered Ebla. He controls a large chunk of my empire that's too important to lose. Remember, we all must make sacrifices for the good of the family. You'll be playing an important role."

I crossed my arms. "Father, I won't do it. My destiny is to be a priestess."

His face reddened. "You most certainly will marry Hidar. He and I have already signed the marriage contract."

I sat down suddenly on a stool without waiting for permission. My father must have been planning this marriage for a while, to have already negotiated and signed a contract. Messengers must have been going back and forth between Akkad and Mari without my having any idea.

Now I was trapped.

"How could you do this without asking me? Inanna doesn't want me to go to Mari as a wife." I left the seal laying abandoned on his desk.

"How do you know? Has She said so? She hasn't told me any such thing." Father stood tall and looked at me with narrowed eyes. "If you are queen of Mari, you can help fulfill my destiny of becoming king of the world, and it may fulfill your destiny as well." He picked up the seal and forced it into my palm.

Hands clenched and face averted, I asked, "What is King Hidar like? Is he young and handsome at least?"

"My diplomats said nothing about his looks. But they did say he had a son older than you."

I felt as if I were going to vomit. "He already has an heir? So my son won't rule Mari one day? Your future grandchildren deserve an inheritance."

Father stood. "You should be happy. I've made you a queen instead of placing you under the thumb of some high priest of Inanna. You'll leave in two days."

He called the scribe back in. "Take her to her mother and explain the contract with King Hidar to them."

"Father, wait. What about Ninsha? Must I leave her behind?"

His expression softened. "Esh, believe me, I want you to be happy. Your servant will go with you."

☙

In the courtyard of the women's quarters, the scribe read the contract out loud. As a bride price, King Hidar would give my father fifty rings of silver. As a dowry, I would take many lengths of wool and linen cloth, my clothes and jewelry, sesame oil, many spices, and twenty cows.

I sat on a stool, fists clenched, my mouth held firmly shut for fear I'd shriek angry words. I could barely hear the scribe over the pounding in my ears, although I didn't care, not even about the amounts of my dowry and bride price.

Mother walked back and forth, grinning like a hyena. After the scribe finished and left, Mother said, "See, it was a good thing I prepared you to be a queen. Now you'll not embarrass us."

My eyes and cheeks got warm. "You should be embarrassed by this arrangement. My son won't inherit the kingdom of Mari. I'm only a tool, a tool that's being wasted."

Mother rounded on me. "Of course you're a tool. All women are tools. You thought you were so special, that you had a destiny better than mine, but now you know your place."

From the corner of my eye I saw Ninsha peeking out of the music room. The cooks began talking loudly. My face burned with humiliation. Everyone had heard what Mother said.

"I still have a destiny," I shouted. "Inanna will open the way for me."

Mother sneered. "So much pride, even now. It was your father who betrayed you. I had nothing to do with this marriage. It was all him."

"At least Father loves me." I bit my lip, but it was too late to hold back the words. My breath stopped. I didn't want to hear her response.

"What mother could love such an unfeminine daughter?" she snapped.

Pain twisted in my chest, and I thrust myself up from the bench. "I'll be in my room packing."

CHAPTER ELEVEN

Ninsha found me after her lesson was finished, sitting blurry-eyed on the floor, staring into the rattan chest at the foot of my bed.

Ninsha knelt next to me. "Esh! What's all this about your marriage? I thought you were going to be a priestess."

"I will be. Somehow."

"Who's this King Hidar?"

"He's king of Mari, in the northwest." I turned toward her, eyes streaming. "Ninsha, he already has a son older than me. What will happen to me and my children when that son inherits?"

"I'm sorry. You must be so disappointed." Ninsha put her arm around me. "Maybe things will work out better than you expect." She looked down and played with her amulet. "Did...did your father tell you what my future will be?"

"Yes. That's the only good part."

She squealed and blushed. "I get to marry Mani?"

I stared at her. A prince might marry a hostage princess. But Ninsha had been a servant for so long, everyone, even I, usually forgot she was the daughter of an ensi. Father had given her to me to take to Mari as if she were another cow.

"I didn't know you wanted to marry Mani."

"I always expected to marry one of your brothers. After all, I was brought up here in your home, just as a girl child destined to be a bride would be. I always hoped it would be Mani."

"I'm sorry. Father isn't going to marry you to Mani. He's sending you with me."

Her eyes glittered with tears. She grabbed my arm. "Will I be forced to marry a stranger in Mari too?"

"No. You'll be coming as my...my friend."

Her mouth twisted. "If I were going as your friend, I would get to choose to go."

"Neither of us has any choice. We must follow the king's orders."

She took her hand back and rubbed her arms. "Maybe we'll enjoy Mari."

I hadn't considered that. But it was true—now we would be the adults setting the rules for the women of the palace. We could choose to sew—or to do something else. We could do our duties to our own standards, not to someone else's. Once I had a child, my husband would likely give me properties to manage, and Ninsha and I would be able to get away from court to oversee them. Being queen in Mari would not be like living under Mother's tyranny.

I smiled at Ninsha. "Maybe we will! But first, we have to get through a long, dangerous trip. We're leaving in two days."

"Two days! What should I take?"

"We need to ask my mother."

"I'm here." Mother stood at the door. I had the feeling she had been eavesdropping. "The scribe was clear. Your dowry is cloth, your clothes and jewelry, oil, spices, and cows. Everything else, take out of the chest and put it aside."

She turned a kinder face to Ninsha. "I'll allow you to take your clothes. Pack them in the chest with Esh's. I'll also give you girls several sharp needles. Who knows whether King Hidar will give you any before you've provided a son?"

No words of reassurance, no account of what I faced as a new wife. Only a gift of needles, which my mother had to know what the last thing on our minds as we faced a future alone in a strange city.

☙

By the next morning, the shock of what was happening had partly worn off, and Ninsha and I wanted to say goodbye to a lot of people. Most of those who lived in the women's quarters already knew I was leaving. The laundresses and cooks were excited about my marriage and asked many questions about my future husband, almost none of which I could answer. Bashtum cried at the loss of the two students she had worked with for so many years, and we cried with her. The guards were surprised and wished us well.

Kalki had a present for me, a tablet demonstrating the proper way to write a letter. "The king expects you to write to him often with news and gossip of the court. He's already talked to me about reading your letters to him."

I felt foolish. I had not even considered that I would be a spy in the household of my husband.

Father must have thought I was too innocent to tell, but I had grown up listening to the adults talk in the sewing room. As usual, my father had layers of reasons for what he did, and I wondered what other plans for King Hidar and his city Father had hidden from me.

We had caught Kalki on his way to Uncle Ubil-Eshtar, so he had little time to talk. But on his way out, elbows flying, he surprised us by gathering us to him in a hug. "Write to me, too, you girls, and let me know how you're getting along in Mari."

"Now we need to see Mani." Ninsha blushed a dark red.

We found him sitting in the warm spring sunlight in a courtyard with frescoes of colorful scenes of battle, polishing his weapons with a whetstone with sharp motions and excess vigor. His face was red, and a vein pulsed in his neck.

"What's wrong?" I thought he might have heard that I'd be leaving.

"You're being sent away to marry a king that Father will want to conquer sooner or later. I'm getting a bride from Nippur, and Rimush, a daughter of the ensi of Larsa. Rimush kept me up all night raging that Father was dishonoring him." Mani yawned and set aside his weapons.

I knelt on the courtyard floor. "We always knew we'd be married to strangers."

"Not so." Mani exchanged a look with Ninsha. "I always assumed Father had Ninsha in mind for me. Uruk is an important city, one that is unhappy under Akkadian rule. A marriage with Ninsha might have quieted their restlessness."

"And you both would have married someone you knew and liked," I said.

Ninsha burst into tears.

Even Mani was red-eyed. He quickly changed the subject. "Father is older than most people ever get. I wonder whether he's trying to get things settled before I become king."

My chest tightened, and my head spun. "Father's not going to die," I blurted out.

"One day he will," Mani said, "as hard as it is to imagine."

Sorrow gripped my heart, and I felt my anger at Father diminish a bit. "Tomorrow may be the last time I ever see him."

We sat silently for a while with our thoughts. Ninsha moved to sit next to Mani, and he clasped her hand.

Meanwhile, I pondered how different my life would be, in both good and bad ways, and I wondered what kind of man Hidar and his son were.

Then Mani called for a jar of beer. "Let's set aside our sadness for this last time together and share a jar. It may be a long time before we do so again."

CHAPTER TWELVE

Ninsha and I stood outside the palace as the caravan formed. We were walking to Mari; a sailboat couldn't hold everyone and the dowry. The cows lowed their distress, and soldiers and cooks milled about, waiting for the donkeys to be loaded with fodder, my dowry, and supplies for the trip. The chilly wind worked wisps loose from our tightly dressed hair. I felt underdressed, having packed away all my jewelry except the simple gold pin on my left shoulder that held my robe together. Behind us stood my father, his hand on my shoulder, and Mani, just as silent as Ninsha and I were, while my little brothers Ilaba'is and Ibarum poked each other and giggled. Birds sang loudly in the trees, and ovens wafted the luscious odor of bread through the city.

Across the street, Inanna shimmered. Goosebumps broke out on my skin. I wished she had come to talk to me. Even so, her upraised fist gave me courage and reassured me that I could still find a way to my destiny. I just needed to figure out how.

As the soldiers moved into formation to protect the caravan, I was surprised to see how many accompanied us. The trip must be more dangerous than I had realized. I caught a glimpse of the tall leader of the soldiers, his arms akimbo, and couldn't tear my eyes away for a moment. He was a handsome Sumerian man who somehow looked familiar. Then it came to me. It was Za-mu-ba-ni-mah. Taller and much broader-shouldered than he used to be, but definitely him. Remembering how Za-mu used to follow Rimush around and imitate his disdain for Mani and me, I resolved to keep clear of him. He must be even more insufferable now that he led soldiers.

Za-mu walked the length of the caravan, checking in with the soldiers, cooks, and animal drivers. Then he came to stand before me but looked over my shoulder at my father. "All's ready, my king."

My father took my shoulders and turned me around. His eyes were glossy. "Write to me often, little bird. And don't worry. Your husband will know he must treat you well or risk my anger."

"I don't want to leave you, Father," I choked out.

"I'd keep you with me always if I could. But you're grown up now, and it's time for you to have your own household and children. It will be an exciting adventure for you."

I pressed my lips together. I turned to Mani, but my throat clogged and I couldn't speak.

He seemed to have trouble getting any words out too. I studied his face, trying to imprint it in my memories.

Za-mu cleared his throat. "My lady, you and Lady Ninsha will be in the center of the caravan."

I took Ninsha's hand as Za-mu led us to two donkeys and helped us climb onto them. Then we rode away from the only home I had ever known.

ॐ

Fields being harvested quickly gave way to scrubby steppe as we followed the road northwest along the holy river Buranun, Whose banks teemed with life. Stout-bodied plovers and lapwings picked their way through marshes on their long legs, grabbing lizards and bobbing for fish. Tall white egrets stalked the shore, catching fish, lizards, and mice between their long beaks. Date trees clustered near the water.

Away from the river stretched bare steppe as far as the eye could see, broken only by clumps of goosefoot or meadowgrass that erupted from the pale ground. The wind blew hard and constantly.

Midafternoon, Za-mu called a halt to the trek.

Ninsha and I were more than ready for a break; riding on a donkey on a rough path had us sore all over. We slid off our donkeys and groaned. "I'll walk as the soldiers do from now on," I said.

"I as well," Ninsha said. "Nothing would get me back on a donkey again."

63

The sun burned hot for early spring, but we sat under it because there were no trees. The donkeys and cows nibbled the scrubby plants until the donkey boy put out some fodder. Cooks caught fish and broiled them and served them with beer and bread. Ninsha and I were famished and ate as quickly as politeness permitted.

Za-mu worked his way from group to group, checking on the people and animals of the caravan. When he reached us, he asked how we were doing.

I wasn't going to admit to throbbing, painful thighs. "We've decided to walk instead of riding from now on." I waved toward the holy Buranun. "I've never seen the river before without fields lining It."

"We won't see fields again until we get near Sippar."

"How far away is that?" Ninsha asked.

"Another three and a half days, if you can walk full days."

Ninsha opened her mouth, but before she could say anything, I interjected, "We can walk. We're stronger than you think."

"Good. We'll continue until early evening and then stop to camp for the night. But if you can't make it until we stop, let me know."

Ninsha smiled. "Thank you for watching out for us."

Za-mu moved on to the next group of people.

I turned to watch him. "He was polite and respectful. I didn't expect him to be."

"It's been several years since we've seen him, and he's been in the army. He must have grown up."

"I guess so. I'm glad. It'll make our trip more pleasant."

Za-mu didn't eat until he had checked on everyone, and I was surprised again. What had happened to the disagreeable boy who idolized Rimush?

☙

Soon the caravan got underway again. Our thighs were even sorer for having had a rest break, but my pride kept me from asking Za-mu to stop. It was twilight when Za-mu called a halt to make camp on a dry rise near the river. Soldiers put up a tent for Ninsha and me to sleep in. The soldiers would sleep on the ground. As before, servants caught fish and served it with beer and bread. I wondered whether such would be our fare for the whole trip.

Ninsha and I were talking about the gazelles we had seen far in the distance when Za-mu approached us.

"May I join you?"

I glanced over at the soldiers joking and singing. "Don't you want to eat with your men?"

"They can't enjoy themselves fully when their commander is with them. They're too concerned about making a good impression."

I scooted closer to Ninsha. "Then please, join us."

He lowered his long-legged form onto the desert floor. "I've been away with the army for a long time. What news of Rimush and Mani?"

"My father has arranged marriages for both of them, Mani to a princess from Nippur and Rimush to the ensi of Larsa's daughter."

"Are they pleased?"

I hesitated a moment. "Let's just say that they were expecting different brides."

"Too bad," he said.

Ninsha brushed back some loose strands of hair set free by the wind. "Have you ever been there? To Mari?"

"Once." Za-mu took a few bites of fish. "It's a bigger city than Akkad, and its city mound stands higher on the plain. It has a wide canal through the center of the city. Otherwise it looks a lot like Akkad."

I finished my bread and brushed crumbs from my lap. "How hard is the Eblaite language to understand?"

"It sounds like someone speaking Akkadian badly. If you pay attention, you'll be able to catch almost all of what is being said."

"That's a relief," Ninsha said.

"At court, some people will also speak Sumerian or Akkadian. Isn't that right, Za-mu?" I thought I remembered that from our lessons with Kalki.

A shadow crossed Za-mu's face, and he looked away. "I don't know. I've had no dealings at court."

I remembered then that he had been a prince before he came to Akkad as a hostage. I wondered whether he, like Ninsha, still smarted from his loss of status.

He changed the subject. "Has anyone warned you of the dangerous animals we might encounter?" 65

"No," we said together.

"You should keep an eye out for spiders, scorpions, and centipedes, which are common out here. They may be small but their bite or sting really hurts. Some are poisonous. Not to mention the vipers and cobras."

Ninsha shivered. "Now I'll be afraid to go to sleep."

"If you don't bother them, they usually won't bother you. Just watch where you step."

"Thank you for the warning." I was going to stop watching the horizon and concentrate on my feet from now on.

"I should go now." Za-mu enfolded his remaining fish within his bread and stood. "Thank you for your companionship." He strode away.

"You're right," Ninsha said. "He has changed."

"I hope he eats with us again. I would welcome a diversion. I spend too much time worrying about how ugly and grouchy my husband will be."

Ninsha took my hand. "Don't worry, Esh. Whatever happens, you'll still have me."

CHAPTER THIRTEEN

"Esh! Esh!" It was the second night of the trip.

I groggily opened my eyes to see in the moonlight that Ninsha wore a look of horror.

"What's the mat—"

"Don't move!" she whispered. "There's a scorpion on your clothes."

The hair on my arms rose. Despite her warning, I immediately lifted my head to see. There most definitely was a scorpion, a large black one. My stomach felt as if it were full of rocks. The creature was longer than the width of my hand, and it had a fat tail with a stinger like a curved needle.

I started trembling and couldn't stop. Would the jiggling irk the scorpion? I could only hope not. I could barely breathe, my chest was so tight. Why couldn't it have been a spider? I wasn't afraid of them.

Ninsha's eyes were round. "What should I do?"

"Don't do anything. It might sting one of us."

"We have to do something."

"Za-mu said, 'don't bother them, and they won't bother you.'"

"You can't just lie there."

I didn't see how I could, either, but calling for help or moving might be interpreted by the scorpion as bothering it. "I think I have to. And you too."

We spent a long time without moving. The scorpion remained where it was. Was it asleep? At last, my fear increased to the point I couldn't bear the animal's presence anymore.

"Ninsha, would you do something for me?" I asked quietly.

"Yes?"

67

"Move away slowly and then go down to the river. Find a plant with a thick stem and bring it back."

She stood and scurried away, letting the tent opening flap, and the scorpion lifted its pincers at the motion. My breath caught. Several moments passed before I could breathe easily again. Then I waited. Ninsha seemed to be taking forever to return with a stalk.

At last she came back inside the tent. "I'm back. What now?"

"What I want you to do is to work the stalk underneath the scorpion and then flip it out of the tent. Can you do that?"

She drew back. "I don't think I can do that at all. I should wake one of the soldiers to do it."

"No, I don't want any commotion that will cause the scorpion to sting." I took a shallow breath. "Give me the stem."

"You're going to do it?"

"I think I have to."

She put the stalk in my hand and closed my fingers around it, then stepped back.

Slowly I brought the stalk up to my chest and lay the tip near the scorpion.

It investigated the stalk and then climbed on it.

I took a breath. I was grasping the stalk so hard, my knuckles looked white. "Great Inanna, guide my aim." I had to be careful that the scorpion didn't land on someone else.

The scorpion scurried toward my hand.

I flung the stalk as hard as I could.

"You did it!" Ninsha whispered.

I panted in the dark. "Thank you, Inanna. Thank you too, Ninsha."

Ninsha lay down and fell asleep almost right away, but I felt as alert as if it were day. I lay awake for a long time, sure that every brush of wind on my skin was another poisonous creature skittering about.

I woke early despite my lack of sleep. I got up and tottered around the camp to work out the pain in my feet. I didn't want to delay the caravan when we got on the road. I was very much looking forward to sleeping in Sippar that evening and eating something besides fish.

The sun was barely above the horizon, and pink and orange tinted the holy Buranun as It flowed sluggishly south to home. Even the cooks were only just getting up. The breeze was chilly, and I wrapped my shawl tightly around me, thinking about joining the cooks as they fed their fires.

"Lady Esh!"

I turned. Za-mu strode toward me. "You're up with the dawn."

"I often am," I told him.

"Me too. A soldier's habit. Care to walk along the river?"

The breeze would be even cooler there, but I didn't want to be alone with my thoughts. "Yes, that would be nice."

We turned and walked toward the Buranun. Only a few egrets waded in Its shallows, but dozens of marsh frogs dared to croak a chorus. Above, the moon still shone brightly, and the water reflected both its silvery light and the sun's harsh pink rays.

"The frogs are having a late night," I said.

"Even more of them were croaking earlier. I'm surprised they didn't wake everyone."

"Ninsha and I were tired enough last night to sleep through anything. Almost anything," I corrected.

His face brightened. "How is Ninsha?"

She's holding up better than I expected."

We walked silently for a while and turned to go back to camp.

"Za-mu, do you know anything about my husband, King Hidar? Did you hear anything when you were in Mari?"

"Don't you know anything?"

"Only that he's old enough to have a son older than me."

His eyebrows drew together. "You're marrying a man who already has an heir?"

My face burned with embarrassment. "Yes. I'm a treaty bride."

"I'm sorry. And I'm also sorry that I don't know anything about him. I'd relieve your worries if I could."

"Lots of women marry men they know nothing about." I tried to keep my voice light, but he glanced at me as if he knew what I was thinking.

As the sun rose, more egrets arrived until the water's edge was crowded with white bodies and the air filled with their harsh calls. Storks too came, and the chorus of frogs ended.

Za-mu looked toward our caravan. "The camp is rousing. I need to check on preparations for breakfast and leaving. May I join you for lunch today if I can?"

"Certainly. We both enjoy your company."

Za-mu strode off, and I thought how much less worried I would be if I were marrying him instead of King Hidar.

CHAPTER FOURTEEN

"Looking forward to sleeping in Sippar tonight?" Za-mu asked.

"We're both looking forward to a soft bed," I said.

"Or even a hard one," Ninsha added. "Although I have to say, I've been sleeping fine on the ground."

"Probably because you're tired. But it's not the luxury you're used to." Za-mu took a long slurp of beer from the jar.

"At home, we spent mornings, afternoons, and evenings sewing or in lessons," I said. "This trip is in some ways a respite before I shoulder the duties of a queen."

"I expect to be busier than ever once we get to Mari," Ninsha said.

"Do you have a husband waiting too?"

Ninsha pressed her lips together. "No."

"She's going as my...my friend." I didn't want to embarrass her by naming her a servant.

"That must be a big relief, to have someone you know with you." Za-mu crammed down his food.

"Yes. I'm lucky I don't have to go alone," I said.

Ninsha tore the last of her bread into pieces and tossed it onto the ground. Immediately two terns landed and squabbled over the crumbs. We all laughed, and the conversation turned to people at the Akkad palace. Too soon we had to get on our way. We had walked until near sunset the first two nights, but this day we got a reprieve, arriving in Sippar while the sun was still high in the sky.

The city's walls and those of its smaller sister city across the Buranun, Sippar-Amnanum, came into view soon after we started walking after lunch, and soon we were among the green fields around the two cities. We were amazed at how high Sippar sat and how big it was. We climbed its steep mound and entered a tall gate in the wall, where Sippar guards led us to the palace.

The queen of Sippar welcomed us with jars of beer, which we drank under an awning in a courtyard frescoed with dolphins frolicking in the sea while making small talk about our journey. Ninsha and I both felt much refreshed after being able to sit and have a hearty drink. Afterward, she had a servant take us to a room so we could rest, wash, and put on fresh clothes. The room was in the palace itself. The servant explained that they didn't have women's quarters in the north. She said, though, that no men should be in the courtyard off our room. "As soon as you want to bathe, we have a tub ready for you. And I'll take your dirty clothes to launder."

"That sounds wonderful," Ninsha said.

Our things had already been delivered But our eyes were drawn to the bed. Laughing, we pulled off our dusty robes and threw ourselves onto the sheets. They felt so soft, and the bed had a welcome give.

Ninsha spread-eagled herself, kicking her feet in the air, leaving me only a sliver at the edge.

I was looking forward to washing my feet and hoped the dirt was not ground in permanently. "Can you believe we've only covered a small part of the distance to Mari? It feels as if we've been in the steppe for weeks."

"Why are you complaining? The longer it takes, the longer you have before you meet your husband."

"I hope I can learn more about Hidar tonight."

The servant returned and, looking askance at our sprawling forms, offered to take our dirty clothes now and to show us to the bathing room.

We quickly accepted on both counts. After washing, we put on clean robes and combed our hair. Then Ninsha put our hair up.

The servant returned to take us to supper. She led us through the palace into a large courtyard where musicians were singing and the king, queen, and several men I assumed were royal councilors awaited us in the shade. The king and queen each sat on a chair on a daïs and were so adorned with gold, lapis lazuli, and carnelian that I felt ashamed of my few ornaments, priceless as they were. Ninsha and I brought our right hands to our noses in front of the king and queen and, at their gesture, took the two empty rattan stools. A servant immediately brought each of us a beaker of red beer.

I took a sip. "This is delicious. Thank you, and thank you for your welcome as we travel to Mari."

The king leaned toward us. "We were honored that your father thought highly enough of Sippar to ask whether you could stop here on your journey."

I had no knowledge of what my father thought of Sippar, so I merely nodded acknowledgement.

Servants refilled glasses. Others brought in delicious-smelling food and placed it on the low table in front of each person. My mouth began to water. "The food smells wonderful. Thank you for your hospitality."

The king continued as if I hadn't spoken. "We pay our taxes on time and send men when your father requests them."

My face heated. It was odd to eat among men, and the king's attention flustered me. "I'm certain my father's heart is gladdened by your prompt responses to his requests." We were being very diplomatic, talking about "requests" instead of "demands."

"You'll be sure to tell him how we welcomed you, won't you?" As he spoke, the queen beamed at me.

"Of course, my lord. He'll be pleased." The king seemed concerned that, despite his support of my father, Sippar might be seized as so many other cities had been.

"Good. Good." The king turned his attention to his bowls, and then so did I. The meal was more splendid than any I had eaten before. One bread was enriched with cheese and dates, and another bread was fermented and steamed with pine nuts inside. The beer was smooth and sweet. The savory dishes smelled of spices and meat: boiled duck in broth with saffron, garlic, and leeks; roasted venison and turnips; and smoked fish with rosemary and thyme. We were also served pears poached in honey with sesame seeds.

While the others ate, I took the opportunity to glance around the courtyard. The frescos depicted a king hunting lions and leopards. Blocks of limestone made up the floor. In the shade, a woodlark in a cage tweeted a song.

"Do you know King Hidar?" I asked.

"I know his reputation," the king said. "He conquered Ebla and now has a huge territory. A worthy husband for you, young Esh-tar-da-ri."

A warrior, at least. "And what do you know of the gods of Mari?"

The queen answered this time. "Their primary gods are Dagan, a god of fertility, and Mer, a storm god. They also worship many of the Sumerian gods, such as Adad, Whom I knew as a child in the south as Ishkur."

"How did you know the two gods were the same?" I asked.

"Adad is the god of rain and storms, and so is Ishkur. They must be the same god."

"Like Inanna and Ishtar?"

"I still think of Inanna and Ishtar as separate gods," the king said. "Inanna is female, after all, and Ishtar is male, or at least He was when I was a boy."

"Indeed, my lord," said one of the hitherto silent courtiers. "But imagine how relations among different states could be improved if everyone believed they worshipped the same gods."

The king nodded.

"Do they worship Inanna at Mari?" I asked.

The queen replied. "Under the name Ishtar-Anunitum, her warrior aspect."

"Then she's not really Inanna, is she?" grumbled the king.

I wondered whether being a priestess of Ishtar-Anunitum would satisfy me. If my husband let me serve the goddess. Or would he insist I stay in the palace and sew?

We left early the next morning. It would take us six or seven days to reach the next city, Hit, and after a night in a bed, Ninsha and I weren't looking forward to sleeping on the ground again. As we tramped along green fields being harvested, I reflected on the conversation at supper the night before about the gods and their names. If I worshipped Ishtar-Anunitum, would I truly be worshipping Inanna?

Soon after we passed the last of the fields around the two cities, Za-mu called a halt for lunch. The cooks hurried to unpack their pots and fishing poles from the donkey that carried them. As one started a fire, others carried their poles to the river.

Ninsha and I futilely tried to brush dust from our robes. The soldiers meandered about, stretching and joking. Birds called in the rushes along the river's edge.

"Dust cloud!" Za-mu shouted. He began bellowing orders. The soldiers formed a half-circle in front of the cooks, donkey boys, and donkeys.

Za-mu ran back to us. "Get in the center and stay there."

Breathless, I ran to where he pointed. Then I saw Ninsha wasn't with me. I whirled around.

She hadn't moved. "Why?" she asked Za-mu.

I ran back to her, grabbed her hand, and dragged her behind the protective line of soldiers.

Ninsha resisted the whole way. "We need to know what's happening."

"No; right now, we need to do what Za-mu says. I think we'll find out soon enough what's happening." Gasping, I stopped when we got to the cooks and followed their example, crouching behind the fire and cooking pots with my elbows tight into my sides. The cooks were clutching their amulets. That seemed a good idea, so I clutched mine too.

Ninsha stood, trying to peer between the soldiers lined up in front of us with their spears raised. "I can't see what's happening."

"Get down," I ordered and pulled on her arm. "It might be a bandit attack."

Eyes wide, she at last crouched with the rest of us.

We stayed down for what seemed both a short moment and a half-day wait. Over the heartbeat in my ears, I heard Ninsha's hoarse breathing. A donkey snorted, and the cows milled about. Knives clanged as the head cook passed them out to the other cooks.

Then the bandits were on us, screaming. Dressed in dirty, dust-covered fleeces, they tried to storm past the soldiers, pushing the battle closer to us.

I grabbed a pot and held it in front of me.

Three bandits were down already. The soldiers shouted as they thrust their spears. At a call from Za-mu, they dropped their spears and pulled their knives. Red blood spattered the sand.

One bandit forced his way past the line. He looked around and grinned when he saw Ninsha and me.

Ninsha sobbed.

I clutched the pot harder.

The bandit lifted his knife and strutted toward us. The cooks stood and swung their knives, forcing the bandit back. He moved to the side and took a step forward, then lunged.

Ninsha and I screamed. I hefted the pot.

The bandit grabbed Ninsha's arm.

Anger filled me and set my blood afire. "No!" I brought the pot down hard on his head.

In the next moment, the cooks surrounded him, swinging their cleavers and knives. I grabbed Ninsha's arm and pulled her away from the tumult. Blood spilled to the ground, and I looked away while Ninsha continued screaming.

By now, our soldiers had killed the remaining bandits. The churned sand around their feet was red, and the soldiers were laughing and shouting. Za-mu moved among them, slapping backs and grabbing arms.

When he finished with the soldiers, Za-mu strode toward us and looked at the bandit at our feet for a long moment, his eyes taking in the cracked pot I held. Ninsha stopped screaming and panted raggedly, her hands on her knees. Za-mu turned to the cooks. "Good job, men." Then he pointed upriver. "We'll march on another league and set up for lunch again. So pack back up now."

My heart continued to pound in my ears. When Za-mu called a halt again for lunch, I was still shaky, and Ninsha couldn't stop babbling. I sat down in the sand and buried my face in my hands until my food was brought. The bandit attack had taken away my appetite, but the smell of freshly baked bread brought it back, and I gorged on broiled fish and bread.

Za-mu came over to us with his lunch and sat down. "How are you feeling now?"

"Still scared," Ninsha said.

"I'm having a hard time settling down," I confessed.

"Everyone's feeling the effects of the fight," Za-mu said. "We'll be walking all afternoon. You'll feel the better for it."

"Good," I said. "Were any of our soldiers injured?"

"Scratches, no more. You have the best warriors in the world protecting you."

"How did you get to be part of my father's army anyway?"

"He saw me training with Mani and Rimush. He must have liked what he saw. I've been in the army five years now."

"And he trusts you, even though you're a hostage?"

"He must. He asked me personally to put together a guard for this trip."

Ninsha put down her bowl. "Don't you want to go home?"

"I don't feel as if I have a home. If I went back to Kutallu, it would be to people I barely remember and a city I don't know."

I thought how close I had always been to my father. "Don't you miss your parents?"

"Not anymore. They're shadows in my mind. And I like being in Sargon's army."

"I still sometimes wish I could go back to Uruk," Ninsha said.

"Did you ever ask King Sargon?" Za-mu asked.

"Me, ask the great king for a favor? Oh, no. Besides, who would take care of Esh if I weren't around?"

Za-mu raised his eyebrows. "I suspect Esh can take care of herself."

Ninsha patted my hand. "No, she needs me."

"She's lucky to have you." He turned to me. "Have you found out anything more about Mari's king?"

"Only that he conquered Ebla, which I probably once learned in lessons anyway."

"I as well. I paid more attention to weapons training than to learning history and geography."

"Ninsha and I are glad you did."

He sat straighter. "Anyone in King Sargon's army could have defeated the bandits."

"But you were the one who did," Ninsha said. "You're our hero."

Blushing, he stood while he finished the last few bites of his bread. "I need to get the caravan moving now." He smiled at Ninsha and left.

CHAPTER FIFTEEN

We reached the town of Hit, notable for its many small pools of bitumen, after several more days of walking. I stopped walking to stare at a pool, seeing my distorted reflection in its glossy black surface. I picked up a stone and dropped it in. It sat on top, slowly dimpling the surface as it sank.

We replenished our supplies in Hit and kept walking. It took another nine days for us to encounter the green fields around Mari. Beyond the fields lay the city, a tall wall curving around it. The tops of temples peeked above the wall.

Za-mu sent a messenger ahead to alert the palace that we were almost there.

When we stopped for lunch, Ninsha and Za-mu ate together, but I was too nervous to eat anything or sit still, so I wandered about while everyone else enjoyed their fish and lentils. I wanted to run away from the caravan then, but I knew I couldn't live on the sparse vegetation. Still, I looked out across the fields to the desert with longing.

After lunch we trudged up to a city gate. The guards allowed our party to enter, and one of them led us on wide, straight streets smelling of bread and chickpeas up to the palace. The building was larger than the Akkad palace, and taller as well. I felt dwarfed by the doorway, which reached to more than twice my height.

Suddenly, time sped up. A rush of servants besieged us. Some led away the donkeys and their bundles; some took charge of the cows; others guided the soldiers away. The remaining servant, a skinny young woman with light brown hair and hunched shoulders, greeted us. "I welcome you to Mari. I'll be your servant. My name is Satpa."

"Thank you for your welcome. I am Esh-tar-da-ri, daughter of Sargon, king of Akkad, and this is my companion, Lady Nin-sha-su-gu, sister of the ensi of Uruk."

"Come, my lady," Satpa said. "Your husband awaits."

"May we wash the dust from our faces and hands first?" We had last bathed and changed our clothes in Sippar, thirteen or fourteen days earlier.

"The king wants to see you right away." Satpa led us through the vestibule and a large courtyard to a doorway with a guard and a man who looked like a scribe. "The king's cupbearer," she whispered then told the cupbearer who we were. He led us into a throne room with two men in it and announced us: "Princess Esh-tar-da-ri and the lady Nin-sha-su-gu."

On a daïs, in a chair inlaid with shell, sat a pale, dark-eyed man in a tufted skirt who looked older than my father's seventy years. To hide my disappointment, I bent my head modestly and brought my hand up to my nose. From under my eyelashes I searched his face for signs of kindness or gentleness but found none. His beard was long and scraggly, and his white hair was pulled back, accentuating his face's wrinkles and sagginess all the more. He was a little plump, with no sign of warrior's muscles.

He looked between me and Ninsha, and then his eyes settled on me, and he studied me as I had studied him. "Princess Esh-tar-da-ri. Did you not think to wash off the dust of travel before presenting yourself to me?"

My stomach fell. "I came as soon as I arrived, as you ordered, my king."

He frowned. "Your servant should have known better."

I responded with care. "I beg pardon, my king. Shall I come back later?"

"You're here now. I only wanted to get a look at you before the wedding banquet. You please me well, dust and all."

"I'm glad you're pleased, my king."

"Allow me to present my son and heir, Ishqi-Mari."

I turned toward the man standing next to King Hidar and saluted him.

Ishqi-Mari gave no smile or greeting in return. His was a cruel face, pinched despite his youth. His lips were pressed together as if he were keeping words tightly locked away. He, too, wore a tufted skirt, which showed off powerful tanned muscles.

I dropped my eyes. *I'm going to avoid being near him, if I can.*

"Now, wife, go to your rooms and prepare. The wedding feast will start tonight," Hidar said.

So soon! I gulped and bowed my head.

ॐ

"So what do you think?" Ninsha asked after Satpa had led us to our new rooms.

I pulled off my robe and tossed it aside. "He's an unattractive old man, as I feared. But perhaps he's kinder than he looks."

Ninsha poured water from a pitcher into a bowl. "His son looks meaner than a hyena."

"Let's hope we have few dealings with him." I dampened a piece of linen and wiped my face then cleaned the rest of me. "Our quarters please me." We had two rooms, a large bedchamber with space to work and a small storage room. Everything was clean and fresh-smelling, and the linens and door hanging were new and nicely stitched. The walls were freshly plastered. The main room, which had a fresco of cows and calves at pasture, opened onto a large shared courtyard.

"Having a storeroom will help us keep the main room neat," Ninsha said. "The servants have already put your chest in there as well as your bride price and the cloth from your dowry."

"We don't have much else to put in it."

Ninsha began washing. "We will. Your husband will want you to show off his wealth. He'll have to give you jewelry."

"We'll see." I wrapped myself in a clean robe and pinned it closed at my left shoulder, suspending the amethyst cylinder seal my father had given me from the pin. I sat on a stool and began combing my hair.

"I'll do that." Ninsha took the comb from me and finished the combing. Then she put my hair up. "There. You look so beautiful that the king will fall in love with you and give you whatever you want."

"We both know you're the beautiful one," I said.

She winked at me. "To an old man, all young women are beautiful."

A striped cat wandered in and sat watching us.

Tears formed in my eyes. To be a bride was to be helpless in a way I'd never experienced. Mechanically I put on a beaded belt and gold earrings. "All I've ever wanted was to be a priestess of Inanna."

Ninsha rested her hands on my shoulders from behind. "Don't give up hope. You haven't even asked your husband yet."

Satpa rushed into the room and set a large, black, hairy object on a stool. "You need this for tonight, my queen." Then she darted out before I could ask what it was.

Ninsha and I stared at the object. She shrank back. "I think it's an animal."

I reached over and poked it with my finger. No reaction. I sniffed it. "It smells like a sheep." At last I picked it up. "It's not as heavy as it looks, and it's hollow inside."

"Is it a basket?" Ninsha asked.

I grimaced, gingerly put my hand inside, and felt around. "It's empty. Perhaps I'm supposed to carry it to dinner."

"Could it be something for your first night with your husband?"

"Mother told me a little of what to expect. She didn't mention a hairy object."

"Let's think about this," Ninsha said. "Could you wear it in any way?"

I mentally went through the parts of the body. There was only one part the hollow space would fit. I picked it up and put it on my head. "What do you think?"

"That can't be right. It looks ridiculous."

Satpa rushed into the room again. "It looks perfect. You didn't need any help with it after all." She left as quickly as she had come.

Ninsha and I looked at each other and broke into laughter.

§

Every head turned in my direction when I entered the torch-lit courtyard where the wedding feast was being held. Even the musicians stopped playing their harps. Satpa had led Ninsha to her place separately, so I had to endure the scrutiny alone.

King Hidar stood up. "Here, wife," he said grandly. "Your place is next to mine."

I edged around the people on stools and made my way to the daïs. I sat on the stool to my husband's left and looked over the sea of strange faces. I didn't see any of my father's soldiers, and I realized with a pang that in the rush when we arrived, Ninsha and I hadn't said goodbye to Za-mu.

As I scanned the guests, I wondered whether I'd ever learn all their names. Or understand the Mari fashions. The women wore their hair in two bulky bundles over their ears, and their robes had unfamiliar embroidery designs. *I must look as foreign to the guests as they look to me.*

Meanwhile, servants were distributing a small stoppered bottle to each diner. I picked up mine and pulled out the stopper, as others were doing. The scent of perfume wafted out. I closed it and set it to the side of the bowl.

Hidar put his spotted hand on mine. "We can't have anyone outshine you at your own wedding feast, can we? This is for you." He handed me a cloth-wrapped bundle, and I unwrapped it carefully. Inside was a beaded collar three fingers wide in which triangles of gold beads alternated with triangles of lapis lazuli beads. Hidar picked up the collar and fastened it about my neck. "Now you have jewelry befitting a queen."

"Thank you, my lord." I put my hand up to touch the collar. The beads were smoothly polished and felt cool to the touch. "It's beautiful."

Hidar puffed out his chest. But on his other side, Ishqi-Mari glowered at me.

I quickly turned my gaze away.

The woman on my left touched my arm. She was about my age, with full lips and body. "I'm Tamma, King Hidar's daughter."

"How odd to think you're my daughter now. I hope we'll be good friends."

"I hope so too. You must feel lost in this crowd. Let me introduce you to my grandmother here on my left, Azzu-eli." The ancient woman turned toward us when she heard her name. Her face was pinched like her grandson's but otherwise was elegant. "Grandmother, this is Esh-tar-da-ri, father's new wife."

"Please, call me Esh. My family did."

"We're your family now, child," the queen mother said reprovingly.

My heart twisted, and tears stung my eyes. I couldn't imagine ever feeling at home here. The king viewed me as a possession, and his son appeared to despise me. What I wouldn't have given to be back in Akkad with Father and Mani.

My mother-in-law peered at me. "Tomorrow, come sew with me."

Relief flooded through me. Perhaps we could be friends. "Thank you, Mother. I will."

"I'll come sew with you too," Tamma said. "Have you met my brother, Ishqi-Mari? He's on the other side of Father."

"Yes, I met him this afternoon." I paused then decided to trust her a little. "I don't think he approves of your father remarrying."

"He doesn't agree with most decisions Father makes. Pay him no mind."

I didn't think it was going to be that easy to avoid his ill feelings.

Tamma nodded her head toward a middle-aged man wearing a lot of gold. "That's Tu-ru-Dagan, Father's most trusted councilor. Beside him is Paila, the high priestess of Dagan."

I repeated the names in my head. "Thank you for your help. I think I'll have to learn the names a few at a time."

Hidar interrupted. "You two will have time to get to know each other later. Tonight I want my bride to myself. Now, my dear, I want to tell you all about Mari."

It became quickly evident that Hidar loved his city and knew its history well but was no storyteller. As we sat most of the evening, being served course after course with wine to wash it down and regularly being cheered and toasted, he told me about his reign and those of his predecessors.

The king excused himself once and left for a couple minutes. As I looked around the room, I caught Ishqi-Mari staring at me.

He frowned and said coldly and softly, "You better not get pregnant. My father doesn't need your brats."

Cold raced through me. Hidar returned, and I turned my attention back to him but found I could no longer follow the gist of what he was saying. Instead, I kept thinking about Ishqi-Mari's comment, which felt like a threat.

CHAPTER SIXTEEN

I dragged myself from the king's bedchamber back to my rooms the next morning. The men I passed in the hall smiled lewdly at me, and my face and ears flared with heat. I kept my gaze down and walked faster.

Ninsha was already up, dressed, and sewing in our main room. She held up the fabric. "I'm making you a new robe from the nicest linen in your dowry. Sit down and tell me all about your night."

"I'd rather forget about it." I gingerly lowered myself onto a stool. "He's not kind."

Ninsha took my hand. "Oh, Esh. Did he hurt you?"

"No more than needed for the task." I swallowed. "But there were no tender words, no questions about me. I could have been any woman." I yawned. "I didn't sleep well afterward."

"You can rest in here today. I'll be quiet."

"I can't. I'm supposed to sew with my mother-in-law. I need to wash up and put on a clean robe, if I have one."

"The ones that were laundered yesterday are back."

"Good. Did you want to sew with us? Someone needs to keep me awake." I went into the storage room to wash up at the basin.

"Yes, I'll go," she called. "I need to learn the Mari embroidery designs."

"Another thing, Ninsha." I lowered my voice. "My new son seems to hate me. At supper last night, when our eyes caught, Ishqi-Mari said, 'You better not get pregnant.'"

"That's horrifying." Ninsha came to the doorway, frowning. "Are you sure you heard him correctly? The room was noisy."

"I'm sure." I shuddered. Remembering his words chilled me through. "I don't feel safe here in Mari." I felt a twinge of homesickness. No one had threatened my life or my future child's life in Akkad.

☙

I asked Satpa how to find Azzu-eli's rooms and learned they opened to the same courtyard as ours did, as did Tamma's. Ninsha and I went across to join Azzu-eli and my new daughter Tamma in sewing. My mother-in-law's main room was spacious, and several oil lamps burned, providing extra light and the scent of meat.

"Mother," I said after the four of us had been chitchatting about minor things for a while, "I need help. I need to start managing the household. Would you please introduce me to the servants and tell me about the properties I'm to manage?"

"You don't need to worry about any of that. I'll continue to run the household. You work on getting pregnant."

My body tightened up, and I could hear my heartbeat in my ears. She had an established high status as the king's mother, and I was only a bride. Managing the household would bring me status. "That's kind of you to offer. But I'm the king's wife, and I must take up my official duties."

Azzu-eli's nostrils flared, and she set down her work. "I was a king's wife before your father was born. I will continue as I have since Tamma's mother died."

Tamma yawned and in an offhand way said, "Grandmother, you complain all the time about your workload. Here's your chance to get rid of it."

"No one can manage the household as well as I do," my mother-in-law said. "I'm not an old goat that can no longer give milk."

"I'm sure everyone appreciates your hard work," I said, "but I'm—"

Ninsha put her hand on my arm. I didn't know why she stopped me, but I trusted her judgment. "I'll think about what you said," I finished.

An uneasy silence prevailed. I racked my brain for something innocuous to say.

"Speaking of your expertise, Lady Azzu-eli," Ninsha said, "I wonder if you could show me some local embroidery designs." She held up the fabric. "I'm sewing Lady Esh a new robe."

Azzu-eli smiled haughtily. "Of course. And I'll have my servant Belizunu teach you how to style her hair in the proper manner."

ṭ

As soon as Ninsha and I returned to our rooms, I rounded on her. "Why did you stop me from insisting on my rights? I am determined to do my duty as a king's wife."

She set down her basket. "Of course you are. But she's a proud old lady. I think you need to approach her differently."

"I need to be more forceful. Make it clear she can't run the household anymore." I paced the room.

Ninsha sat on a stool. "I think it might work better to do the opposite. I think you should make her happy to get rid of these duties."

"Flattery, you mean. Or trickery."

"Not at all," Ninsha said. "Acknowledge how hard she's worked since the king's first wife died. Say that it's time for a well-deserved rest. Let her know that you'll need her expertise to help you get started."

I stopped pacing. "My admitting ignorance would give her another reason to insist on doing everything herself. But I have no status here unless I manage the household."

"You heard Tamma. Azzu-eli complains about how much work she does. She probably would be glad for you to take it over if she can keep her pride. And a softer approach means no hard feelings among the people we have to live with for years to come."

I sighed, my anger draining away. Ninsha was right: We needed to stay on good terms with the king's relatives or our lives here would be unpleasant and lonely. "I'm more used to giving orders than begging favors."

"I haven't had the luxury of being able to order people around," she said dryly. "I've had to figure out other ways to get what I want."

I sat down next to her. "You should tell me when you need something. I can always give an order on your behalf."

"That's not the point, Esh."

"I'm going to try your way tomorrow." I patted her hand. "For now, we need to get ready for the second night of the wedding banquet."

ॐ

During the first evening of the banquet, I had been too overwhelmed by the new sounds and sights and smells of Mari's palace to pay much attention to the food. The second night, I could enjoy the various dishes. Meltingly soft leeks. Tender goat in a stew. Several kinds of bread; my favorite bread contained cheese. Stewed goose. Dried fruits.

More people attended the banquet than had the previous night. I asked King Hidar to tell me who they were. He identified the priests and priestesses, the general of his army, leading citizens, and governors of towns under his rule, the last of whom had only arrived today. After the meal, the king had the guests presented to me, and I endured their scrutiny and accepted their presents as I tried to memorize their names and relationships.

Afterward, King Hidar tucked my hand into his arm and led me back to his bedchamber. Tonight I noticed the brazier in the middle of the room, his weapons in the corner, and the aromatic cedar bedstead. "I trust everything went well when you took up your new duties."

My stomach dropped. "Your mother wants to continue running the household."

"She's old and deserves to spend her days listening to music and walking in the gardens. You need to take over." His face hardened. "Your father assured me that you're not lazy."

"He spoke truly. Tomorrow I'll try again to get her to relinquish her duties."

"See that you get them." His words held a warning.

Softly, I asked, "Would you speak to her?"

"I don't involve myself in domestic matters. You must take care of it."

I dropped my gaze. "Yes, my king." *What would I do now?*

ॐ

The king's orders were the first thing in my mind when I woke up the next morning. I had to take over my duties as soon as possible.

When Satpa brought breakfast, I asked her to show Ninsha and me around the palace. I met the cooks, the bakers, the laundresses, the musicians, the barbers, the physician, and the jesters. I gave each their orders for the day and instructions for meeting with me each morning from now on. I still needed to talk with the craftspeople and the managers of the weaving facility and the farms, but I was pleased with my progress toward wresting my duties from Azzu-eli.

Ninsha kept her lips tightly pressed together on the tour, but when we were back in our rooms alone, she asked, "What are you doing? We discussed waiting just yesterday afternoon."

"The king gave me an order last night. He said I must take charge of my duties. It can't wait."

"At what cost to your relationship with Azzu-eli? You've forgotten everything we talked about."

I drew myself up to my full height. "I didn't forget. The king gave me an order. I have no choice. What else can I do?"

"Talk to Azzu-eli again."

"I can do that now." I pushed aside the door curtain and glanced out into the courtyard to see the angle of the sun. It was midmorning already. "Let's get our sewing. It's time to go."

"This won't be pleasant," she muttered under her breath, picking up her basket.

My chest was tight as I took up my own basket, and we walked across the bright courtyard to Azzu-eli's rooms, where Azzu-eli and Tamma already sat sewing.

Azzu-eli stood up when she saw me, her face an angry red. "What did you think you were doing, undermining my authority? All morning, servants were coming by to tell me you gave them orders."

"I had no choice. The king ordered me last night to relieve you of the tasks."

Azzu-eli put her hands on her hips. "He doesn't have the right. My son doesn't run the household; I do."

"I'm the king's wife. It's my responsibility. You know that."

She made a dismissive gesture with her hand. "Get out. I don't want to see you again."

My chest tightened even more. I saluted her, then Ninsha and I turned to go.

"Ninsha, you may stay," Azzu-eli said.

Ninsha sat on a stool and unpacked her sewing. I swallowed hard and returned to our rooms to fume.

CHAPTER SEVENTEEN

"Why did you desert me and stay with Azzu-eli?" I said when Ninsha returned that afternoon.

She set her basket down next to a stool. "I didn't desert you. You need a spy there. You'll be glad I stayed."

"I don't think so."

"I found out that the servants are loyal to her and won't follow your orders without her say-so. She also complained about managing the household, and each time, I mentioned that she didn't have to if she didn't want to. She called me impertinent, but I'm invited back tomorrow to sew."

"I'll be bored here by myself. Why don't you stay with me?"

"Now that you've been banished, I'm your only chance of convincing her to turn over your duties to you."

I clenched my jaw as I thought over her words. At last, I admitted, "You're right, Ninsha." I picked up the cat and stroked it, trying to calm myself. "What am I going to tell the king?"

"Don't tell him anything."

"He might ask."

"Rulers don't follow up. They assume people will do as ordered." She picked up her basket again and headed toward the door. "In case he does ask, lie."

❦

After the acrobats finished on the third night of the banquet, I went back to our rooms, thankful that the king did not desire my presence that night. Ninsha hadn't arrived yet, so by lamplight, sitting on the bed, I took down my own hair and combed it, reflecting on how strange it felt to wear it over my ears.

In the dim room, Inanna's sudden appearance half-blinded me. She shone the silver of the moon, and her arrows reflected the golden light of the lamp. Sweet smells wafted from her.

"Greetings, my lady." I stood and saluted her. "I'm so relieved to see you. I've been afraid of a lot of things here in Mari. I was even afraid you'd abandoned me."

"Never. You haven't needed my encouragement for a while."

I certainly needed it now. I toyed with the ends of my hair. "I haven't played my role here well. Now I'm in a pit of my own making, and I don't know how to climb out," I admitted. "I can't persuade my mother-in-law to turn the household duties over to me, and now she's forbidden me her rooms."

"Watch for your chance. Grab it when it comes. I've counseled the same before."

"What will my chance look like?"

"You'll know it when you see it." The goddess stroked my face, and I leaned into her cool hand. "I sense your despair. But you've only been in Mari a few days. Things will settle out soon. You're not as helpless as you feel."

I felt worse than helpless. I felt alone, despite having Ninsha with me, and trapped. "Can't you visit me more often?" My voice trembled.

"You are stronger than that, child. And I have battles to fight, taverns to visit, and lovers to encourage." Her form lost its substance and melted away.

☙

On the fourth night of the wedding banquet, Hidar drank heavily and was in a good mood. He described in detail how he had conquered Ebla, complete with how he had cut the heads off the leaders of the city.

I made appreciative noises. When he finished telling me about his conquest, I worked up my courage. "My lord, does Mari have a temple to Inanna?"

"No, I don't think we do. But we do have a large temple to Ishtar-Anunitum, the warrior aspect of Ishtar." Hidar knifed a chunk of venison and put it in his mouth. He took a long sip out of our shared beer pot.

I took a drink as well to wet my parched mouth. "May I ask a favor of you?" I asked, heart in my throat.

He looked at me with narrowed eyes. "What favor?"

"I would like to be a lay priestess at Ishtar's temple."

Hidar frowned. "You're a queen. You should be a high priestess, not a subordinate to the high priest, who ranks below you."

"I don't mind being a subordinate. I want to honor Ishtar."

"I'm pleased with your piety and love for the gods, but you should do nothing that diminishes your rank."

I dropped my head. "Yes, my lord."

Hidar turned toward Ishqi-Mari on his right, and I stared at nothing. My request had been for naught. Perhaps I should have listed reasons my being Ishtar's priestess would benefit Hidar. I needed to get to know my husband better before trying again. I needed to know how to move him.

Loud voices distracted me from my thoughts. Hidar and Ishqi-Mari were arguing.

Ishqi-Mari brought his fist down on his table. "I want a bride now, not later."

"Don't be in such a hurry. You're still young."

"I'm old enough to be a man and have a wife. Old enough to sire heirs."

"Don't worry about heirs now. I'm planning to live a long time and enjoy my young wife."

My face heated. Although I wasn't hungry, I started eating my food so Hidar wouldn't notice I was eavesdropping.

"Accidents can happen," Ishqi-Mari said.

Goosebumps popped up on my arms.

Hidar pushed back his chair and stood. "Are you threatening me?"

There was a frightening pause. "No, Father. I'm just pointing out the obvious."

"Be patient. I've married off most of your sisters, but I need to find a husband for Tamma. She's already sixteen. Once she's married, I intend to find a bride for you."

"Yes, Father," Ishqi-Mari muttered. He kicked his stool back and left the room.

CHAPTER EIGHTEEN

Azzu-eli sent her servant to fetch me late the next morning. As I followed the servant across the cool courtyard, my stomach twisting, I wondered why I had been sent for. I had thought she no longer wanted anything to do with me. When I entered Azzu-eli's room, I found her alone with Ishqi-Mari.

"Please repeat what you just told me," Azzu-eli said. Her severe face showed no emotion.

Ishqi-Mari's gaze danced between Azzu-eli and me. He cleared his throat. "The servants are complaining about Esh-tar-da-ri. They say that she makes bad decisions, isn't in her rooms when they arrive for instructions, and shouts at the staff. Grandmother, you should talk to the king about these problems."

I felt like laughing at his obvious lies until I realized he might be telling them to the king or people around him who didn't know better. I maintained as serious a face as Azzu-eli. "What surprising complaints."

"Grandmother, you should talk to the king," he repeated.

"I'll take appropriate action," she said. "You may go now, grandson." He walked out of the room with a confident stride.

He thinks he's sabotaged me. But instead, Azzu-eli knows the truth.

Azzu-eli turned to me. "So you've made an enemy of your son already."

I refused to drop my head. "He seems not to approve of his father remarrying."

"Your marriage makes good political sense for Mari. We need Akkad as an ally. I don't know why my grandson doesn't see that."

I picked at the fabric of my robe. "I wonder whether he fears my future sons as competition."

"Or maybe he thinks you should have been *his* bride. The minds of young men are hard to understand. Please sit down, Esh."

I took a rattan stool near her and dared to speak honestly. "I don't know how to protect myself from him."

"I will be your protector. I'd like you to come sew in the afternoons with me sometimes."

A weight fell off my shoulders, and I leaned toward her. "Thank you, Mother. But why have you changed your mind?"

"Ishqi-Mari's complaints about you reminded me that I was once a new bride here, alone and friendless. There were those who tried to undermine me at first." She lowered her chin. "I know what you're going through."

Here was the opportunity Inanna had told me to seize, this moment of honesty and sympathy. But I let the chance to ask her to relinquish the household duties pass by. I needed her as an ally in this hostile household.

☙

Four busy months passed before I realized I hadn't written to anyone in Akkad. I found Satpa and asked her to take me to the scribes' workshop. She led me through the palace to a pleasant courtyard with several potted trees. It was a late spring day, and the sweltering heat was oppressive. Yet three scribes knelt on woven reed mats in the shade and copied documents. All wore skirts of linen; two had beards and one was bare-faced and bare-headed like a Sumerian. I had met them already, early on.

The scribes jumped to their feet and saluted. "How may we help you, Queen Esh-tar-da-ri?" asked the oldest of the men, the beardless one, Gig-be.

Hearing his accent, I switched to Sumerian. "I'm in need of prepared tablets and reeds."

Gigbe said, "We do all the writing in the palace."

"I need to write some letters."

He scratched his chin. "Previous queens dictated their letters to me."

"Perhaps they couldn't read and write. Since I can, I'd rather write my letters myself and not take up your time."

"My lady, I'm sending our apprentice out tomorrow to collect clay from the river bank. We can make your tablets and reeds afterward and take them to your quarters. Is that soon enough?"

"Thank you. That will be satisfactory."

He saluted me. "I need to write up a requisition form." He set aside the tablet he had been working on and took a fresh one out of a pot. As I stood in the heat of the sun, Gigbe filled the tablet with characters and then handed it to me.

I read over the document and then rolled my cylinder seal across the bottom. I handed it back to the scribe, and he rolled his seal beneath. "You'll have your tablets and reeds tomorrow."

The next afternoon, Ninsha and I came back from Azzu-eli's quarters to find a basket waiting in our doorway. I took off the cloth covering it and saw fresh clay tablets inside. "Now I can write to my father and Kalki," I said.

"I wonder how Kalki is." Ninsha set down the basket with her sewing and sat on a stool. "I miss him, and I miss our lessons too."

"I do as well. And I miss my father terribly."

"Are you going to write in here or in the courtyard?"

"Here. It's cooler and more private." I put the basket next to a stool and sat down. The cat immediately jumped on my lap, and I had to put him on the floor, where he acted affronted. I took a tablet and a reed from the basket and set them on my knee. I had studied the tablet Kalki gave us with the sample letter, but I had to think for a moment to remember the scheme.

From Esh-tar-da-ri, Queen of Mari, to her father and lord, King Sargon, king of Akkad. May the gods Ilaba and Inanna keep you forever in good health! On our way here, the king and queen of Sippar were eager hosts and expressed their loyalty to you. We were attacked by bandits, but your soldiers, led by Za-mu, protected us and killed them. Mari is larger than Akkad, with a circular wall around the city and wide, straight streets inside. Our marriage banquet lasted several nights and had fifty people in attendance. The king presented me with a beaded collar of gold and lapis lazuli. Despite my months in Mari, I have not yet settled into my place here. However, Queen Mother Azzu-eli has made us welcome. We often sew with her and my new daughter Tamma. My husband is an old man. I sense that his son, Ishqi-Mari, is discontent and eager to replace him. They quarrel. Ishqi-Mari has tried to undermine me. Ishtar-Anunitum is worshipped here, but my husband forbids me to be her priestess. Please let me know, whom in Mari can I trust?

I rolled my seal across the bottom and set the tablet aside on a reed mat to dry. I would set it out in the sunshine the next day while I inquired whether any traveling merchants were going to Akkad. My father must have spies besides me here, and they would be the safest people to help me dispatch my letter. But I didn't know who they were or whether they would risk exposing themselves.

The light was dimming, and I went into the courtyard to tell Satpa to bring us two lamps.

Once she had, I wrote a letter to Kalki in Sumerian while Ninsha, squinting, continued her sewing by lamplight. I rolled my seal across the bottom of the tablet and then read both letters aloud to Ninsha.

"The letter to your father could be dangerous for us if someone reads it. Imagine what mischief Ishqi-Mari could make if he saw it."

"I need to find someone trustworthy to carry these letters to Akkad." I went to the door and called for Satpa, who came quickly. "Satpa, where do merchants stay while they're in Mari?"

"There's a caravanserai outside the north gate."

"Tomorrow morning, you'll take us there."

She wrung her hands and spoke to the floor. "Tomorrow I wash the royal linens. Queen Azzu-eli orders it."

It was clearly an excuse. The palace had laundresses to do laundry, and they weren't frail things like Satpa. "Then find another servant to guide us."

97

"We're all washing laundry," she said quickly. "Lots of laundry."

"Even the guards and the scribes?"

"They, uh, they have something else to do."

"The morning after, then. We'll expect you early."

"I can't then, either."

"What aren't you telling us?" Ninsha asked.

Satpa dragged her toe across the floor. "We're not supposed to let you out of the courtyard."

I exchanged a glance with Ninsha. "Who gave you those orders?"

"I can't tell you."

"Was it the king?" I asked.

"No."

"As queen, I outrank everyone in the palace except the king and his mother. That means if I command something, it takes precedence over what anyone else tells you. Do you understand?"

"But...does that still hold now that you're going back to Akkad?"

Heat rushed through my body. Someone was spreading rumors about me. "I'm not going back to Akkad. Whoever told you otherwise was lying."

"Oh." Satpa burst into tears. "But if I don't do what he says, he'll hurt me."

Ninsha stood and offered Satpa her chair. She fetched the servant a mug of water.

I had an idea who had threatened her. "Was it King Hidar's son, Ishqi-Mari?"

Her eyes widened. "Ishqi-Mari's servant. How did you know?"

"We don't want you to be hurt," Ninsha said.

"But we don't want to be trapped here either," I added. "Can you arrange to be busy tomorrow morning with Azzu-eli or Tamma?"

Ninsha's mouth fell open. "You don't mean for us to go to the caravanserai by ourselves, do you?"

Satpa wiped her eyes with her hand. "I do have to help with the laundry tomorrow. Two of the laundresses are sick."

"Ninsha, we'll slip out tomorrow morning and find a guard to go with us," I said. "Get a ring of silver from my bride price."

Satpa said, "My lady, did you know you already have two guards assigned to you? They were transferred from Ishqi-Mari when you first came."

I clenched my fists. They should have reported to me months ago.

Ninsha put her hands on her hips. "We haven't seen them. They certainly haven't earned their keep."

I sighed in exasperation. I might be queen, but no one seemed inclined to help me make Mari my home. "Satpa, take a message to our guards. Tell them to report here early tomorrow morning."

CHAPTER NINETEEN

One guard—Asqudum, who was tall and skinny—walked in front of Ninsha and me, and the other guard—Bad-su-bad, who was short and on the plump side—walked behind us. We moved single file through the busy city on a pleasant morning. I kept a sharp eye on the two overdue guards, but I could find no fault with their behavior.

The cool breeze on the warm morning kept us feeling alternately too cool and too warm. This was my first look at Mari since the day we arrived, when I was too tired to notice much.

Not only was Mari bigger than Akkad but it also seemed to have more of everything—more people in the streets, more shops, more places to get ready-made food, more temples, more markets and bakeries. The shops displayed luxury products from distant places: ivory and pearls from Meluhha, carnelian from Dilmun, and chlorite beads and vessels from Elam, among others. Birds in cages sang rival tunes, interrupted by the occasional bray of a donkey. Sacrificial animals huddled together in pens.

We could not get a good look at the shops, though, because our silent guards walked fast. Asqudum had excused their long absence by saying that Ishqi-Mari had still needed them. Ninsha and I had exchanged glances at this news, and we looked at each other again when they made a sixth turn in this city laid out in a grid.

Ninsha shifted the cloth-covered bundle of letters on her hip. "You're queen of a rich city."

"I knew Mari was a crossroads of trade routes, but even so my imagination had not stretched so far."

"Once we get settled, it would be fun to walk around the city at a slower pace."

"And I'd like to go to the temple of Ishtar-Anunitum soon and pray for my father's success in battle. We'll need a sacrifice-worthy sheep."

"That looks easy enough to find."

We were in a neighborhood of small houses now, with few shops or temples. It was a relief from the hubbub of the commercial streets, but a little suspicious—usually city gates are on a major street. Somewhere nearby, bread was baking, and my stomach rumbled. Then I saw the bakery up ahead.

"Guards! We'll stop at the bakery."

Ninsha and I stepped into the house. Arrayed before us on a table were several kinds of bread, flat and risen, dark and light, barley and wheat. I chose a flatbread with pieces of dates in it, and Ninsha chose some light, fluffy rolls. I cut off a small piece of silver and gave it to the baker, and we exited the house.

The street was empty.

"Bad-su-bad! Asqudum!" I shouted, but the only response was that a woman came out of her house to shake her fist at us.

Ninsha stamped her foot. "I thought it a bad omen that they formerly worked for Ishqi-Mari."

"We should wait here. They may have gone to get something to eat or drink."

Ninsha looked at me with an expression approaching pity. "I doubt it, Esh. They would have told us. Now we have to find our way home on our own."

I took a deep breath. "No clouds obscure the sky. The sun will tell us which way north is. We should be able to bumble our way to the north gate and then to the caravanserai."

"The sun won't keep us away from the taverns and other places of ill repute."

I linked elbows with her. "Come. Don't grumble. Let's eat our bread and head east until we find a major road."

"If we get murdered, it's your fault."

"We won't get murdered. We'll have an exciting adventure." Despite my brave words, my heart was racing. I wiped a drop of sweat from my forehead and told myself it was because I wore the tall felt hat of the royal women of Mari.

101

Like gerbils, we crept along the walls of the houses in the shade, peeping around corners before we crossed an intersection. After a short time, we reached a main street, and I breathed a sigh of relief even as we plunged into the noise and smells of humanity.

"You beautiful women look lost." A man thrust himself in front of us, standing too close and blocking our way. His breath reeked of cheap beer. "I'll help you."

"For silver, no doubt." Ninsha's voice was tart, but because of our clasped arms, I could feel her shaking.

The man shrugged. "You have it. I need it."

"You're not going to get any from us," I said. "Now stand aside."

He closed the distance between us. His flesh pressed against mine, and I flinched. Clearly he had no idea who I was, despite my distinctive hat, but if I told him, he might decide to kidnap us for ransom.

He grabbed Ninsha and me by the arms in a painfully tight grip and started pulling us toward an alley.

Ninsha screamed.

My heart raced, and my knees felt wobbly, as if they couldn't hold me up. I shouted "Help!" but it came out as a squeak. I tried to pull away, but he was too strong. We were going to be robbed and probably raped or beaten, and there was nothing we could do.

"Let them go!" a man's voice ordered.

"Get your own women," our captor rasped. "These are mine."

"The king of Akkad charged me with protecting them. Release them."

I turned to look at our would-be savior. "Za-mu!" Hope blossomed in my chest.

"We have our own king here."

Za-mu's fist crashed into our abductor's face, who bellowed and let go of our arms to cradle his nose.

I shoved Ninsha out of his reach and scrambled behind Za-mu. Now, at last, some passersby stopped.

Za-mu pulled his knife. "Get out of here! Now!"

Our captor glared up at Za-mu, his face tight and red. "You better hope I don't see you again." He pushed his way through the crowd.

Za-mu turned toward us. "Are you hurt, my queen, my lady?"

102

"We thought you were in Akkad," I said, rubbing my arm where it had been squeezed. "What are you doing here? And please call us 'Esh' and 'Ninsha.'"

He gestured for us to follow him to the alley. "I'm keeping an eye on things in Mari for your father," he said softly.

"You're a spy," Ninsha whispered.

"What are you two doing wandering the city without guards?"

"We had guards," I said, "but they abandoned us. We're on our way to the caravanserai to find someone to carry some letters to Akkad."

"Give me your letters. I have couriers who go back and forth from the palace in Akkad."

Ninsha glanced at me for confirmation then handed Za-mu the tablets.

"From now on, give your letters to the cook Bel-i-a-mi, and he'll get them to me. Now I need to make sure you get back to the palace safely. This way."

We turned to follow him back to the main street. "We're so glad to see you," I said. "We never got to say 'goodbye' or 'thank you' after we arrived here. Thank you for rescuing us today as well."

"Thank you," Ninsha echoed.

"How is it being a queen?" he asked.

I shrugged my shoulders. "Lonely. Boring. Sometimes scary, like today. At least Ninsha and I have each other."

"Being a spy is lonely and boring most of the time, too."

"And exciting the rest of the time?" Ninsha asked.

"As my cover, I pretend to be a scribe, and I write letters and petitions for people. It's a good way to hear gossip. Today was the first day with excitement."

"You should come visit us at the palace," Ninsha said.

"That's not a good idea. People might guess I'm more than a scribe. In fact, I should leave you now before someone sees me with you. The palace is two blocks farther up this street."

Ninsha's face dropped. "We've barely said hello, and now it's time to say goodbye, maybe forever."

"You'll make friends here soon." He turned and went the other way down the street. Just before he disappeared, he turned around to look at Ninsha and caught us watching him.

103

When Ninsha and I entered the foyer of the palace, the chief councilor was headed out. "Good morning, Tu-ru-Dagan." I saluted him and then stopped short at his look of astonishment.

"What are you doing here?" he asked.

Now it was my turn to be surprised. "Where else would I be?"

He stroked his beard. "Most of the guards are out looking for you. The king told me that you ran away."

"He did?" I was shocked for a moment then pretended outrage. "We went out to run an errand."

"If I may make a recommendation, my queen—go to the king right away and let him know you're back."

"Yes, I will. Thank you."

Ninsha and I hurried our steps.

"You're back!" King Hidar rose from his chair.

"Councilor Tu-ru-Dagan told us a strange story, that we had run away and that you had guards searching for us. My lord, we went on an errand."

"An errand? Your guards came back and told a different story."

"Bad-su-bad and Asqudum deserve to be punished. They got us lost and then abandoned us. We were accosted by a thief. We were lucky to find our way home."

"Those two have worked in the palace for years. I can't believe they lied."

I kept my voice level and soft. "If I may be so bold, my lord, the guards were previously assigned to Ishqi-Mari. Perhaps he is playing a joke on me. Or on the staff." I kept quiet about the possibility that the target of any "joke" was Hidar himself. "In any case, I would like new guards."

His lips pursed and he leaned back in his chair. "My son is not known for the best judgment. I'll talk to him. In the future, let your servants run your errands."

"Yes, my lord."

"You'll come to supper tonight. I'll send a servant for you. You're dismissed for now."

"Yes, my lord." I left the room and rejoined Ninsha, who waited outside with the king's cupbearer. "The guards who abandoned us came back here and told lies. I've informed the king of the truth." I purposely spoke loudly enough for the nearby servants to hear. They might prefer the more interesting story that we ran away, but perhaps some would spread what really happened.

We started walking toward our rooms. "What a morning!" Ninsha said. "I'm looking forward to a nice, quiet afternoon of sewing."

"I'm having supper with the king tonight. Do you think it's too early to bring up being a priestess of Ishtar-Anunitum again?"

"Probably not. But wait until he has had some wine to do so."

CHAPTER TWENTY

The sun was low when King Hidar's servant came to get me. I was glad; no matter where we ate, we would be out of the hot sun of late spring. The servant led me to the courtyard where the wedding feast had taken place. This time, only a decorated wooden chair for the king and a rattan stool for me as well as two low tables with a beer jug between them occupied the space. I stood next to my stool, waiting for the king. We would be alone except for the harpist in the corner, who was singing a hymn to the king.

King Hidar arrived soon afterward, his beard newly trimmed. I saluted him. After he sat down, he gestured to me to sit down. "How are you, my dear?"

"I'm well, my king. And you?"

"Healthy as a bull." He puffed out his chest.

Servants began carrying out the food and placing it on the tables. I took a sip from the beer jar and tasted that it was sweetened by honey. We ate silently—lamb in beet broth and beer, leavened barley bread, spiced cheeses, and dried dates. Everything was delicious. For the first time, I was able to see the walls of the courtyard and their frescos of battles, with Hidar himself prominently depicted killing enemy warriors.

After the meal, King Hidar cleared his throat. "I'm relieved that you didn't run away, that the story was a misunderstanding."

"My king, I wouldn't leave Mari. I'm Sargon's daughter and guarantor of peace between our kingdoms."

"Before you returned, I wondered to myself why you would leave. I realized that I haven't been doing my duty often enough. I'm sure you're eager for a child, so I'll have you brought to my bed more often."

"Yes, my lord." A child would strengthen the peace between Mari and Akkad. Still, Hidar remained old and ugly, and I had been relieved to visit his bed infrequently. Now that situation would change.

"My dear, I also have a surprise for you. I know you are pious and were disappointed that I wouldn't let you become a priestess of Ishtar-Anunitum."

I felt light enough to rise up into the sky above. "You've changed your mind? Oh, thank you, my lord! I am so grateful."

Hidar frowned. "You've misunderstood. I haven't changed my mind. I'm making you high priestess of Shamash, the sun god. The position is elevated enough for my queen."

"Pardon me?"

"You're going to be Shamash's high priestess at His temple."

I grabbed the sides of the stool to steady myself. Breathe, I told myself. I forced a smile. "Thank you, my lord. I will be diligent in my duties."

I worshipped Shamash occasionally, of course, but He wasn't my patron god; Inanna was. Being Shamash's high priestess would be a time-consuming task. The time I would need to spend on my duties at His temple would cut into the time I could spend honoring Inanna in her guise of Ishtar-Anunitum. "When will I be invested?"

"In seven or eight days."

"Father, I need to—" Ishqi-Mari strode into the courtyard and stopped dead when he saw me. His eyes turned as cold as stones. "You've returned," he said flatly.

"She didn't leave us. She was running errands with her servant."

"I see." Ishqi-Mari continued to stare at me.

Hidar added, "Whatever you've come to see me about, it will have to wait until tomorrow."

Ishqi-Mari's gaze turned toward Hidar. "It's important, Father."

"Not as important as my spending time with my wife. I'll see you first thing tomorrow."

Ishqi-Mari's color heightened, and he spun and stalked out.

Hidar didn't watch him go but kept his eyes on me. He stroked my cheek. "And now, my dear, to bed, as I promised you."

☙

I slept late the next morning, and Ninsha was gone, as well as her sewing basket, when I got back to our rooms. I wished Inanna would appear. I was now firmly on a course counter to what She wanted. After rinsing my face and hands, I picked up my sewing basket and went across the courtyard to Azzu-eli's rooms. Ninsha and Tamma were animatedly discussing their favorite breads while Azzu-eli sat white-faced and silent, listening to them. Red spots decorated each of her cheeks.

I walked to her side. "Mother, are you ill?" Her hands were trembling.

"No, of course not." She lifted her head to an arrogant tilt.

"Ninsha and I can leave if you like." I wasn't in the mood for sewing anyway.

"Stay! I told you, I'm not sick."

"Yes, Mother."

"What's this about your running away?" my mother-in-law asked.

"A ridiculous rumor. We ran an errand."

"Rumors tend to spread quickly in the palace," Tamma said.

I sat on a stool and pulled a length of linen from my basket. I planned to hem it for a diaper for my future firstborn. It was a fine, tightly woven linen that would be absorbent. I couldn't help but sigh; I was still disappointed about the previous night's surprises.

Ninsha looked over at me. "Any news?"

"I'm to be high priestess of Shamash," I said woodenly, trying to keep the disappointment out of my voice. "My investiture is in seven days."

"Try to sound a little happier," Azzu-eli said. "You've been given a great honor. Although I'm not sure how my son thinks you can handle those duties when you have so many here."

"Mother, what duties here?"

"Why, managing the servants and the household, managing the weaving shed, and dealing with our estates outside the city."

Those were certainly my responsibilities, but ones she did and refused to give up. I took a breath to calm my voice. "Mother, you handle all of those tasks."

"I'm thinking of giving them over to you." She paused for a breath. "Someday."

I wondered whether I should press Azzu-eli to stop usurping my responsibilities now. Again it seemed the wrong time. *I should be content for now with today's concession that she will turn them over someday.*

Azzu-eli coughed, and the cough wracked her body. When she finished, her face was red with exertion. She drooped on her stool.

I stood and motioned to Ninsha. "Mother, Ninsha and I are leaving so that you can rest. We hope you feel better soon."

"I'm fine," she insisted then lapsed into a coughing spell.

☙

A frowning Satpa came to me early the next morning with a message from Azzu-eli. "The queen mother will not be receiving visitors today."

Her cough the previous day came immediately to mind. "Is she sick?"

"She says she's not. But she's lying in bed looking pale."

"Is anyone else sick that you know of?" In the crowded quarters of a palace, illness could spread easily and fast.

"Two of her servants."

"Who's taking care of them?"

Satpa answered that one of the queen mother's servants, Belizunu, wasn't sick.

Ninsha's eyebrows drew together. "That's a load for one person."

"You're right," I said. "We and Satpa will have to help out. We also need to prevent transmitting the illness elsewhere in the palace." I turned to Satpa. "First, set some servants at the entrance to the courtyard and don't let anyone in or out."

Satpa wrung her hands. "What will we do for food?"

"Have the servants set the food down at the entrance to the courtyard, and our servants here will distribute it."

109

Ninsha spoke up. "We need to alert the cooks to prepare broth and porridge for the sick ones."

"I haven't been around Azzu-eli," Satpa said.

"Then let the cooks know and also tell the king's cupbearer that the king's mother is ill and that I'll tend her. I will alert Tamma."

"I already told Tamma." Satpa's face twisted with worry. "Are we going to get sick too?"

"As the gods will," I said. "But we should pray and stay as far away from the sick ones as we can and still care for them."

We sent Satpa off for our last contact with the outside world and went to Azzu-eli's rooms. We found her in bed and the sick servants curled up on pallets on the floor. The room already smelled of sickness and sweat. Belizunu held a wet linen cloth to Azzu-eli's forehead.

I explained to her the measures I had put into place, and she sagged against the wall in relief. I sent her to rest and took over holding the cool cloth to the queen mother's head while Ninsha did the same for the two servants. Satpa returned from her errands and fetched a pitcher of cool water. When food arrived, we helped the three patients sit up and spooned broth into their mouths. The servants seemed not fully aware of their surroundings, but Azzu-eli held my gaze and croaked a request for beer. Ninsha and I murmured prayers to Bau, the Sumerian goddess of healing.

As the day wore on, Belizunu returned, and she and Satpa took care of the two sick servants. Ninsha and I split the care of Azzu-eli. The queen mother remained thirsty, and we needed to refill the pitcher of water several times. Supper came, and again we fed the sick.

As I spooned porridge into Azzu-eli, she grasped my arm. "No one...giving...orders. You must."

"Don't worry, Mother, I'll take over management of the household. But I won't relinquish my duties when you are well."

"Won't be well."

"Ninsha and I are taking care of you. You'll be well again soon if you eat your broth and porridge."

"Tamma?"

"Staying safe in her room, I hope. We can't all be sick at once."

The queen relaxed into my arm and swallowed the porridge I fed her.

Despite my orders that no one come in or go out of the courtyard, an ashipu priest and an asu doctor whose assistant carried a basket of remedies arrived to see the sick queen mother.

"The king sent us," the asu doctor said. "How long has the queen mother been sick?"

"Since yesterday," I said, relieved that the king had sent his physician and summoned a priest from a temple.

The asu turned to Azzu-eli and asked about her symptoms.

The ashipu priest stood close, watching and listening.

"I have a headache and I keep coughing. Also, my throat is sore and I'm tired," Azzu-eli said feebly.

The asu doctor rummaged in his basket, pulled out a tiny cloth bundle, and said to her, "My lady, you have been touched by the hand of the god Shamash. You must repent the sin that angered the god." Then he turned to me and handed me the bundle, which smelled of thyme. "Make an infusion of these herbs and make her drink it four times a day. If she repents, the herbs will heal her. Also make her drink beer for nourishment." He motioned to his assistant, and they left the room.

The ashipu priest stepped forward to the bed. He felt Azzu-eli's forehead and the place in the wrist that pulses, and he looked in her mouth and ears. "My queen, who is your patron god?"

"Ninhursag, the lady of the mountains," Azzu-eli rasped.

"I agree with the asu that you have been touched by Shamash. You must confess how you have sinned against the god."

Her gaze darted to me and back to the ashipu healer. "I don't know."

"You have hurt or offended no person in Shamash's favor?"

The queen mother looked away. "My son's wife. She will be the new high priestess of Shamash. I prevented her from doing her duties in this household."

"Do you repent?"

"Yes."

The ashipu priest lay his hands on her and recited a long prayer to Shamash. When he finished, he chanted a long incantation to expel the demon that had made her sick. Then he turned to me. "When she is well, she must sacrifice a ram to Shamash."

"I will see that it is done."

111

CHAPTER TWENTY-ONE

The next several days passed as one, with Ninsha and I constantly in the sickroom mopping foreheads, infusing herbs, and encouraging Azzu-eli to recite the chant. We lost all sense of time and season. The room took on a resiny scent from the herbs. Ninsha and I remained healthy, as did Satpa, but all three of us felt dazed. Belizunu came down sick as well, and after that the work load increased for the rest of us. I also had to give orders to the servants every morning and, once, talk to the accountant.

One evening, I fainted in the sickroom. I wasn't sick; I had skipped some meals for lack of time. But Ninsha, taking her duty to me seriously, insisted that I go back to our rooms and rest. I went back and lay down but couldn't get to sleep. So I got up, wondering how many days were left before I became Shamash's high priestess and lost hope forever of being a priestess of Inanna in any of her guises. I looked in the basket of tablets. Despite my neglect, the remaining one was still damp, and I put it on my lap and picked up the stylus. My cultic and household duties would keep me busy, and this might be my last chance to write a hymn to Inanna. I had been waiting to be consecrated as a priestess in Her temple first, but now I feared that would never happen.

I looked at the tablet and thought how easy it would be to praise Shamash and his jurisdictions. He rose each morning to shine His light on the world. He dispensed justice. He protected soldiers, sailors, merchants, and travelers, all those who had cause to leave their home city.

His twin, Inanna, was a different story. In some sense, everything and its opposite were in her purview. She was not limited as the other gods were to a small list of attributes. She flouted the rules and caused humans to do so as well. I felt overwhelmed by the task of reducing her and her attributes to a few lines. But slowly I began to prick out some characters, focusing on her aspect as Ishtar-Anunitum.

Queen of Heaven astride Your lion,
Arrows in Your quiver, bow at the ready,
Chaos is in Your eye.
Your lips sing war.
Storm clouds clothe you,
The winds do Your bidding,
The thunder is Your drum.
Hail Inanna! Praise be to the Queen of Heaven.

When I finished the hymn, I sang it softly for the goddess. Then I lay back down on my bed and cried for my future that had been destined, yet denied.

I woke up in my bed, refreshed but chastising myself for leaving Ninsha and Satpa to care for the sick all night. As I patted my hair into some semblance of order, a messenger arrived from the king. He was putting off my investiture as Shamash's en-priestess another seven days so that I could continue caring for Azzu-eli.

I exhaled a sigh of relief. I had time, at least, to start to pack away my sorrow and gather my courage for a future so far from what I expected and wanted.

I went out to the entrance to the courtyard, where already servants gathered to hear their orders for the day. For safety's sake, I stood well back from them while giving them their instructions. Then I went to Azzu-eli's room. She was visibly better, but Ninsha looked exhausted. After asking whether Azzu-eli had already drunk her herbal infusion, I sent Ninsha and Satpa to our room to get some sleep.

"Mother, you look much better today. Are you feeling better?"

"I'm fine. I don't need you girls in here fussing about." Her voice was strong but still a little raspy.

"I'm glad to hear that. Just let me see you walk."

She swung one leg out of bed, took a rest, and then swung the other leg out. She pushed off from the bed and wobbled on shaking legs. She tried to take a step but lost her balance. She would have ended up on the floor if I hadn't caught her. I helped her to sit on the bed.

"Mother, perhaps you need a little more time to get your strength back."

"There are things I need to do."

"I've taken charge of the household. The only thing you need to do is get well."

A man shouted in the courtyard. Then he pushed aside the door curtain and came into Azzu-eli's room. It was Ishqi-Mari. "What fool gave orders that I couldn't see my grandmother?"

I turned toward him. "Her illness is contagious. I gave instructions that no one leave the courtyard and no one come in."

"I am the king's son. You can't keep me out."

"Yes, I see."

"Now where's my grandmother?"

I stepped away from the bed so he could see her behind me.

He walked to her and grasped her hands gently. "I only just heard that you are sick."

As they talked, I went over to check on Belizunu and the other servants. They still looked sick and had trouble keeping their eyes open. I poured water from a pitcher into a cup and urged each one to drink. Now that Azzu-eli was better, perhaps I should move these three into the courtyard to finish getting well. It would be easier to attend them without annoying the queen mother. I went to the doorway and looked out to see where they would be least in the way.

"Grandmother fell asleep," Ishqi-Mari said close behind me.

I jumped.

"She says you took care of her while she was sick."

I turned around and backed away. "Yes, of course I did."

"I'll hold you responsible if she doesn't get well."

"She'll get well. She's doing much better today than she was."

"Make sure of it." He strode past me out of the room, his arm brushing mine.

Although his arm was warm, a chill ran through me, and I was glad Azzu-eli would soon be well. The fewer the encounters with Ishqi-Mari, the happier I would be.

☙

Ninsha and I were up early seven mornings later to ready me for my investiture as high priestess of Shamash. The sun was shining, and I could tell that before noon it would be scorching. Today would be full of rituals, starting with purification ceremonies and ending, finally, in a meeting with the god Himself. I was worried about making a misstep, and, as Ninsha dressed my hair, I fussed with the edges of my robe.

Satpa, carrying a pitcher of water, slid into our room between the curtain's edge and the doorway. She went into the storeroom, set the pitcher down, and motioned for us to join her. We did.

"What's going on, Satpa?" I asked.

"My lady, speak softly." She moved closer to me. "There are two palace guards outside your rooms. Bad-su-bad and Asqudum."

My stomach turned over. "The ones who got us lost and deserted us." The ones whose loyalty seemed to belong to Ishqi-Mari.

"It's not just you," Satpa said. "There are also guards outside the doors of Azzu-eli's and Tamma's rooms."

Ninsha grabbed my arm and spoke in a trembling voice. "Are we prisoners or are we under protection?"

"I don't know," Satpa said. "Your guards let me come in without any questions."

"I'm going to find out." I pulled free of Ninsha and headed toward the door. I pulled back the curtain and walked out.

The guards crossed their spears in front of me. "You can't leave," Asqudum said roughly, smirking.

I swallowed. "I am the queen. Today I become the high priestess of Shamash. I can go where I want."

The spears stayed crossed. "Not today, you can't," Asqudum said.

"On whose orders?"

"Ishqi-Mari's."

"My orders take precedence over his."

"Not anymore. Now get back inside."

115

I slunk back into our rooms and pulled the curtain across the doorway as wide as it would go. I rejoined Ninsha and Satpa in the storage room. "They stopped me from leaving. Ishqi-Mari's orders."

Ninsha wrapped her arms around herself and dropped her head. "We're trapped."

That wasn't the worst of it. "And we don't know why or for how long. I need to see King Hidar."

"But we can't get out." Ninsha's voice was unsteady.

"I need to think," I said. "Meanwhile, we don't need to huddle in the storeroom." I went into the other room, picked up my sewing basket, and sat on the bed. I took out a sheet and continued hemming it.

Ninsha joined me with her own sewing, and Satpa lit a couple more oil lamps before sitting on a stool. The smell of cooking meat filled the room.

Ninsha picked up her needle, colored threads, and fabric then set them down again. "Will we get lunch? What do you think is going on?"

I kept sewing. "I thought maybe Ishqi-Mari wanted to disrupt my becoming high priestess of Shamash today. But that wouldn't explain why he has his grandmother and sister under guard too. Satpa, did you notice anything else strange this morning?"

"No, nothing," Satpa said. She twisted her hands in her lap then got up and walked about the room.

I focused on my sewing, trying to let the repetition of stitching calm my beating heart and frantic mind.

After a while, Ninsha looked up at the servant. "Satpa, hold this robe up in front of you. I want to see how the tassels hang before I attach any more."

Satpa did as instructed. She brought her hand up to the bodice and stroked the embroidery.

I smiled at her enjoyment. "You look like a princess." My eyes widened as my own words echoed through my head. "That's it!" I whispered.

"What?" Ninsha asked.

"Satpa and I will change clothes. You will do her hair up like mine and mine like hers. As a servant, I can leave and find the king. Meanwhile, if the guards look in, they'll see two princesses sewing."

Ninsha looked doubtful. "What if the guards recognize you?"

116

"Then they won't let me leave, and we won't be any worse off than we are now."

Satpa and I traded clothes. I tugged her robe down, not used to having so much of my legs revealed. "What do you think, Ninsha?"

"Give Satpa your necklace and earrings, and hide your amulet under your robe." She tilted her head and looked at us critically. "Esh, if you want to pass for a servant, you'll need to stand like one. Lower your head, and hunch your shoulders a little."

I did as she suggested.

"Now walk across the room. No, not like that. Take small, quiet steps. Look hesitant. You want to be ignored. And Satpa, you need to stand straight with your head up."

Satpa and I practiced, and after a while, Ninsha was satisfied with our disguises. "You'll need to be careful, Esh. What if the palace is under attack? You could run into murderous enemy soldiers."

I sat down suddenly. She was right. We had no idea why Ishqi-Mari was keeping the palace women under guard. I had simply assumed he was executing some trick. A wave of fear rolled through me, and I sat on my hands so that Satpa and Ninsha wouldn't see them shaking.

When I could breathe with ease, I stood and retrieved the pitcher of water Satpa had brought in earlier. I filled the mugs and poured the rest in the washing basin. I let myself slump and drew my shoulders forward. I tucked my head down. "Don't draw the guards' attention," I whispered, and slipped out between the curtain and the door frame.

"Where are you going?" Bad-su-bad asked.

"To fetch more water for the queen," I answered in a timid voice. I kept walking forward, careful not to look up. No spears stopped me. When I was halfway across the courtyard, I realized I had gotten away with it. I went into the washing room and hid in the darkness, peeking out around the doorway. Leaning on their spears, Bad-su-bad and Asqudum resumed their conversation, facing each other.

I set the pitcher quietly on the floor and left the courtyard.

It was immediately clear that something unusual was happening. The rooms rang with soldiers' voices, and several times soldiers striding down the corridor forced me to the side. Making myself as unobtrusive as I could, I made my way to Hidar's courtyard, where soldiers tromped back and forth chaotically. In front of Hidar's door, his cupbearer lay sprawled on the ground, face down.

My first thought was that if he didn't get up, he'd be trampled by the soldiers. A moment passed before I took in the awkwardness of his splayed limbs and the red pool spreading from under his body. The king's cupbearer was dead.

Frozen, I drew in a harsh breath and attracted the attention of a soldier, whose eyes wandered off as soon as he saw my servant clothes. I ducked my head deeper and forced myself to resume walking. I had to find Hidar. I got as near the doorway to his throne room as I could and waited until all the soldiers were looking elsewhere. Then I slipped into the room and was blinded in the much darker space. "My lord?" I said quietly.

I heard no sound except a fly buzzing.

Slowly, my eyes adjusted to the dimness. The room was disordered, with furniture tipped over. Although no lamps burned, I could see the king's chair was occupied. I made my way around the furniture and closer to the daïs. I gasped. Hidar was propped in his chair, his head hanging at an odd angle. His throat was cut from ear to ear.

I couldn't believe he was dead. I went closer and put my face close to his nose, waiting to hear his breathing and feel his breath on my cheek.

Nothing.

The king was dead. My husband and protector was dead.

Dizzy, I collapsed onto the nearest stool. Ninsha and I had to get out of the palace. Right away, before we ended up like Hidar and his cupbearer.

But where should we go? Where was safe?

I put my elbow on my knee and rested my head in my palm. I was lucky to have gotten this far, lucky in the confusion and hubbub of the soldiers. Now I had to get safely back to our room and get Ninsha. Somehow. Or should we trust Ishqi-Mari's guards to keep us safe?

"Girl! You don't belong in here!"

I looked up and straight into Ishqi-Mari's eyes for a moment before remembering my disguise. Recognition flickered.

I stood, crumpled into myself as best I could and still walk. "Sorry, my lord," I said softly and tried to walk by him.

He grabbed my arm. "Who are you, girl?"

I froze. "Satpa," I forced out.

"Whom do you serve?"

"Esh-tar-da-ri the queen and Nin-sha-su-gu her lady."

"Get out of here. Attend your ladies." He released my arm.

"Yes, my lord."

"Wait." He grabbed my arm again and forced my chin up with his hand. He studied me for several moments. "You're not Esh-tar-da-ri's servant. You're the queen herself."

I said nothing.

"I set guards to keep you safe. You shouldn't be here."

I lifted my head and straightened up. "Why would you care whether I'm safe? Especially now?"

He frowned. "That should be obvious."

"I have no idea."

"Now that I'm king—"

I shuddered.

"—I need to stay allies with Sargon of Akkad, which means I need to keep you safe and marry you."

My heart thudded in my chest, and my thoughts slipped out as words. "But you hate me."

He shrugged. "No matter. I'll have to get children on you, of course, but otherwise I'll leave you to yourself. You'll stay in your rooms and not bother me."

"As your prisoner? Do you have any idea what my father will do to you when he finds out?"

"He won't find out. The scribes will write only what I tell them to."

He doesn't know that I can write or that Father has an agent here. I need to go along with Ishqi-Mari for now and get a message to my father.

Ishqi-Mari shouted for a soldier. When one came in, he ordered him to take me back to my room and stay there as a third guard.

When the soldier shoved me into my room, both Ninsha and Satpa jumped up. I motioned toward the storeroom. We crowded together.

Ninsha put her hand on my cheek. "Where are you injured? I'll take care of it."

"I'm not injured," I said, looking down at the evidence of King Hidar's brutal death.

"There's blood on your feet."

Satpa shrieked and then clapped both hands over her mouth.

"It's not my blood. Listen—King Hidar is dead, and Ishqi-Mari is in charge. He wants to marry me to maintain the alliance with Akkad."

Ninsha and Satpa stared at me with wide eyes. Ninsha recovered first. "What do we do now?"

"I must write to my father and tell him what has happened."

Ninsha bit her lip. "It will take at least a month for a messenger to go and an army to come back."

I wiped my damp hands on my robe and leaned against the wall for support. "I must put off the wedding as long as possible."

Ninsha asked, "Will he wait that long?"

I could only stare at the floor.

CHAPTER TWENTY-TWO

I changed clothes with Satpa and put my jewelry back on. Ninsha and I alternated sewing and staring at the walls, while Satpa paced. After the morning passed, we heard clanking in the courtyard. Ninsha and I jumped, clutching our sewing to our chests. "The guard is changing," Satpa whispered.

Before our hearts could calm down, a soldier burst into our room. "Come with me!" he shouted. "King Ishqi-Mari wants to see you all right now."

Satpa started crying. Ninsha and I linked arms and, at the soldier's gestures, went out into the courtyard.

"You two," he said to the new guards who had replaced Bad-su-bad and Asqudum. "Reinforce the other guards until I bring these women back."

"If you do bring them back," one guard said and guffawed.

The soldier pushed us out of the courtyard and hurried us through the palace. Sweat ran down my back as I breathlessly tried to keep up with him. I couldn't think of any reason that we would be summoned that didn't fill me with dread. Did Ishqi-Mari want to marry me right now? Or had he changed his mind and decided to kill us?

Unexpectedly, we were herded outside into the city street. I blinked hard against the light. The sun shone sharply. Despite the heat, many people thronged the street.

"Keep moving!" the soldier said.

Now that we were out of the palace and away from the other soldiers, I saw a chance to save Ninsha and Satpa. "When we reach the next intersection, Ninsha, you run down the cross street and Satpa, you

121

run back this way," I whispered. "One man can't catch three women going in different directions."

"I can't leave you," Ninsha said softly.

"I'll get away if I can. Let's meet up at the temple of Ishtar-Anunitum."

"Don't talk. Keep looking scared," the soldier said, much softer than before. "Pretend you don't know me!"

Pretend? I was so surprised that I stumbled. I looked the soldier full in the face for the first time. Ninsha did as well and gasped. Our captor was not a Mari soldier; he was Za-mu in a Mari army sash and helmet.

"Don't look. Keep moving," he said. "We need to go a lot farther before we're safe."

I was full of questions that I had to tamp down for many blocks until we came to a bakery and climbed the stairs to the apartment above. Za-mu pulled off his copper helmet and tossed his sash and battle axe on the bed. "Paila, the high priestess of Dagan, is dead. Murdered. Same for your husband's advisor, Tu-ru-dagan. Sooner or later, someone will discover you're missing and come looking for you. We need to get out of the city and head toward Akkad."

"We'll need bread, cooking supplies, and a fishing net." I remembered how bare the steppe was. A donkey perhaps could live off the scrubby plants but not a person.

"I have no fishing net, but I bought bread and a bag of barley at the bakery this morning. We can load it on my donkey. Before we leave here, though, take off all your jewelry, and put your hair up in an Akkadian style. We need to look like common foreigners going home."

"But I don't want to go to Akkad," Satpa said. "My family is here in Mari."

Za-mu turned toward her. "If you go back to the palace, Ishqi-Mari may punish you as a collaborator in the escape."

Satpa started to cry again.

I put my hand on her shoulder. "You don't have to stay in Akkad. You can come back to Mari with a merchant caravan."

The reassurance didn't calm her. To be honest, it wouldn't have calmed me either in her place.

As I took off my beaded collar and earrings, Ninsha redid Satpa's hair in an Akkadian style. Then she arranged mine and, finally, her own.

Za-mu gave us each a narrow sash of undyed wool. "Tie the sash around your waist. You'll look poorer and more foreign." Meanwhile, he put flatbreads into the sack of barley and slung it over his back. He picked up the battle axe again then changed his mind and left it. "My knife has to be enough. I need to look like an ordinary citizen. Let's go." He went down the stairs first and checked outside for pursuit. Then he waved us down and into the street.

I wanted to run. Instead, we walked at what seemed a funereal pace three blocks to a stable, where Za-mu's donkey was peacefully eating hay. Za-mu loaded the food on it and led it out into the street.

"We'll head for the southeast gate. If soldiers stop us, you're my younger sisters. We're returning to Akkad after selling linen here, and we're meeting up with a caravan along the canal. Our being linen merchants would explain the high quality of your robes."

"Do you think we'll be stopped?" Ninsha asked.

"Given the coup this morning, supporters of King Hidar may try to flee the city. The guards at the gates may have orders to question everyone leaving...and may also have been told of your escape."

Despite the heat, a chill ran down my spine.

We started walking, Za-mu and the donkey in the lead. We stopped at a market to buy a bag of dried apricots, another of dates, and a pot for cooking, all of which was added to the donkey's back. Then Za-mu took us down quiet residential streets, zigzagging through the city. We saw no soldiers or guards and only a few citizens. At last we reached a gate that pierced the inner wall. A long line of people waited to go through.

Za-mu led us to the side. "In case they're looking for three women, possibly with a man, we should split up until we get to the other side. Esh and I will go through first. Ninsha, you and your servant will go through behind us." He and I and the donkey got in line, and after two men joined the line behind us, Ninsha and Satpa got in line.

The line progressed in starts and stops. I pulled my shawl over my head to protect my head and neck from the sun. As we waited, we saw a man yanked out of line by soldiers and then marched back the way

123

we had come. My stomach twisted at the thought that we might follow that man's fate.

At last, only one family stood in front of us. I could finally see that two men guarded the gate and more soldiers stood to the side, scanning the faces of people in line. I dipped my head modestly and drew my shawl close. The guards looked at the family and let them through.

Our turn. The guards stared at us then they stared at the donkey. "Reason for leaving the inner city?" asked one.

Za-mu was ready with an answer. "My sister and I are returning home to Akkad."

"Mighty few supplies for a trip that long."

"That's because we're joining up with a caravan that's waiting by the canal."

The guard eyed us again then motioned us through the gate.

As soon as we were beyond the inner wall, I let out a big sigh.

"Too early for that. We still have the gate in the outer wall to go through," Za-mu said.

"We got through this gate easily. Maybe we'll do so again at the next gate."

We moved to the side to wait for Ninsha and Satpa. I looked around. The houses and shops were less dense on this side of the wall. Toward the canal that ran through the city there were no buildings at all, only orchards and small fields. The outer wall looked imposingly tall, and the line to leave seemed shorter.

Za-mu stood looking at the gate we came through, a frown on his face. "Only one group of people separated us from Ninsha, but three groups have come through after us."

My head turned toward the inner gate. "We have to go back for them."

"No. We stay right here and wait."

"And what if they don't come through?"

"Then we go home on our own."

"You can't mean that. We can't abandon Ninsha."

He crossed his arms. "King Sargon would want you back safely at any cost."

"If they were turned back, they'll probably go to the temple of Ishtar to wait for us to join them."

124

"The temple is in the middle of the city, and we're almost to the gate of the outer wall. We can't go back to the center of the city and start over again."

"Why not?"

"Going back will put you in danger again. If I were a soldier of Mari, I would have already traced us to my apartment above the bakery by now."

"I won't go without Ninsha."

"Yes, you will, even if I have to throw you over the donkey and hold you down."

My chest grew tight. Why did men take advantage of their size? I stared at the gate, willing Ninsha and Satpa to come through.

When Ninsha finally appeared, I didn't know it at first because I was scanning for two women. But Ninsha was by herself. Her hair had fallen into waves down her back. She saw us and walked over.

I threw my arms around her and gave her a tight hug. "Thank the gods! I was so worried about you. What happened?"

Ninsha made a futile pass over her hair with her hand. "As soon as you two went through the gate, Satpa took off running. I chased after her for a few blocks but then I was afraid I'd get lost. So I went back to the gate and got in line."

"Not good," said Za-mu. "She can tell Ishqi-Mari our plans."

"She won't do that," Ninsha said.

"If she's tortured, she'll speak. We need to get moving and get out of Mari fast." He tugged on the donkey's lead and started striding toward the next gate. Ninsha and I followed at a fast walk.

When we approached the gate, there were only a few groups in line. We soon saw that the guards were asking questions only of the guests with an urgent air. Za-mu put on a manner of utter calm, and we went through the gate without a problem.

I started to sigh, but Za-mu interrupted. "This road will take us to the canal, which links to the river. We need to hurry now to stay ahead of Ishqi-Mari's soldiers."

By the time we reached the canal, I was ready to sit down for a rest. But Za-mu, glancing back at the outer gate repeatedly, urged us on. As we headed downstream, we saw a caravan ahead of us. I thought we should catch up and travel with them, but Za-mu said no. He looked back again and ordered us to wade into the reeds, and he led the donkey in among us.

"Are they coming? How long do we have to stay here?" The mountain chill of the water from the holy river Buranun made me shiver, and I recoiled every time some slimy thing brushed against my legs.

Za-mu pulled his knife and parted the reeds in front of him slightly. "There are six soldiers, and they're looking around....now one is pointing to the caravan....They're running this way. Stay low and be quiet."

I sank further down until the water was at my waist. I could see nothing, and I hoped that meant the soldiers would not be able to see me.

Ninsha stretched out her arm toward me, and I caught her hand and held it. When we heard running feet, we both jerked at the same moment. The sound grew louder quickly until the soldiers were right by us. Ninsha and I squeezed hands. Then the soldiers passed without slowing, and the sound of feet softened and disappeared altogether. I heard only the cries and splashes of birds.

"Za-mu, I'm so cold," Ninsha said. "I want to get out now. Please?"

Za-mu rubbed the back of his neck. "I'm sorry, Ninsha. Not until after they've come back and gone within the walls. First, they'll probably search the caravan and then go farther downstream to look for us."

We stayed in the water until we all were shivering uncontrollably and making the reeds rustle. At last we heard the tromp of feet, marching this time, and we forced ourselves to crouch down lower in the water. The soldiers were talking, and as they passed us, we could make out their words.

"They probably went to the wharves and took a boat."

"No, more likely, they went out the north gate and found a caravan to join."

"Soldiers were sent to both places and others besides. We'll catch them."

A frog squawked, and the soldiers stopped walking.

I held my breath.

One of the soldiers laughed. "You city boys. Don't you know a marsh frog when you hear one?"

A soldier grumbled, and they started walking again. Soon, we couldn't hear their steps anymore.

I stood up to get some of me out of the cold water but otherwise didn't move, waiting for Za-mu's instructions. A long time seemed to go by. My teeth were chattering, and my knees were knocking.

Finally he said, "We're safe. They've gone inside the gate."

"Thank goodness." I shoved my way through the reeds to dry land, expecting Ninsha to follow behind me.

"My legs are wobbling too much to take even one step," Ninsha said through tears.

Za-mu forced his way through the reeds to her. "Are you ill?"

"I'm too cold to move."

"I'll help you." He put an arm around her waist, and she slumped against him. He helped her toward dry land. The donkey galumphed after them. When Ninsha was on dry land, Za-mu took each of her hands in turn and rubbed it gently between his own.

Once back on the path, the heat of the sun felt glorious. Even so, we all shivered for a while, the donkey included, but the sun gradually warmed us up and removed some of the moisture from our wet clothes. The donkey's eyes were wide with fear, and Za-mu scratched it under its chin as we headed downstream on the path.

After a short time of fast walking, we saw the caravan ahead. I nodded toward it. "They're not making very good time."

"The soldiers may have stopped them for a while." Za-mu pointed ahead. "Look—there's blood on the path. Someone's been injured."

I shivered, and not from cold this time. We had escaped, but someone else had paid the price. I hoped Satpa's return to the palace was less violent.

CHAPTER TWENTY-THREE

When we reached Hit, a sailboat crew agreed to carry us the rest of the way to Akkad, and we rode the river to the docks of home.

News of the coup had not yet reached Akkad, and people in the palace were astounded to see us. Before we had a chance to change into clean, dry clothes free of sand, Father called us to his office and enveloped me in a long hug before directing us to sit on the stools in front of his desk.

"Tell me everything," Father demanded.

"My husband, Hidar, has been killed," I said. "His throat was slit by his son, Ishqi-Mari, or on his behalf. I saw my husband's dead body myself. Ishqi-Mari now rules Mari. He planned to marry me to encourage you to maintain the truce, but Za-mu rescued us."

"I had made several useful contacts in Mari," Za-mu said. "As soon as a servant escaped from the palace and spread the news of the coup, I heard about it and went to the palace to find the queen."

"Your bride price?" Father asked me.

"Left behind. Ninsha and I escaped with only the clothes and jewelry we were wearing."

Father drummed his fingers on his desk. "What sort of man is this Ishqi-Mari?"

"Treacherous," I immediately answered.

"My sources named him vicious, ambitious, and hot-headed," Za-mu added.

Father turned to me. "Do you carry Hidar's child in your belly?"

My face heated, and I dropped my head. "No, Father."

"Too bad. We could have claimed the kingship on the child's behalf."

"Ishqi-Mari killed your daughter's husband and held your daughter hostage," I said. "Surely that's justification for war."

"No more talk of war," Father said. "If I do attack Mari, I want it to be a surprise to Ishqi-Mari. Now what should I do about you, Esh?"

My stomach felt full of rocks. "I still long to serve Inanna and write hymns to Her. Please, let me be one of Her priestesses," I begged, casting dignity to the winds. "I don't care which city you send me to."

"I already have Inanna's support. It would be a waste to give you to Her temple. I'll have to think about where you could be valuable."

ﻉ

After I had cleaned up from our trip home, I went to see Mani. I found him polishing his helmet in the courtyard by his bedroom.

"You're home!" He set his helmet down and embraced me. "Is your husband with you?"

I wondered how many times I would have to explain what happened in Mari. "Hidar's dead. Murdered. At his son's order and maybe by his hand. Ninsha and I had to flee Mari to avoid my being forced to marry that son."

Mani called for a servant to bring us a pot of beer. "Are you and Ninsha all right?"

"Za-mu protected us, and Inanna must have been watching over us."

"Thank the gods. You must be sad to be widowed."

I sighed and sat on a stool. "I was horrified to find Hidar's body, as you might imagine. He didn't deserve to die like that. But I hadn't wanted to marry him, and I didn't like him."

"Well, I'm glad you're home. Did you meet my wife in the women's quarters?"

"No, not yet. Are you happy with your marriage?"

"She's been a good wife so far. Esh, she's going to have my baby!"

"Congratulations!"

"And soon I'll be leaving on campaign to the island of Dilmun, in the gulf. Father's letting me lead it myself."

"You must be very happy."

"Life is going well for me. And now to have you back home!"

129

"I don't think Father will let me stay home for long."

The servant brought in a beer pot with two straws and set it down between us.

"Why?" Mani took a sip of the beer.

"I worry that he'll marry me off again." My throat tightened against the words.

Mani gave me a worried look. "Maybe he'll finally send you to be a priestess of Inanna."

"He's already said he won't, that there's no advantage in it for the family."

"What will you do?"

"I'll have to appeal to Inanna."

Ninsha and I were settled into our former room, which felt almost as foreign as Mari had at first. Ninsha went to say hello to various servants, leaving me alone with my thoughts. My only hope of becoming Inanna's priestess was the goddess Herself.

To buy a sacrificial animal, I would need something to pay with. I looked under the bed and in the corners for silver or jewelry but found none. At last I went to my mother's work room and asked the servants to leave.

"I had heard you were back," Mother purred. "The gods have not smiled on you."

I was a queen now. I wouldn't let her make me feel guilty or humiliated. I shrugged. "The gods freed me from marriage to an elderly man with a treacherous son. That's good fortune."

Her smile held. "Your father will send you somewhere else. I'm sure of it."

"I still want to be a simple priestess of Inanna. I came here to ask you for a ring of silver so that I can buy a sacrifice for Her. I need Her help."

"You're trying to trick me. A sacrificial animal costs much less than that."

I sighed. "I'll bring back the ring, of course. Please, Mother." No matter how many times Mother was spiteful to me, it still felt like an arrow to the heart.

She stood and went to her chest. From it she pulled a cloth bag that jingled. She pulled out a ring of silver and handed it to me.

I slid the ring onto my arm like a bracelet. "Thank you, Mother."

I took my leave. I left the palace and headed upward toward Ulmash House, the temple of Ishtar, through the remains of a sandstorm. The street was nearly empty. I could understand why; my eyes immediately felt scratchy from the wind and dust.

Still, as I neared the temples of Ilaba and Ishtar, the road was edged with animal keepers selling animals for sacrifice. I purchased a pretty nanny goat with a sleek white coat and brown ears, and the seller clipped off part of the silver ring as his payment. He tied a rope around the goat's neck and handed the end to me.

I set off again for Ulmash House, this time with the goat following. At the temple gate, a priestess stopped me.

"I'm Esh-tar-da-ri, the daughter of the king."

"I'm sorry, but you're filthy. You can't come before the goddess like that."

I was wearing the only clothes I had. "I apologize. Please, take my sacrifice and ask for Ishtar's blessing on me."

"Certainly. You'll have my prayers."

I went back to the palace. In the women's quarters, I found my mother still in her work room. "Here is what's left." I handed her the ring of silver. "I have to ask another favor. These are the only clothes I have. May I borrow a robe?"

Smirking, she went to her chest. She took out a robe and handed it to me.

"Thank you. I'll stop bothering you now." I went back to our room. I resolved to no longer care about earning Mother's praise; doing so was clearly impossible.

❦

The next morning, I was playing a game with my little brothers. In the months I had been gone, both had grown taller, and Ilaba'is' voice had dropped. It startled me each time he spoke. They told me about the weapons training they were doing and how hard it was to sit still for their lessons.

"Father says he'll make us each an ensi of a city when we get older," Ibarum said.

"When you're ensis, you'll be glad to know how to read and write," I said, remembering as I said it how I had disliked adults dismissing my feelings thus when I was a child. I felt a yawning distance between us. I was now a dowager queen, and they were just boys. But I shouldn't speak down to them. "Knowing so doesn't make your lessons any more tolerable now, though."

"That's right!" Ilaba'is said. "*You* understand."

"Esh, don't indulge them!" Mother had sneaked up behind us. "I need you in the sewing room now. I have new linen to be made into sheets."

"I'll help you out tomorrow or the next day," I said. "Today I plan to recuperate from the trip home and catch up on my sleep."

"Don't speak impertinently to me! I'm in charge of the women's quarters, and I'm telling you to sew sheets today."

My stomach turned over, just as it so often had when I was little. But I was no longer a child. I had the rank to speak up and be heard. "I'll be glad to help you with your tasks while I'm staying here, Mother. But I'm a queen now. You can't order me about anymore."

Her face turned white then red, and she sputtered before she got any words out. "As long as you're staying in *my* domain, wearing *my* clothes, you'll do what I say."

"In that case, I'll ask Father for another place to stay." I unpinned my robe and let it drop to the floor in a puddle of fabric. I stepped out, picked it up, and handed it to my mother. "I'll also ask him for some clothes." I walked to my room, ignoring the diatribe that erupted behind me.

CHAPTER TWENTY-FOUR

It took a week before my father had time to see me.

I walked into the room and saluted him. "Thank you for making time for me."

"Your mother is quite unhappy with you."

I clasped my arms and pulled them tight to my chest. "Some things never change."

"Little bird, for my sake, will you try to get along with her?"

"Father, I try, but she makes it impossible. She gives me orders as if I were a child, not a sister queen. Would it be possible for Ninsha and me to stay in another part of the palace? And may I have another robe? This one is the only one I have, and it's ragged and stained from our escape from Mari."

"I think it's best if you leave Akkad."

My stomach dropped, and I stiffened. "Please don't marry me off again." I'd only gotten free of King Hidar the week before.

"I have something more interesting and prestigious in mind. I received a messenger yesterday who reported that the temple of Nanna in Ur, House Sending Light to the Earth, needs a new zirru, which is what they call their high priestess."

Not again, I thought numbly. "I don't even know which god Nanna is."

"God of the moon. An ancient, high-ranking god. Similar to our Suen."

Most princesses would be delighted to be named high priestess of Nanna. But I'd had my heart set on serving Inanna since I was little, even before She first appeared to me. I wanted to yell, as I had when

133

he told me to marry Hidar. But I was a queen now and needed to behave with dignity and calm. "Father, I don't want to be priestess of Suen. Besides, last week you said it would be a waste to make me a priestess."

"A waste to make you a priestess of Inanna. It would be different if you were zirru of Nanna—or rather, Suen. You would have influence throughout the empire. And you would be my eyes and ears in Ur as well."

I was intrigued in spite of myself. "How much influence?"

"Enough to help me unify my kingdom. You would be the spiritual leader of Sumer and Akkad. The people of Ur consider Nanna to be the chief of the gods."

I blinked. I would be the most powerful woman in the empire...if I could handle it. I would have much power after a lifetime of powerlessness. "How would I unify the cities under you?"

"That would be your choice."

I swallowed. "Father, allow me to be a priestess of Inanna, and I will pray for you and our family night and day."

"Your duty is to follow my wishes. You'll be the priestess of Suen."

I sat in silence for several moments. Being zirru of Suen wasn't my first choice, but it was better than most of my other options. It gave me a chance to make a mark on the world. "As you wish, Father. I'll be zirru. When do I go to Ur?"

"We'll leave in five days."

ह

Ninsha and I found Mani in his favorite courtyard with a barber, getting his beard trimmed, curled, and oiled.

We stood in front of him so he could see us without moving his head. "We'll be leaving in a few days, Mani."

He spoke out of nearly closed lips. "Has Father found you a new husband?"

I sighed. "In a fashion. I'm to be high priestess and wife of Nanna the moon god—he's like our Suen—in the House Sending Light to the Earth in Ur. Ninsha is going with me."

"It's not what you wanted, I know, but being zirru is a high honor."

"I know. I'm disappointed anyway."

134

"Even gods must give way before the will of Sargon, King of Akkad and Sumer, King of the World."

I stifled a laugh. "Don't be irreverent! I have to say this for being zirru, at least it gets me away from Mother. We've been clashing."

"Like finger cymbals," Ninsha added.

"So I've heard," Mani said. "If Father allows it, I'll go with you to Ur to your investiture and offer a good sacrifice to your new divine husband."

I grabbed his hand and squeezed it. "I'd like that."

ে

As everyone else was eating supper, I stood in the courtyard of the women's quarters praying to Inanna.

My skin trembled. Amid the smell of incense, a glowing cloud materialized next to me. The bright afternoon sunlight seemed dim by comparison. "My daughter, you are troubled," Inanna said.

A tear fell from my eye. "My destiny is to write hymns to You. I've known it since I was a child. But my father refuses to let me be Your priestess. I'm to be priestess of Suen instead. I've failed You."

"Your father has failed Me, not you, child."

"Can you help me?"

"You've already written one hymn to Me. When you are in Ur, continue to write more."

My eyes burned. "But why? Who will sing them to You?"

"You will, child. And take them to the House of Heaven, My great temple in Uruk, so the priestesses there can sing them too." She stroked my hair. "It will work out, you'll see." She vanished.

Section III

City of Ur

Age 16

CHAPTER TWENTY-FIVE

Ninsha and I traveled downriver to Ur by sailboat, accompanied by my father, his advisors, Mani, and what seemed like half the palace staff, with Za-mu and four dozen soldiers as our guards. The twenty boats were crowded, and the soldiers had to take turns standing under the hot early-spring sun. Awnings protected Father, Ninsha, and me from the sun's rays.

Ninsha and Za-mu spent a long time talking, while I covered my hair with a shawl and watched the busy shoreline. It teemed with shore birds, and I saw a flock of wild goats and even once a porcupine, all coming to the sacred river Buranun to drink.

Father had rented a large house in Ur near the temple. Some of the ceremonies during the seven days of ritual were supposed to take place at the new zirru's father's house, and Akkad was too far away.

The morning after we arrived, I met with a priest, Me-zi-da, to learn what I would be expected to do and say during my installment. He was a stuffy man, middle-aged and stiff, but I appreciated his attention to detail. I didn't want to make a fool of myself.

Because I was marrying a god, the consecration rituals to install me as zirru of Nanna were modeled on wedding customs. Suen, of course, already had a divine wife—the goddess Ningal—but needed an earthly wife—me—to pray, run His temple and estates, and make offerings. I learned that, in addition, I would be in charge of the Gipar House, which contained Ningal's temple and living quarters for the priestesses. If I had been someone who craved power and influence, being the zirru of Suen would have satisfied me.

139

Instead, my heart sank lower and lower as I listened to Me-zi-da. Unless I did something greatly immoral, there were only two opportunities in the seven days for the temple to reject my candidacy. I briefly considered doing something immoral, but my pride—and my love for my father—kept me from destroying my reputation.

That afternoon, Mani and I went for a walk to see Ur. The city itself was ancient, one of the oldest cities in Sumer. We went to the temenos, the enclosure that contained religious buildings including the Gipar House and the House Sending Light to the Earth. I couldn't stop staring. Suen's temple was built of mudbrick that glowed in the sun and stood on its own flat mound. Built in three tiers, with each tier smaller than the one below it, the temple culminated in a small sanctuary at the top. To see it, I had to lean my head so far back the sun glared in my eyes.

On the first day of the initiation, Father, Mani, Ninsha, and I went to the courtyard of House Sending Light to Earth, where a diviner would announce the name of the new high priestess. We joined a murmuring crowd that included many priests and priestesses.

"Hear that?" Ninsha whispered. "They're saying that a priestess named Sim-tur will be chosen."

My heart rose. I turned away from Father and prayed softly to Suen to choose Sim-tur and to Inanna to save me from being zirru.

A hush fell over the crowd. I stood on my toes and saw that the diviner, whom I had met the day before, was mounting the steps of Suen's house. Naked except for a cap on his shaved head, he climbed all the way up to the top tier, where he went inside the small building that was the god's private domain to consult with Him about His choice.

It felt like a long time until he came back out. My heart was pounding hard, and I had trouble catching my breath. I grabbed Ninsha's hand.

The diviner walked down to the first terrace. "The great god Nanna, lord of wisdom, has chosen. His new zirru will be Esh-tar-da-ri of Akkad."

Father cheered, but much of the crowd whispered to each other. I caught the name "Sim-tur" several times.

The diviner held up his hands to silence the crowd. "Zirru, approach!"

140

Ninsha squeezed my hand, and then I was moving through the crowd toward the temple building. It took all my willpower to climb the first step, then the second, then the third, until I finally reached the terrace where the diviner stood. Despair and excitement warred within me.

The diviner took a small jar of oil and poured some on my head, and I smelled cedar. "Behold the new zirru of Nanna: Enheduanna, high priestess of the ornament of the sky."

I cringed. I had not reckoned on giving up my name and receiving a title in its place.

An incantation priest came up the steps leading a white ewe. That priest, the diviner, and I walked to the altar. As the diviner chanted, the priest lifted the sheep onto the altar and with a quick motion, slit the sheep's throat. Blood gushed over the altar and over the edges, and I backed up to keep from being splattered.

Next, the diviner and I went to the edge of the platform facing the courtyard. The diviner announced, "Behold: Enheduanna, the embodiment of Ningal!" In front of the gathered priests and priestesses, I sang a hymn I had learned from Me-zi-da the previous day.

The incantation priest, the diviner, and I then went to the Gipar House. Again, as the diviner chanted, the priest sacrificed a sheep.

The diviner said, "Behold Enheduanna, she who will bring offerings in baskets, bring about rejoicing, make the god's house comfortable, and put in order the place of the holy purification rites."

I recited the words I had learned the day before. "Nanna, I shall praise you. Suen, I shall glorify your name."

Then the incantation priest and three priestesses—Sim-tur, Buru, and a novitiate named Ningbanda—took me back to the bathing room in my father's rented house. As the incantation priest waited outside, the senior priestess, who unfortunately was Sim-tur, coldly said, "Undress now."

I did. The priestesses walked around me, counting my fingers and toes, looking for scars, and otherwise checking for any flaws that would displease the god Suen. I meanwhile evaluated my rival, Sim-tur. She was older than me by perhaps a dozen years. Her hair was black, like most Sumerians', and hung straight down her back. Her face showed no emotion. Nothing physical about her explained why she was a senior priestess already and had been expected to be zirru.

I brought my mind back to the present. The bathing ritual was my last chance to escape being high priestess, and when Sim-tur said, "Her hair's too curly," happiness shot through me. *Could my escape be this simple?*

But Buru said, "I think she's suitable," and Ningbanda said "yes" in a soft voice.

Sim-tur harrumphed and agreed.

There was no more way out for me. I was no longer Esh of Akkad but Enheduanna of Ur.

Next, while the exorcist priest chanted incantations, the priestesses washed my body and hair. Then they trimmed my fingernails, known to accumulate evil, accompanied by a special incantation. More incantations were said over my new regalia—a flounced red robe and a rolled-brim wool hat—to purify them, and at last I was dressed and bejeweled. The robe was heavier than I had expected and gave off a faint scent of incense.

The priestesses led me outside, where musicians, singers, sacrificial animals, and naked priests waited. When they saw me, they formed into groups in a line. Buru led me to my spot in the parade, in front of one white cow and nine black ewes, and we processed to Suen's house, accompanied by forty priests and priestesses banging drums. Citizens lined the street and shouted "hurrahs" as we passed.

I was not yet permitted to go to the sanctuary on top of the ziggurat; I needed further purification. The incantation priest asked, "What offenses have you committed against the gods?"

I stood silent for a moment, not wanting to confess to a stranger. "I argued with my father, I did not grieve the death of my husband, and I'm becoming priestess of Suen even though I promised myself to Inanna."

The priest stiffened at the last sin, then regained his composure and recited incantations to clean me of my offenses and to clean my feet from the contamination of the street.

The incantation priest mixed beer and water in a bowl, and I rinsed my mouth with the mixture to make it pure enough to speak to the god. Then the ten animals were sacrificed to Suen, and the incantation priest led me up to the sanctuary on top.

My mouth went dry as we climbed the stairs. I would meet a god face to face in His sacred place. Who wouldn't be frightened under such circumstances? I had to stop and breathe for a moment before I went into the sanctuary.

Inside, Suen stood in a dim room off the vestibule surrounded by a fog of frankincense. I took a deep breath and saluted Him with my hand to my nose. After my eyes adjusted, I could see His face, hands, and feet were made of gold, his eyes were glossy dark stones, and his body was silver. He wore a robe made of fine wool ornamented with precious stones and silver embroidery. He was magnificent. I could understand why the people of Ur believed He was the most important deity of all.

A bed stood at the back of the room, where I would sleep with the god on certain feast nights. In the space between the bed and the god, votary statues with large eyes crowded, and there were so many they overflowed into the vestibule.

After I had prayed, the incantation priest and I, woozy from the incense, went down the stairs of the ziggurat to the courtyard, where a feast was laid out. A throne draped with red cloth awaited me. But all the rituals had taken their toll. My head pounded, and I had little appetite. I was relieved when at last the diviner again anointed my head with oil, and my family returned to my father's rented house, where priests placed a red cloth over my bed. As soon as they left, I fell asleep immediately.

The second day, there was again a procession from Father's rented house to the temple, a lamb was sacrificed, and a feast followed.

The next several days ran into each other. Each day, my father hosted a feast in his rented house. All the priests of Suen and priestesses of Ningal attended, as did the ensis—governors— and councilors of the cities of Ur and Uruk, which was three days' walk upstream. Ninsha was able to see her eldest brother, Lugalanne, the ensi of Uruk, after many years apart.

I disliked Lugalanne right away. He drank too much, laughed too loudly, and stood too close. His slipshod salute to my father caused whispers around the courtyard. Ninsha didn't say what she thought of him, but she looked both disappointed and embarrassed.

Kaku, the ensi of Ur, was easier to like, but I worried about his tendency to laugh with Lugalanne and to let Lugalanne speak over him.

143

I had hoped to talk to Mani, but every night he and Father spoke with officials from Uruk and Ur, getting their measure and gauging their loyalty. Silent, I sat with them, trying to get a sense of both cities and their leaders. I was introduced to the priests of Suen and priestesses of Ningal, but there were so many that I remembered only a few of their names.

On the last day of my consecration, I awoke dull-witted and still full from the feast of the night before. Ninsha looked even more sluggish, but she helped me wash and dress in my red flounced robe. I took part in one final procession to the temple. After reaching it, I visited the sanctuaries of Nanna and Ningal, offering cuts of roasted lamb.

I sang one last song, and at last I could go to Gipar House and my rooms there for the first time. They consisted of a day room off a courtyard, with an adjacent sleeping chamber and a bathing room. Ninsha had followed behind the procession and joined me once the priests and priestesses left my room.

I sat on the bed and leaned back on my elbows. "Here we are again, in a strange city where we don't want to be."

"I thought I would feel at home in Sumer, but I don't." Ninsha sat beside me and started taking her hair down. "I guess I lived in Akkad too long."

I had something I needed to say to her. I took a deep breath for courage. "Do you want to stay with me here, as my friend and aide? We are no longer under the authority of a man. You could return to your family's house or become a priestess of Ningal here. Or even a priestess of Inanna in Uruk."

She thought for a long time. "I've never been as devout as you. Being a priestess doesn't appeal to me. I want to marry and have a family. But after seeing what my brother is like, I worry about moving home and having him choose my husband. Something about him reminds me of Ishqi-Mari."

I sagged with relief. "So you'll stay with me?"

"For now. I think you'll need me more here than ever before."

I hugged her tightly. "We'll have to get another stool then, and another lamp." Even though a high priestess would have at least one servant, the small room was set up with only one person in mind: one stool, one chest, one low table with an oil lamp, and a basket of jewelry.

A brazier constituted the rest of the furnishings, an unexpected luxury. We would stay warm in winter.

CHAPTER TWENTY-SIX

Although I was tired from the rituals, Father and Mani were sailing home the next day, and that evening was my last chance to see them. I grabbed a shawl and headed to my father's rental house, Ninsha chattering alongside me. She and Za-mu were going for a walk.

Father's guards stopped me at the door. In my flounced red robe, hat, and loose-hanging hair, they didn't recognize me at first. I wasn't surprised. I felt like a different person—one weighted down by more than all the heavy jewelry my zirru-ship provided me.

At the house, Za-mu was waiting outside. He and Ninsha headed away. Inside, I found Father and Mani eating supper with a Sumerian man I didn't know. We exchanged greetings, and a servant brought me a platter of sliced boiled lamb and cheeses. I devoured it hungrily. None of us spoke until we had finished the meal and the men were having a glass of wine.

"I thought you'd be too tired to come by tonight," Mani said.

"I wanted to say goodbye before you all go home and Mani heads off for Dilmun."

Za-mu slipped into the room and sat down at the table with us.

Mani and Father exchanged looks. "Change of plans," said Mani. "I'm off to Mari to avenge you."

"Oh." I thought about the people I knew in Mari—Azzu-eli, Tamma, Satpa, Belizunu, Bel-i-a-mi—who didn't deserve to die because of Ishqi-Mari's actions. "What will happen to the royal women and their servants? And Bel-i-a-mi?"

Mani was quiet for several moments. "Controlling a victorious army is nearly impossible. Many soldiers join the army so that they can kill

146

and steal with impunity. I'd like to promise I'll protect your friends, but I can't."

"I know Mari well," Za-mu said. "Esh, I'll bring your friends out before the attack, if that is acceptable, Mani."

Mani frowned. "You could spoil the surprise of our attack."

"Please, Mani, let Za-mu try to rescue them." I took Mani's hand and squeezed it.

"All right, as a gift to you. But the attack goes as planned, whether or not he succeeds."

"Thank you!" I got up and hugged Mani. "And thank you, Za-mu."

Father stood. "Esh, I've chosen a shaperum for you." He put his hand on the shoulder of the stranger. "This is Adda of Ur."

I blinked. "What's a shaperum?"

"My lady," Adda said, "If you agree, I would take over some of your managerial duties. I could supervise your estates; manage the sale of temple animals, grain, and wool; and collect rents from temple properties. I could also coordinate disbursement of food and products. Whatever you don't wish to do yourself."

"I've started installing shaperums in many of the cities I conquer to ensure honest dealings by loyal people," Father explained. "It occurred to me that you could use one to help with your work at the temple."

I hadn't thought that far ahead. I could use someone I trusted, but I hadn't chosen Adda. "To whom would Adda report?"

"To you, of course, little bird. My part was only to find an honest person with experience for you."

"Thank you, Father." What else could I say? Even though I was seventeen, I didn't know how to go about finding employees. "Adda, I would be pleased to have you as my shaperum."

"I have something else for you too," Father said. He went into another room and came back with a bundle of cloth, which he handed to me.

I opened it and found several gold bracelets, each set with a different stone. I slipped them on my arm and watched them flash in the lamp light. The temple provided the zirru with lots of jewelry to wear, but these would be mine, even if I were no longer zirru. "Thank you, Father. These are beautiful."

"Have you thought about the mission I gave you, to unite the Sumerian and Akkadian gods?" Father asked.

"Yes. I'm thinking of writing some hymns."

"I'm looking forward to whatever you come up with."

Reluctantly, I acknowledged to myself it was time to go. "Oh, Father!" I wanted to throw my arms around him, but that would lower the king's dignity in front of others. "I'm going to miss you so much."

His eyes shone. "Little bird, you're a woman. It was always fated that you would leave home and start a new life elsewhere."

"That doesn't mean it doesn't hurt being apart from you."

"I'll pray for the gods to watch over you," he said softly. "We can write letters as we did before."

Writing letters was the only thing I had to look forward to.

☙

"How much of the liturgy for Nanna and Ningal do you know?" the priestess Sim-tur asked accusingly.

"None," I answered, feeling a tightness in my chest. I feared some of the priestesses would be disrespectful because of my ignorance. "And from now on, Nanna will be known as Suen. My father wants it made clear that the Akkadians and Sumerians worship the same deities." It would be the only change I made to the rituals of the temples of Suen and Ningal; I thought as part of my mission to unite Sumer and Akkad that it was important for the Sumerians to see that we of Akkad continued their traditions.

Her eyes went cold, and her face turned red. "Is that why he bought you the zirru-ship?"

Sim-tur's anger reminded me that she had been the favorite of the priestesses to become high priestess. "That's one of the reasons, yes." I ignored her jibe that my father had bought the office I now so reluctantly held. He didn't have to buy it—as king he had the right to fill offices with people he trusted.

"All the priestesses of Ningal have lived in the temple since they were chosen as children. We all know the liturgy by heart."

"If all that mattered were training, any one of you would make a better zirru than me," I admitted. "But the moon god Suen chose me over all of the priestesses. We have to bow to His desires."

She snorted. "You don't even pretend to be qualified for your position."

"Why pretend? We both know the truth. I'm honest with you because I hope you and I can work together."

She made a sour face. "I need to take you to Nanna's temple for you to be shown your duties there. Then you'll come back here to learn your responsibilities to Ningal."

"While I'm at the temple, please take an extra stool and an extra lamp to my room."

Sim-tur's face became stormy.

Ninsha remained quiet throughout the conversation, but her face showed the worry I hoped my face was hiding.

Sim-tur didn't speak as she led me from the Gipar to the courtyard in front of Suen's temple, where she left me in the care of the priest Me-zi-da. I wondered whether he would be as hostile as Sim-tur, and my stomach tightened. My time as zirru would be unpleasant if everyone shared Sim-tur's attitude.

Me-zi-da saluted me. He was bare chested and wore a red skirt. "Come. I'll show you around the temple grounds and tell you what happens in each area. I'm sure you're eager to get started." He gestured to the buildings around the edge of the courtyard. "These are mostly storehouses, and we have larger ones in the countryside. The large building at the back holds the kitchens, and the rest are offices, including one for you."

He led me up the first set of steps of Suen's ziggurat. Today, without the rituals to distract me, the temple's platform seemed dizzyingly high, and we were only on the first terrace. We walked over to the altar and lustration jars in the corner. A servant was scrubbing blood from around the altar.

"The god is fed two meals on most days, one at daybreak and one at sunset," Me-zi-da said. "A priest sacrifices five sheep and one steer for each meal on the altar and performs the appropriate rituals. Then the offering is taken to the kitchen for the butcher to cut it up and the cooks to cook it. Now let's go to the sanctuary on top."

We climbed to the second terrace and without stopping continued to the third level. A stiff breeze pushed against us, and I dreaded the idea of going to the top in the near-dark. From up here I could look over the whole city of Ur and see the encircling wall and the fields and orchards beyond. Although the city sat on a tall mound, from the top terrace it looked almost flat. The view was so absorbing, I could have stared forever, but Me-zi-da led me into the small sanctuary building, a respite from the aggressive wind.

He spoke softly. "After the cooks prepare the meal, you place that table in front of Nanna. Then offer water for washing and step outside while the god cleans Himself. Light enough incense to last throughout the meal. Priests carry the food up from the kitchen, and you set out the roasted meat, ten loaves of bread, and fruit on the table and pour mugs of milk and beer for the god to drink. Then the priests sing a hymn, and you say an incantation, and everyone leaves so that Nanna can eat His meal in peace."

"Six animals and ten loaves of bread is a lot of food. Does He usually eat it all?" I asked.

"No, He eats the essence of the food but very little of its earthly form. After a certain interval, the priests return and take the leftovers away."

I felt foolish for assuming that gods ate as humans did. "What happens to the leftover food?"

"The food is divided up among the priests according to their assigned share. Some priests have sold some or all of their share to outsiders, so you will see city folk collecting food along with the priests."

"What happens on festival days?"

He was visibly pleased that I had asked. "The Eshesh festivals take place on the first, seventh, and fifteenth days of the month. Nanna receives two additional meals on those days, which might include geese, dormice, doves, and ostrich and duck eggs. In addition, each month on the Day of Lying Down, the day Nanna is dead and absent from the sky, we make special offerings. Same for the Akitu and Ezen-mah festivals. The rituals for both ordinary and festival days are written down. I'll send a scribe to read you these tablets."

"Thank you, Me-zi-da, but there's no need to send me a scribe. I'll read the tablets for myself. What other responsibilities do I have as zirru?"

"You make sure Nanna and Ningal are wearing the appropriate clothes for the day, feed Ningal in her temple, perform purification rites, maintain the buildings, make sure the priests of Nanna and priestesses of Ningal behave appropriately, and manage the estates of both gods. You accompany Nanna in processions and when he goes to Nippur each spring to visit His father, Enlil, at the House of the Mountain. You have so many duties, it's hard to list them all."

I was glad Father had thought to get me a shaperum. "From now on, Nanna will be known as Suen. My father wants people to know that the Akkadians and Sumerians worship the same gods."

"But...but," Me-zi-da stammered, his eyes wide. "You can't change a god's name."

"It's not really a change. The moon god already had the name Suen in the north."

"But...but..."

If Me-zi-da's reaction was any indication, the new policy would not be popular. "When do the priests gather together next? I need to let everyone know to call the god 'Suen.'"

"We gather before serving the god's evening meal."

"I'll tell them then."

"I'll take you back to Sim-tur now. You'll find that the rituals for Ningal are similar to those for Nanna...I mean, Suen."

"Thank you for showing me around. I'll see you again a little before sunset."

CHAPTER TWENTY-SEVEN

Me-zi-da was right: The rituals for Ningal at the Gipar House were similar to those in Suen's, although as a minor goddess, She received less food. In fact, the Gipar shared a butcher with Suen. A stair inside the Gipar led to the roof, where I would be expected to watch the moon and stars nightly to discover the dates of the festivals. The Gipar House tablet room had tablets I needed to study, and I borrowed them, to Simtur's obvious scorn. I could tell already she would be a thorn in my side.

I returned to my rooms with my head spinning with information. It was already midafternoon, so I went through the tablets until I found the instructions for serving an ordinary evening meal and began to memorize procedures and the words I needed to say.

Ninsha returned, her sewing basket in hand, and sat down next to me.

"Did you find enough to do while I was gone?"

"Yes. It turns out there is much more sewing to do here than in a palace—clothes for both Ningal and Suen, as well as clothes for all the priests and priestesses and novitiates. It seems to be a never-ending job. The priestesses were glad to have me join them, and I was glad I could so easily make them happy."

"What about you? Will you be happy here?"

"I'm with you. Why wouldn't I be happy?" She glanced at the tablets in my lap. "What are you studying?"

"Instructions for rituals and incantations for Ningal. When I memorize everything on them, there's another set waiting for me at Suen's temple."

"How are you doing with that?"

"I think I have the ritual for the evening meal down."

"Give me the tablets. I'll test how you're doing."

I gave her the tablets and pointed to the section about ordinary meals. Then I talked myself through the ritual and repeated the incantations needed when serving Ningal her food.

"You missed some steps."

I sighed and looked over her shoulder, reading through the instructions again.

"Why don't you try it again?" Ninsha asked.

I described everything correctly that time and then another time.

"You've got it."

"Good." I took the tablets back. "Now I need to study for tomorrow's dawn offering."

"First, I should tell you something." Ninsha bit her lip. "Many of the priestesses think Sim-tur should have been chosen zirru. They grumbled about it while sewing."

I winced. "The faster I can learn the rituals, the better."

"That may not be enough for Sim-tur, after hearing what she said this morning."

"She was short with me this afternoon too."

"I'm worried the other priestesses won't like you."

"As long as they respect me and obey my orders and instructions, I'll be happy."

"Just as your mother was?"

I stiffened. "I'm nothing like my mother."

"She didn't care to make friends either. I see it even if you don't."

A bell clanged.

"It must be time for Suen's evening meal." I was glad for the excuse to leave. I got up, straightened my robe, and pulled on my rolled-brim hat. "First I'm meeting with the priests."

I walked over to the god Suen's courtyard. Some priests were already there, and others were streaming out of the various buildings surrounding the courtyard. I waited until I saw no more stragglers and then climbed up the first two stairs of the temple. The priests saluted me.

"I have a brief announcement before we perform our holy duties. From now on, we will refer to the god not as Nanna but as Suen."

The priests turned to look at each other, and grumbling filled the courtyard.

"He's the same god as before, and his rituals remain the same, except that where you would have said 'Nanna' you now say 'Suen.'" I stepped down to the courtyard and looked for Me-zi-da. I needed his help for my first evening serving Suen.

☙

The next morning, after the offering to Ningal and presentation of Her meal, I repeated my announcement to the priestesses of Ningal except for Sim-tur, who was missing. The Akkadians didn't have a counterpart of Ningal, so Her name would remain the same. Afterward, the priestesses introduced themselves to me again. There were only ten priestesses altogether; Ningal, lady of the reeds, was a minor goddess, notable only for her powerful husband, the moon god Suen, and her children, Ishtar and her twin, the sun god Shamash.

Adda was waiting for me, and I took him to my office off the courtyard and got him settled in. Then I sent a priest to the Gipar to look for Sim-tur. She had taken over the zirru's duties after the last zirru died, so she seemed the best to explain the records and contracts.

The priest came back without her. He couldn't find her, he said.

Adda and I sorted through the tablets on the table. A merchant came by to introduce himself as someone who bought our best-quality wool cloth. Adda found his contract, and we all went over the terms together and the changes the merchant proposed.

The afternoon dragged by reading tablets. I was glad when the sun began to set and I could feed the gods. And gladder yet when I could go back to my room at the Gipar, throw myself on a stool, and talk to Ninsha.

"I can't believe the rest of my life will be repetitions of today," I said.

"I'm surprised you're discontented. You've wanted to be a priestess your whole life," Ninsha said, sitting on the edge of the bed.

"An ordinary priestess of Inanna. One who praises the goddess all day. Not an administrator, not the one in charge of scores of details."

"I have some news that may distract you."

"What's that?"

"I saw Sim-tur in a dark corner of the Gipar talking to my brother Lugalanne. I didn't think anything of it until they saw me and immediately went outside. Lugalanne put his hand on her waist, and she let it stay there for several moments before she stepped away."

"Sim-tur didn't show up this morning for the meal for Ningal. Later I sent a priest for her, and he couldn't find her."

"I wonder what she and Lugalanne had to talk about," Ninsha said, taking out her hairpins.

"I wonder why they didn't want you to hear them. You're his sister, after all."

"Will you reprimand her?"

"Lugalanne broke the rule against men in Gipar House. I don't know that Sim-tur did anything against temple rules by meeting him, though." I frowned. "I need to look it up. Something else I have to concern myself with that a priestess of Inanna wouldn't."

"When I was sewing with the priestesses today, some of them talked about Sim-tur's not showing up this morning. They thought it was unusual, and they didn't even know about Lugalanne."

"I'll keep an eye on her."

"You seem out of spirits tonight."

"I had different plans for my life." I paused, thinking how Inanna hadn't visited me in a long while. "And to top it off I forgot to tell you that Mani is on his way to Mari to conquer it."

Eyes wide, she sat up straighter. "Azzu-eli. Tamma. Satpa. What will happen to them?"

"I don't know. Za-mu will try to rescue them. What if he is caught?"

She brought her knuckles to her mouth. "That's a terrible thought. Now I won't be able to sleep tonight."

"I'm sorry for burdening you. A princess should do her duty without complaining. I will strive to do better."

CHAPTER TWENTY-EIGHT

I gradually memorized the liturgies over the next month until they were second nature. One afternoon, it was time to move on. I collected some blank tablets from the scribes and sat down to think about the mission my father gave me to unite north and south in one religion. What if I wrote hymns that praised the gods' houses instead of the gods? By praising both Sumerian and Akkadian temples, I would be showing that they were all part of one religion and that the Akkadians recognized the importance of the Sumerian temples.

I picked up a tablet and a stylus and started recording some notes. "Suen lives in the House Sending Light to the Earth in Ur. Ea lives at the House That Is A Ziggurat in Eridu. Enlil lives at the House of the Mountain in Nippur." I kept writing until the front and back of the tablet were full of city, god, and temple names.

I had a lot of blank spaces in the temple name column. I would have to go to the scribes and ask for information. My knowledge about most of the temples began and ended with the city and the god's name.

Tablet in hand, I walked next door to the courtyard of the House Sending Light to the Earth. The summer sun blazed, and no clouds softened the rays. I found two scribes in a scribal office and was glad to get out of the sun. After greeting them, I asked, "If I wanted to know the names of temples in other cities, would you be able to help me?"

"I can," one said. "I had to memorize them when I studied at the tablet house."

I lay the tablet on his table. "The blank spaces are the ones I don't know."

He filled in the missing names on the front, turned the tablet over, and filled in the back. "Here you go, high priestess. May we help you with anything else?"

"How would you suggest finding out information about the temples?"

"That could be hard," the first scribe said. "We may have information on some of them in our records, but we would have to go through hundreds of tablets."

The second scribe spoke up. "The easier way would be to find someone who's been to the various temples. For example, I grew up in Eridu, so I'm familiar with the House That Is a Ziggurat."

"What an excellent idea! Would you be willing to talk to me about it sometime?"

"How about now?"

I sat on a stool in front of his table.

"The House that Is a Ziggurat sits high on its own mound. There's a canal near the temple from which the priests collect pure water. People say that the temple is so well built that no light leaks into the rooms inside." He paused, thinking. "Are you familiar with the plant that is burnt to produce potash?"

"No."

"It grows in the salty marshes near Eridu. The priests use the potash plant to clean the temple. The temple is well known for its large banqueting hall and huge bread oven."

"Thank you. That's just the kind of information I need."

"The priests of Suen come from all over. You should talk to them to learn about the temples in other cities."

"I will, thank you." I turned and went back out into the heat. I stopped by my office to see Adda and then, jostling phrases in my mind, hurried to the Gipar. The thick walls made my room an oasis of coolness. I took another tablet from the basket under my table and began writing. At dusk, I had to stop to tend to the gods, then, after eating, I continued writing by the light of an oil lamp, which scented the room with a meaty smell. I stopped when the hymn totaled a little over 20 lines. I read it through and knew I'd have to revise it, but I thought I had made a good start. I felt lighter, with a sense of contentment I hadn't known in a while.

Oil was left in the lamp, so I took out another tablet and wrote a quick letter to my father. I informed him of finding Lugalanne in the Gipar House and told him I'd started writing a series of hymns to Sumerian and Akkadian temples. As the light sputtered out, I quickly added that Adda was working out well as my shaperum. Then I set my tablets on a reed mat to dry.

I sat in the dark thinking over recent weeks. I had been so unhappy. But I was alive, unlike Hidar. My life wasn't dangerous, unlike Mani's. I didn't have the world's greatest army attacking my town, unlike Azzueli and Tamma. Other people were worse off than me—the thought didn't make me joyous, but I had to admit that the gods had granted me a good life. I'd found contentment in writing the first temple hymn. Perhaps there were other priestly duties that could give me the same satisfaction. After all, if my life had gone as I had planned it, I would be doing some of the same tasks for Inanna and enjoying them.

I would throw off my sadness and write more hymns. Perhaps by the time I finished and sent them to Father, I would be happy.

❦

I put away the bread baskets in a storage room of the Gipar and dusted flour from my hands and robe. It was an unusually cool morning for early summer, and I thought I would take a walk outside the temenos, the walled enclosure that contained the temples of Suen and Ningal and the gods' warehouses. I adjusted my hat on my head and headed for the door, chitchatting with the other priestesses I passed.

I turned a corner and there he was, a man who filled the corridor, blocking the light.

"You're not allowed in the Gipar," I said firmly. What audacity this man had! "I'll show you the way out."

The man didn't move. "I'm looking for Sim-tur."

"She can meet you outside." By this time, my eyes had adjusted to the darkness, and I realized the man was Lugalanne, ensi of Uruk. He was carrying a large wool sack. What was he doing skulking around the women's quarters? "Next time you want to visit the Gipar, write to me ahead of time so I can make arrangements to welcome you in a manner

158

appropriate to your rank." I walked closer so that he would be forced to back up or turn around.

Instead, he set down his bag, put his arms around me, and grabbed my hindquarters. A squealing noise issued from the bag.

"How dare you?" I twisted my way free and pointed toward the exit. "Leave immediately!"

He roared with laughter and ambled out, and I was forced to walk behind him like a servant.

When we stepped outside, he asked me to send Sim-tur out to meet him.

"I'm not a servant," I snapped.

A panting messenger approached the door. "Lady Enheduanna. Thank goodness you're here. I have an urgent message from Akkad."

I reached out my hand for the tablet, and he gave it to me. I skimmed it, gasped, and sagged against the wall. I read it from start to finish slowly. My heart dropped. "No! It can't be."

"What news from Akkad?" Lugalanne asked with an insolent grin.

Rude as the ensi was, he needed to know this news. I read the letter out loud.

To Enheduanna, daughter of Sargon, queen of Mari, and zirru of Suen in Ur, from Kalki, scribe of Ubil-Eshtar. May the gods watch over you and keep you in good health. I regret to tell you that your father, King Sargon, has gone to the Underworld. Manishtushu was fighting in Anatolia, and Rimush has usurped the throne.

I wiped my free hand on my robe. How could it be that Father was dead? Yes, he was old—he was in the fifty-sixth year of his reign, and he had been an adult when he conquered Sumer—but his death didn't feel real. My heartbeat pounded in my ears, and my shaking hands made the tablet jiggle.

Lugalanne's face turned somber. "This usurper. What's he like?"

"Ruthless and cruel. How could he do this to his brother?" I gestured to the messenger. "Come. You can stay tonight with the priests."

"I must take this news to your ensi," Lugalanne said. "Kaku must know."

"I'll join you there soon." My knees felt week, and I leaned against the wall.

Lugalanne went on his way, and I was left to reflect on my father and his death. "Sargon the Great," many people called him. He created an empire from dozens of feuding city-states. Could Rimush hold the empire together?

Light glared next to me, and I smelled sweet incense. The goddess Inanna appeared. She extended her hand to me, and I grabbed it. We stood silently for a long time, mourning the end of Sargon. A tear sparkled on the goddess' bright face before she disappeared.

I took a deep breath. The last time I had seen my father was when he had brought me here to Ur. I had missed him terribly since and looked forward to seeing him again, but it was not to be. My hands shook, and I struggled to breathe. I felt as if I had a sucking hole in my chest, and I knew it would never be filled. I was an orphan. Never again would I have a father. I had to stand alone now. I longed for him with a strength that threatened to tear me apart.

CHAPTER TWENTY-NINE

"Some cities will rise up against the new Akkadian king." Kaku looked up from Kalki's letter and at Lugalanne as if to judge his reaction.

Lugalanne smashed his fist into his palm. "Should we be among them, that's the question."

"No, you shouldn't be among them," I said. "What are you thinking? The Akkadians won the right to rule you." I was angry, and a little frightened too. My office was as much a political position as a religious one. "That the wrong son of Sargon sits on the throne doesn't negate that the gods gave Sargon the land of Sumer."

"No one in Sumer wants to be under the thumb of Akkad," Lugalanne said.

"Akkad has a standing army of thousands. Whom can you put into the field? Potters, scribes, farmers? You have no chance against him."

Lugalanne rubbed his chin. "Tell us more about Rimush, zirru."

"As I said, he's ruthless and cruel. He's also deceitful and cunning. He won't let Sumer fall away from his empire. He will crush you."

Kaku squirmed in his cedar chair. "Maybe this isn't the right time to rebel."

"Don't you want our freedom back?" Lugalanne asked.

Kaku looked askance. "I like being ensi. If we challenge the way things are, we could lose our positions."

"Or you could be an independent king of Ur," Lugalanne said.

Kaku brightened.

"If you rebelled, Rimush wouldn't just replace you," I interjected. "He would execute you. I'm going to stay out of his way, and you should too."

Lugalanne looked hard at me. "That's not how a sister should talk about her brother."

"He wasn't a very brotherly brother." I clenched my mouth shut to avoid saying more.

Lugalanne stood. "Kaku, high priestess, you make good points. I will not involve Uruk in a war." He left abruptly.

"There could still be unrest in Ur," I said to Kaku. "And rebels from other cities might pass through. I'm going to order the gate of the temenos closed."

Kaku wiped sweat from his forehead with his hand. "I'll put extra guards on the city gates. Perhaps it would be in order to have a festival to celebrate Rimush's ascension to the throne."

"If he ever heard of it, he would look kindly on Ur."

Kaku raised his eyebrows. "Of course he'll hear about it. Akkad has several spies in Ur besides you."

The accusation, so casually made, rocked me backwards. "I'm not a spy."

He shrugged. "Maybe you are, maybe you aren't. News of a festival will get back to Akkad either way. That is, if I decide not to go to war."

I left, my heart racing so hard I could hear it in my ears. War would put the gods and the city in danger. I stopped by some shops on the way back to the temple, ordering barley flour, butter, and cheese to augment what we ourselves produced. I didn't trust Kaku not to do something foolish. We needed to be able to feed the gods even if we cut ourselves totally off from the rest of the city. The temenos needed more guards, too, but I would let Adda handle the hiring.

When I got back to the temenos, I ordered the guards at the gate not to let anyone in except those who lived or worked there.

"Are we at risk, lady Enheduanna?"

"Akkad has a new king. Some citizens may celebrate and some may talk rebellion, but either way, they'll be in taverns drinking a lot of beer and arguing. We need to protect the gods and their houses from disruption."

I went to the Gipar and found the priestesses and servants in the sewing room, clustered together and exclaiming over something that on first glance looked like the tall wool hat I wore in Mari. I called for their attention and explained about the new king and what we needed to do to protect the peace of Ningal's sanctuary. "You'll need to stay inside the temenos for a while, until any wildness in the city calms down."

A loud screech followed. Some of the priestesses laughed.

How wrong, that my father is dead yet laughter still exists in the world. "Death and rebellion aren't funny. Anarchy could infect the people of Ur."

"We're not laughing at your news," Buru said, wiping tears from her eyes.

I went rigid. "What, then?"

The hatlike thing galloped over the heads of the priestesses, and they shrieked and batted at it. Then it jumped onto my head and chattered its teeth.

I whirled and shook my head, trying to dislodge it.

The thing tugged at my hat. I grabbed the animal and held it out in front of me.

It looked like a tiny, hideous old man but its body was covered in coarse fur. It pursed its lips.

A noise erupted from its bottom, and warm feces dropped onto my sandalled feet.

I turned my face away. "What is this thing? Whose is it?"

No one moved or said anything. Then Sim-tur stepped forward. "It's called a monkey. Ensi Lugalanne gave it to me."

I shoved the monkey into her hands. "Well, give it back. We can't have it in the Gipar House."

She tilted her head down and frowned. "It won't be any trouble."

"It already is," I said.

With as much dignity as someone with feces on their feet can muster, I went back to my rooms to clean up.

I wanted to stay in my rooms and mourn, but I needed to talk to the priests. I sat on the edge of the bed and put my head in my shaky hands. My heart was so heavy I thought it might drop into my stomach. "Father," I muttered. "Oh, Father. How could you leave me?"

At last I could put off my duties no longer. I went to Suen's temple and gave similar instructions to the priests and workers as I had given to the priestesses. Then I went to my office to see Adda. I told him about everything that had happened that day. We talked about the measures I had put into place and then turned to his work. At last my heart calmed down, slowed by recitals of rents and receipts, amid the heavy weight of grief for my father.

༂

I woke to find Ninsha already gone. I assumed I had overslept and hurried to dress myself before sunrise. I went outside and was surprised to see no hint of light in the sky. It seemed a good time to talk to the temenos guards, so I wrapped a shawl around me against the early morning chill.

"How was the night?" I asked.

"There were more people out than usual. Laughing drunk, angry drunk, all other sorts of drunk."

"Did any try to enter the temenos?"

"A few. It was enough to turn them around and push them in another direction."

Suen, round in the night sky, had been watching out for his own. I would keep precautions in place for a while—it would take time for rebels from other cities to arrive here—but so far the citizens didn't seem rebellious.

I wrote letters to all the ensis of Sumerian cities, giving reasons for them to accept Rimush as their king and warning them of the might of the Akkadian standing army.

That night, I went to sleep early and again rose after Ninsha. I wondered what Ninsha was doing so early in the morning, and, after the gods were fed, I went looking for her.

I went first to the courtyard where the priestesses and seamstresses often sewed on nice days. I found them there, but Ninsha was not among them. "When was the last time anyone saw her?"

"I saw her two mornings ago," Buru answered. Others murmured their agreement.

"She didn't sew with you that day?"

"No, and not yesterday either."

My mouth went dry. I had assumed she had been coming to bed late and leaving early in the morning these past two days. But what if she had never come to bed at all?

I next checked with the cooks and brewers of the Gipar. They hadn't seen her. I had to hold myself back from running when I hurried to the House Sending Light to the Earth to question first Adda and then with his help an endless list of temple workers: guards, accountants, bakers, butchers, gardeners, priests, messengers, leather workers, potters, carpenters, basket weavers, jewelers, metal workers, and stone masons. Never had the temple seemed so populous. And yet, no one had seen Ninsha more recently than two days earlier.

Even the temenos guards said they hadn't seen her. If she left the compound, one of them had to have seen her. I said so to Adda.

"There was no reason for them to remember her. She belongs here, and the guards are there to protect us against outsiders."

I worried my necklace. "I must go tell the ensi that she's disappeared."

"What should I do?" Adda asked.

"Search the temenos, including all the storerooms." I rushed out of the gate and through the streets to Kaku's palace. For once I didn't stop to admire the sculptures. I went right to his reception courtyard and paced at the back, waiting my turn.

When he called me up, I didn't have to say anything.

He half-rose from his chair. "What's happened?"

"My companion, Nin-sha-su-gu, is missing. No one has seen her in at least two days."

Kaku relaxed back into his chair. "Perhaps she's gone back to Akkad."

"She would have told me if she had any such plans. Besides, she's not a fool to travel through Sumer when armies are marching."

"Servants run away all the time. It's nothing to be upset about."

"She was my friend, not a servant. I need you to send guards around the city to look for her."

"I can't spare them."

"You have to."

This time he stood fully up. "No, I don't. I am ensi here. What authority do you even have now, with your father dead? Will your brother support you as zirru?" 165

I was shocked into silence. Rimush had always copied Mother's disdain of me. What if, out of spite, he gave my position to someone else? But wouldn't it serve Rimush as well as it did Father to have me in the highest religious position in Sumer?

"I see you're not so sure either." Kaku crossed his arms. "Have your priests search, if you must. My guards and the men of Ur are joining the city of Lagash in marching against Rimush."

"What?" I stared at him for several moments. "But you can't. He'll destroy your army and then come to do the same to Ur."

He chuckled. "I don't think so. We'll win our freedom."

"Don't be foolish!"

"You've worn out my patience, zirru. Leave me. I have much to do to prepare."

CHAPTER THIRTY

I hurried back to the temples. I saw things now that I'd missed on my way to the palace: a line outside a metal smith's, men fletching arrows or sharpening axes. The men of Ur were preparing to rebel against Rimush.

I stopped dead and put a hand against my mouth. Would the rebels of Ur come for me in their anger against first my father and now my brother? The high priestess of the moon god traditionally came from among the young noblewomen of Ur. Some might consider me an interloper.

As soon as I entered the temenos, I called the priests and workers together. "The city of Ur is rebelling against the new king. For safety's sake, you should stay within the temenos whenever possible. However, I would like a few volunteers to search the city for Nin-sha-su-gu."

Several men stepped forward. I hadn't realized that Ninsha had made so many friends among the priests and workers.

Tears sprang to my eyes. "Thank you. Please report to my office and speak to me or Adda for instructions."

I went to my office immediately afterward, and volunteers showed up soon after.

"We want to help Ninsha however we can," a burly butcher said.

"What do you want us to do?" asked Me-zi-da.

I sent the volunteers off in twos to canvas the city and then climbed to the top of the temple to pray for a long time to Suen's effigy in His sanctuary. He gave me no sign that He would help me—and He had never appeared to me, as Inanna had—but I felt calmer afterward.

167

The following days dragged by. The would-be warriors marched out. The men searching for Ninsha determined that vendors who knew Ninsha hadn't seen her recently. After two weeks I called a halt to the search.

"Ninsha's being kept against her will somewhere, I know it. But no one has seen her."

Adda said, "If she's not here in Ur, she may be in a nearby city."

"You're right. I'll ask the volunteers if they are willing to search Larsa, Eridu, and Uruk." I immediately went to look for the men who had searched Ur. Most agreed to look elsewhere, so I sent them off, temporarily assigned others to their duties, and then waited and fretted.

Ninsha had been part of my life as far back as I could remember. I had taken her for granted, as if she were another eye or arm. I had assumed she would always be nearby, taking care of me. But now that she was gone, I thought of nothing but her. I was lonely and blamed myself for her disappearance. If I had organized a search the day she disappeared, she might be home now. She wasn't one for staying up late. I should have known she was missing the first night.

But I couldn't worry only about her. I was a citizen of Ur now. For the next three weeks, I walked the streets of the city, encouraging those who remained to flee. Many were willing to take my advice, but some outright laughed at me. In the evenings, I worked on the temple hymns.

I also instructed the guards to start training the priests in both the bow and the spear. I hoped we wouldn't need to defend the temenos, but we needed to be ready. My father had sometimes destroyed temples and taken their gods back to Akkad. Knowing Rimush, I expected him to be even more vindictive.

Meanwhile, the men who went to Eridu to look for Ninsha came back first, with no news. A day later, I was disappointed once again when the men who went to Larsa came back empty-handed. Four days went by before the men who went to Uruk came back, again without Ninsha. I walked toward them, feeling nearly too heavy to move. Another disappointment. Where should I look next?

"High priestess, we have some possible good news," Me-zi-da said. "A couple servants of Lugalanne's reported seeing a new woman in the palace for several days about the time Ninsha went missing. We couldn't find her though."

I took a deep breath. "I must go to Uruk to talk to Lugalanne." I thanked the men then turned and headed to my office.

"Adda, the men who went to Uruk heard rumors that suggest Ninsha was in Lugalanne's palace. I must go there and talk to him. Can you find me a guide?"

He frowned. "I don't think you should go during such a troubled time."

"You always give me good advice. But I have to rescue my friend, no matter how dangerous it is."

"Even so, I would be remiss if I didn't recommend you stay here."

"Noted. But I'll go by myself if I have to."

He scratched his chin. "I'll go with you, Esh. I'll order some guards to accompany us. Even by boat, the trip to Uruk isn't safe for two people alone right now."

"Do whatever you think is necessary, as long as we can leave soon." I left him to arrange the trip and went to the Gipar House. Despite Simtur's continuing disrespect, she was the senior priestess after me and had handled the zirru's duties before I arrived. So I put on her the burdens of feeding the gods and accomplishing my other duties while I was in Uruk.

Adda and I left the next morning. He had found a troop of sorts of six former guards and soldiers. They were gray-haired and moved stiffly; everyone younger and spryer had marched off in Kaku's army. But their armor and weapons, seen from a distance, would deter some wrongdoers. I tried not to think about the bandits we encountered on the way to Mari, when neither our large party nor the many armed young men in it had prevented the attack.

We rented a sailboat to take us up the holy Buranun to one of Uruk's harbors. The wind blew from the southeast for a change, and we sped up the sluggish river.

At the gate by Uruk's harbor, the guards didn't want to let us in until I pulled on my rolled-brim hat to prove that I was zirru of Suen in Ur. Adda visited his aunt, a widow, who offered us rooms for the night.

The next morning I dressed in my priestly finery and jewelry and presented myself at Lugalanne's palace, a sprawling building of mud brick that shone golden in the early sunlight. "I am here to see Lugalanne."

"The ensi doesn't see anyone without an appointment."

"I'm the zirru of Nanna in Ur."

"Makes no difference."

"Then may I see Lugalanne's vizier?"

He turned and gestured to a servant, who approached and asked me to follow him. The servant led me to an office in the outer wall of the palace.

"I'm the Enheduanna, zirru of Suen in Ur. I've come to see Nin-sha-su-gu, the sister of Lugalanne."

The vizier didn't look at me but kept searching through a basket of tablets. "She's not here right now."

I felt suddenly more alert. Ninsha had been here! I clasped my shaking hands. "Then I need to speak to Lugalanne. Can you arrange it?"

"Yes. If you will wait in the courtyard outside, he should be able to see you this morning."

I sat on a stool in the courtyard, which was decorated with frescos of battles. I tried to sit still, but my whole body thrummed with excitement. I was close to finding Ninsha and taking her home.

After a long while, a servant came to call for me, and I followed him to a long room where Lugalanne, dressed in a blue fringed robe and many rings and bracelets, sat on a throne of cedarwood new enough that the scent still lingered in the room. His large cylinder seal of red jasper hung from a gold chain pinned to his robe. He smiled at me. "Welcome, my dear. What brings you here?"

His smile was friendly, but I didn't trust him, and I bristled at his disrespectful address. "I'm looking for your sister Ninsha. She disappeared from the Gipar about two months ago."

His grin turned to a snarl. "And you didn't notify me, her nearest kin, about her disappearance?"

I blinked. He'd never shown any interest in her. "I didn't think you'd care."

"She was my responsibility."

"No, she was mine. She came to Ur as my companion."

"She was a royal hostage, and your family treated her as if she were a servant."

I winced. Did Ninsha tell him that? Or did my father say something when they met? "Not anymore. She's now my companion, by her own choice."

He glared, all politeness gone. "You kept her from marrying and having a family of her own."

"She chose to be with me." The words came out louder than I had intended.

He leaned back in his chair and steepled his hands. "You think so, do you? Why did you wait so long to look for her?"

"I've been looking for her for two months!" I stopped and took a couple of deep breaths before speaking again. "My men reported three days ago that she had been seen in Uruk, and I came here right away to take her home."

"This should have been the first place you looked, here in her real home with her real family."

I bit back a retort. "I don't want to argue with you, Lugalanne. Where is Ninsha? I'll take her home to Ur now."

Lugalanne grinned nastily. "You've come too late. She's in the city of Lagash."

My mouth fell open. After the first moment of shock, I thought perhaps he was joking. But his unfriendly smile made it clear he wasn't. "Lagash? What's she doing there?"

"Her husband, Lu-Ab-u, lives there."

Her husband? Lugalanne must have kidnapped Ninsha and forced her to marry for some benefit of his own. *Poor Ninsha! The faster I get to Lagash, the better.* I turned my back on Lugalanne and stalked out of the room to find my traveling companions.

☙

Back at Adda's aunt's house, I recounted my meeting to Adda. "We must leave for Lagash first thing tomorrow to rescue Ninsha."

"Esh, I must point out that Lagash is at war with your brother," Adda said. "Going there would be dangerous."

"We need to get Ninsha out of there before Rimush takes the city."

171

He threw his hands up in exasperation. "And then what?" His voice was loud. "Ur is in just as much danger."

He was right. "As the zirru, I have to go back to Ur. But Ninsha doesn't. We could send her to Akkad."

"If we split up your guard, neither of you will have enough protection. And the battlefield is between Lagash and Akkad."

I was getting tired of his worries. "Do you have a better idea?"

The widow peeked into the room. "When I said you could stay here, I didn't know there would be loud arguments."

"We'll be quieter," I promised.

The widow looked skeptical, but she left us.

Adda stroked his beard. "My lady, what about Ninsha's husband?"

"He deserves to be beaten," I said softly.

"But if they're legally married—"

"She must have been forced into it. I'll rescue her whether or not he approves."

Adda sighed. "What are your orders?"

"Find us a caravan to travel with to Lagash. If you think it's going to be as dangerous as you said, hire some mercenaries. I want to leave tomorrow morning if possible."

"I'll go take care of things now."

CHAPTER THIRTY-ONE

Caravans to Lagash were few and far between because of the fighting, and we couldn't leave Uruk for three days. No one knew where exactly the armies were now or whether one side had already won, and few merchants were willing to risk their cargo or their lives going from Uruk to Lagash.

Mul-la was an exception. His trading routes were between cities along the two holy rivers, the Buranun and the Idigna. This week he intended to take grain and cloth from Uruk across the desert to Lagash and bring back beads, gold, and silver imported from Meluhha. He welcomed our company, especially our eight newly hired mercenaries.

Mul-la had been a soldier in his younger years but now made a humorous figure: Although armed with sword and knife, he had a large round belly that would interfere with drawing either. He was still strong, though. His caravan consisted primarily of other former soldiers, who quickly formed a bond with our guards, and two other merchants.

During the preparations, I went to the House of Heaven, Uruk's great temple of Inanna, with three white sheep as an offering and prayed for Ninsha's safety and our success in reaching her.

"You did a good job finding an experienced merchant for us to travel with," I told Adda.

"If we encounter an army, our gray-haired guards will be quickly mown down, and the mercenaries will run away," he said flatly.

"Inanna will protect us. We're acting in the cause of righteousness."

"Few would consider it righteous to take a man's wife away from him."

Stung by his rebuke, I sharpened my own tone. "I've made my decision. The gods are sure to be on our side."

❦

Once we passed the farms on the outskirts of Uruk, we saw no more canals. The caravan followed a path through unchanging dry, scrubby steppe. Now I understood why Mul-la had packed so many water skins and wineskins, and I hoped there were enough to last us until Lagash. I wondered whether we'd be eating dried fish the whole trip.

In the late afternoon, we passed a bachelor's herd of eight male gazelles, and I heard the twang of a bow. A moment later, the largest gazelle crumpled to the ground, and the others fled. Mul-la walked out to the body still holding his bow. He checked that the animal was dead then motioned for a cook to come get the carcass.

"We'll camp here tonight," he said.

The two cooks got busy digging a fire pit and butchering the gazelle. A black vulture circled overhead. Soon the smell of roasting meat wafted through the camp, accompanied by the shouts and moans of the guards gambling. Before the sun had gone completely down, the meat was done and served in bowls, and wineskins were passed out.

That first day set the routine for the days to follow. Starting with the fifth day, however, deserters from the armies of Ur and Lagash began crossing our path. Some were wounded; all were hungry and thirsty, with desperate eyes. Mul-la began carrying his bow at all times, and the guards marched in a tighter, quieter formation around the wagons. My chest was so tight, I could barely breathe, and I kept close to the guarded wagons. I waited until my bladder was painfully full before leaving the caravan to relieve myself.

Some of the deserters destined for Lagash fell in behind us. The guards occasionally routed them, but they caught up with us again. I glanced over my shoulder often at the staggering, bloody men.

"Perhaps we should go talk to the deserters," I said. "I want to find out the status of the rebellion."

"It would be safer if you stayed with the caravan," Adda said. "I'll go." He patted his knife as if reassuring himself he had it then went to talk to Mul-la. He then went to the wagon that held the water skins and loaded himself with several before heading toward the deserters.

He returned after a long while without the skins. "They deserted after only a few skirmishes among the advance guards. The real battle hadn't happened yet. But they said it was clear the Akkadian army would triumph."

"So Rimush must be on his way to Ur or Lagash. The men following us shouldn't be heading home."

"I told them that."

I glanced back. "They're still there. No one believed you."

"The more important matter is, where should we go?"

I raised my eyebrows. "Lagash, to find Ninsha, of course. Rimush and I may not be on the best terms, but I doubt he would hurt me when I act in our family's interest as the wife of Suen."

"Rimush may not be able to control his rampaging army."

"Then we need to talk to Mul-la about going faster."

☙

After Adda spoke to Mul-la, we traveled only far enough to find a herd of gazelles to supply us our supper. Mul-la shot two animals in quick succession. Black vultures arrived and circled while a cook dragged one animal toward the caravan. He left the first gazelle by the other cook, who was digging a firepit, and went back for the second.

I saw movement from the corner of my eye. Before I could call out, a lioness charged the cook and a second stalked from the side. Growling, the first lioness grabbed the gazelle on the opposite side from the cook, who was frozen with fear. Eyes wide, he held tight to the carcass.

The lioness tugged harder. The cook fell, still holding on, and the lioness dragged away the gazelle and the cook both.

I was standing next to the wagon holding water skins and wineskins. I grabbed a skin and hurled it at the lioness.

After it hit the lioness' head, she took a couple sideways steps but kept her hold on the gazelle.

"Let go!" Mul-la yelled to the cook. He shot an arrow. It landed in the lioness' hindquarters. She began shaking the gazelle and wrested it from the cook. She turned and dragged it away.

The second lioness took a step toward us and snarled. Her fetid breath made me gag and turn my head.

Trembling, I backed up against a wagon.

Then she spun and followed the first lioness.

Dizzy and with a tight chest, I dropped to my knees and sucked in air.

"What kind of idiot are you?" Mul-la yelled at the cook. He strode to him and hit him over the head with his bow. "A man can't win against a lion."

The cook stood up, his face scarlet with embarrassment. "I was too scared to move. I'm sorry I lost the gazelle."

"He's sorry he lost the gazelle," Mul-la muttered. "At least I didn't lose a cook too." He grabbed the cook's shoulders and turned him back and forth. "Are you hurt?"

The cook started shaking as if it were a cold winter's night. "I don't think so."

Mul-la slapped him on the back. "You'll have a story to tell your grandchildren." He walked over to Adda and me.

I hastily stood.

"Tell me again what the deserters told you," Mul-la said.

Adda did. "We have to assume that King Rimush has conquered both armies and is now set on punishing Lagash and Ur."

Mul-la pursed his lips. "The Sumerians could have won."

"Rimush has thousands of well-armed professional soldiers," I said. "Ur's army was made up of craftsmen, farmers, and bureaucrats."

"Whether we continue to Lagash or go home, we could encounter an army bent on destruction," Adda said.

"I am determined to go to Lagash and rescue Ninsha," I said.

"My situation is different." Mul-la scratched his stomach. "A city preparing to be besieged won't want to buy cloth. I might as well head back to Uruk and wait for news."

"But people in Lagash will want the grain you carry," I said.

"Yes, but I'd be selling only half my goods. It's not worth the danger."

Adda stroked his beard. "The high priestess and I and our guards will keep going ahead to Lagash. Can you spare some water skins for us?"

"Yes, and maybe some of tonight's gazelle. You're two days from the city."

I clasped my arms. We would be on our own now.

CHAPTER THIRTY-TWO

Without the wagons, we made better time. At the end of the first day after the caravan left us, we saw three city mounds at a far distance. "Lagash and Girsu," Adda said.

I strained to see flames or dust clouds but saw neither. Rimush's army had not yet arrived.

"Why are there three mounds instead of two?" I asked.

"Lagash covers two hills," Adda said.

As we got closer to Lagash, we were astonished to see how huge it was, at least ten times as big as Ur, and that it was set among marshland on the edge of a sea. Cows grazed among the reeds. Gardens of date palms lined the sea's edge, and tamarisks and poplars grew on the levees. Gulls squawked overhead, and clusters of flamingos scooped up their suppers with upside-down heads. Boats were entering and exiting the harbor.

We arrived in Lagash hungry and thirsty, thanks to the deserters who had followed us and with whom we had shared our water. They scattered as soon as we went through the unguarded gate to the city. Although it was midafternoon, the streets were nearly deserted, with mostly women out. Of the men we did see, almost all were too old or too young to fight. I wondered how the deserters would fare at home. Their youth and sunburned skin made them stand out. It would be clear to all that they had deserted the city's army.

The two mounds of the city were even higher than Ur's. The men we saw did not shave their heads but wore their hair over their ears. Otherwise I could have been in Ur or Uruk, with the streets lined with adjoining mud-brick houses and shops.

When we saw a street vendor, we stopped to get some roasted meat, bread, and beer. I regretted leaving Lugalanne angrily and not questioning him further. As a result, I knew nothing of Lu-Ab-u, Ninsha's husband, so I had to ask strangers where he lived, starting with the street vendor. She, however, knew neither Lu-Ab-u nor Ninsha.

Our bellies full, Adda and I walked toward the temple of Ningirsu, the god of agriculture and healing, questioning people on the way. At last, a prosperous-looking merchant said he was a friend of Lu-Ab-u and gave us directions to his house.

As we headed there, my stomach became tighter and tighter with worry. I wasn't sure what to expect, but it seemed possible, perhaps even likely, that Ninsha had been injured during her kidnapping and her forced marriage. I hoped that she would be well enough to travel and worried that she would be deeply embarrassed for me to see her in her degraded state.

We reached the reed door. I took a deep breath and knocked.

A woman I assumed was a servant opened the door. "Yes?"

"I'm here to see Nin-sha-su-gu. Please tell her it's Esh."

"Wait here, please." The woman went deeper into the house.

Ninsha came to the door, her eyes wide with disbelief. "It *is* you. Come in! Come in! What a surprise to see you!"

"I've been searching since I discovered you were kidnapped."

She tilted her head. "Kidnapped?" As our guards waited outside, she led Adda and me through a courtyard with a fresco of boats on the sea. The sunlight sparkled on her jeweled belt, necklace, and head ornament. Her arms each had several silver bracelets. We continued to a reception room that was painted blue. We sat on stools.

The servant came in after us, carrying a jug of what smelled like juice and placed it on a table. She left and returned with mugs and a plate of cheeses and almonds.

I looked carefully at Ninsha. There were no bruises or cuts on her anywhere that I could see. In fact, her face seemed to glow.

"A lot has happened in the past two months," she said. "I hardly know where to start."

"Don't worry. Your ordeal is over now. We can leave here as soon as you pack. Your servant can come too, if you like."

"Leave? Whatever for? I have a home here now." She beamed at me.

"You can't stay here. Rimush and his army are coming to destroy the town."

Her brow wrinkled. "I have to wait for my husband to return."

"Come with me, Ninsha. I'll protect you from him."

"Esh, you misunderstand what happened. I wasn't kidnapped. Didn't you get my letter?"

"Letter? No, I didn't."

"Lugalanne came to the Gipar to tell me that he had arranged a marriage for me. I went with him back to Uruk to meet Lu-Ab-u and found him to be a decent man. I wrote you a letter, which Lugalanne promised to send to you by messenger, and Lu-Ab-u and I were married."

I sat stunned. It took many moments before I could form words. "But you can't stay here. I need you."

Ninsha patted my hand. "You knew this would have happened someday. I told you I wanted marriage and children. I'm happy with Lu-Ab-u. I look forward to having his babies."

"Is he with Lagash's army now?"

"Yes."

"Rimush's army will win," I said urgently. "Rimush won't let the people of Lagash go unpunished. Please, you have to come with me."

She pursed her lips. "You don't know that. Your father knocked down the walls of rebel cities. Surely that's all Rimush will do...*if* he wins."

"You've forgotten how mean and vindictive Rimush is."

She breathed audibly. "I have a husband now," she said slowly and deliberately. "It's unworthy of you to try to frighten me into abandoning him."

"But Ninsha—"

She put her fingers on my lips. "Shhhh. I've made my decision."

I buried my face in my hands. "I can only stay a little while. I need to return to Ur before Rimush's troops arrive there."

"Esh, everything will turn out better than you expect."

Adda leaned forward and cleared his throat. "My lady, we should leave now."

"So soon?" This dangerous rescue mission had been in vain. It hurt my heart to leave Ninsha here in jeopardy, but she had the right to make her own decision, much as I wanted to do it for her.

Adda said, "We don't know how fast Rimush's troops will travel."

We all stood. I put my arms around Ninsha, and we hugged a long time. At last I broke away. "I wish you joy in your husband and children." I hurried outside without waiting for the servant. When Adda joined me, I was leaning against the outside wall, crying.

He sent the guards and mercenaries to fill the waterskins. He said nothing to me as we left the city and went back into the desert. The northwest wind was blowing hard, and we staggered against it. Dust flew in my eyes and blurred my vision.

"You must think me a fool," I said. I certainly felt like one.

"Not at all." Adda's mouth quirked. "But you were rather resistant to the idea Ninsha wasn't kidnapped."

My ears burned. "I knew she wouldn't leave Ur of her own free will without letting me know."

"If only her letter hadn't been 'lost.'" Adda cleared his throat. "I suspect Lugalanne purposely disposed of it."

"He does seem to relish causing me problems. If I didn't need his good will, I would ban him from the temenos." After a moment, I asked, "Do you think I did the right thing, not forcing Ninsha to come with us?"

"If you had forced her, she would have never forgiven you."

"But at least she'd live."

"There's no guarantee that you and I will survive Rimush's attack on Ur. Only the gods know whether Ninsha would be safer in Lagash or with us."

181

CHAPTER THIRTY-THREE

We beat Rimush to Ur, although we didn't know by how much. It was late afternoon when we arrived, too late for the mercenaries we had hired in Uruk to go home, so I promised them beds in the temenos. The sixteen of us reached at the main gate to the temenos hungry and tired.

"Please state your business here," one of the guards said. His broken-nosed face was unfamiliar, as was the face of the other guard.

"I am Enheduanna, zirru of Suen," I said sharply. "These men work for me."

The guards crossed their spears in front of me. "You can't come in," Broken Nose said.

My brow shot up. "I am the zirru of Suen."

"Not anymore, you're not," Broken Nose said.

I took a step forward. "Of course I'm the zirru. Let us in immediately. I order it."

"Sim-tur is now the zirru. You are no longer welcome here."

My face heated up, and I knew it must be flushing. "Who are you to tell me so?"

"We work for Lugalanne, ensi of Uruk. Now please, move away from the gate. Others are waiting to come in."

I stepped to the side, and my entourage followed suit. I approached a priest who had been waiting behind us. "What is going on?"

"My lady, Sim-tur has made herself zirru."

My heart pounded, and I glared at the priest. "How could you let her?"

He dropped his gaze. "My lady, we're only priests. We can't stand up to Lugalanne's soldiers."

"Lugalanne." *That man truly enjoys interfering in my life.* "How many of the guards are his men?"

"Eight or ten. My lady, I need to tend to my duties."

"Of course. Go, then." I turned to Adda. "If the ensi were here, he would object to Uruk soldiers taking charge of Ur's holiest spot. But the ensi went off with the army. We're on our own."

"What should we do now?" Adda asked.

"Let's try the other gates. With luck, one's not guarded."

We encountered more of Lugalanne's men at the next three gates. I didn't hold out high hopes for the fifth and last gate, but when we arrived, both guards were men I recognized. How foolish of someone to have let them guard together.

"Let us in!" I said.

One guard looked down at the ground. "I'm sorry, my lady, but we can't, or we'll be murdered as the other guards were."

I stepped aside so they could see my men. "I have six soldiers from Ur and eight mercenaries from Uruk. Add you two, and we have sixteen men to their eight or ten."

His mouth dropped open. "You mean to fight on holy ground?"

"Not unless we have to," I said. "Are you with us?"

They let us in, and I led my men to the Gipar House. It had only two entrances, so I sent Adda with half the men to one entrance and I led the remaining men to the other entrance, where we crouched down on either side of the doorway. The sun would be setting soon, and Sim-tur would need to leave the Gipar to feed Suen.

Sure enough, soon she came out. As she took a couple steps toward the temple, we sprang up. My men pulled their weapons out.

She gasped and stepped back, then drew her eating knife. "Don't you dare touch me!"

My men circled her.

Waving her knife, she glared at them.

The men behind her nodded at those in front and then rushed her, grabbing her arms from behind. The other men closed on her.

"Drop the knife!" I ordered.

"No!" Sim-tur thrashed but couldn't break free. One of the guards forced the knife from her hand. It dropped into the dirt.

Blood pounding in my ears, I stepped forward and yanked off the rolled-brim hat she wore.

"How dare you!" she said. "I am zirru now. You are nobody."

"I am the one Suen chose as His high priestess, and I am the one who's been consecrated. It's you who are nobody. For your rebellion, I'm expelling you from the Gipar. You are no longer one of Suen's priestesses."

Adda cleared his throat. "My lady, perhaps you should execute her. She's bound to cause trouble in the future."

"I think casting her out is punishment enough. She has wits enough to know to leave Ur." I pointed at two of the mercenaries. "You and you, remove her from the Gipar by the gate we entered."

"Guards! Guards!" she shouted, struggling again.

The two mercenaries took her from those who held her, and I removed Sim-tur's sash and gagged her with it. The mercenaries left.

I motioned for the rest of the men to follow me, and I walked around the Gipar to join up with the rest of the men. "Sim-tur is on her way out of the city. Now we must send Lugalanne's guards back to Uruk. Ready your weapons and follow me."

I led them to the nearest gate and had them line up in two rows the width of the gate. Settling the hat of the high priestess on my head, I walked up to the guards. "I've had the scoundrel Sim-tur ousted from the Gipar House. There's no longer any reason for you to be here. Go back to Uruk!"

One looked at the two lines of armed men and scratched his nose. "She's gone, you say?"

"Yes. You may catch up with her if you leave now. She left by the north gate. Lugalanne might appreciate your escorting her to Uruk."

The other guard muttered, "Bad enough we weren't able to keep her safe here. Lugalanne will be boiling if she walks to Uruk by herself."

They left their posts and headed off. I left two of my men to guard that gate in case anyone came back, and the rest of us went to the remaining three gates. Guards at the first two gates were easily convinced to find Sim-tur and accompany her to Uruk. But at the main gate, we ran into trouble.

"I don't believe you," Broken Nose said.

"If you don't leave, you'll have to fight my men. Meanwhile, Sim-tur is getting farther away."

In response they brought up their spears.

I skittered to the side, and my men closed on Lugalanne's guards. Neither side wore armor or a helmet, so the confrontation was bound to be bloody. Adda joined me at the side, and the remaining six men slowly closed.

Lugalanne's guards shouted for their comrades, but no one responded. They still held their spears at the ready.

I shouted, "Now!"

Yelling, my men leapt forward, jabbing their spears. Lugalanne's men jumped back, but not fast enough. Broken Nose was stabbed in the chest, and the other man run through the shoulder. The latter dropped his spear and grabbed at his wound.

"Halt!" I gestured toward the man with the spear in his shoulder. "We'll take care of your wounds if your companion will drop his spear."

Broken Nose looked at my six men, all uninjured, and spat on the ground. He dropped his spear.

The priests now crowding the courtyard cheered for me. I lifted my arm and waved to them. Sim-tur must not have run things well.

Adda stepped forward. "I'll make sure an asu healer sees them. Come with me, men."

My heart still pounded, and I felt as if I needed to run around the temenos. It was long past time for Suen to eat, so I started toward the House Sending Light to the Earth.

"High priestess! High priestess!"

I turned around and saw one of the priests leading a dusty man with cuts up and down his legs and arms. I recognized him as a leatherworker from town.

When they reached me, the priest said, "Tell the zirru what you told me."

He stared with empty eyes. "I was in the battle with Rimush's troops. They killed most of us and captured almost all of the rest. I was one of the few men of Ur to escape."

"Rimush won the battle?"

"Yes. He crushed us."

"Rimush will come here to punish the city. You need to flee to Eridu. Take your family and friends with you. Go now."

The soldier's eyes widened, and he grabbed the sides of his head. Then he turned and ran into the city.

I wondered how I could get the rest of Ur's citizens to leave.

❦

Preparing for Rimush's arrival consumed us. I hired the eight mercenaries from our trip to join the temple guards. I set the mercenaries to training the priests and workers on the bow and spear. Meanwhile, Adda hired a hairdresser for me, Ilum-pal, and I spent much of my time at the sanctuary on top of the House Sending Light to the Earth, praying to Suen to protect his city and watching for the dust cloud that would travel with Rimush's army.

Once I saw it, far in the distance, there was no question whose army it was. The dust cloud was many times the size of the one Ur's troops made leaving the city. A chill ran down my back, and I clasped my arms tight to me.

While the priests and guards prepared, I charged Adda with sending messengers to all the temple's farmers, fishermen, and weavers and other craftspeople who lived outside the temenos wall and ordering them to leave the city or shelter at the temple. We would be crowded, but if anything was spared in the city, it would likely be the temples.

Then I put on my regalia and went door to door again through the city urging people to flee to Eridu or to the swamps just beyond it. Many people refused to leave before their son, father, or brother came home. Some men of Ur's army had straggled in, but many, I knew, wouldn't be coming home.

I came across a fletcher's shop still open and went inside.

An elderly man sat by a pot of bitumen, attaching bronze arrowheads to poplar shafts. He looked up when I entered. "Good afternoon, high priestess."

"Grandfather, the army of Rimush is on its way here to punish Ur. You should leave the city. Go to Eridu."

For his answer, he stuck out his withered leg. "I can't leave."

"Do you have some family to help you?"

"Three sons, but they all went to fight the Akkadians." He spit into the dirt.

I winced. Losing three sons would be a great blow. "Can any of your neighbors help you?"

"They've already left."

"The House Sending Light to Earth is crowded, but we have room for you. We'd like to hire you to make arrows and spears for us."

"Priests need weapons about as much as they need baby rattles."

"We must protect Suen and his house. The priests are preparing to fight anyone who tries to breach the temenos wall. Shall I send a wagon for you this afternoon?"

"I didn't say I'd do it."

"Rimush's army is not like a Sumerian army, coming to raid and leaving once they have some booty. You'll likely be killed if you stay here."

He scratched his chin. "I have three daughters-in-law and grandchildren."

"If you love them, send them away now."

"I want them in the temenos with me."

"I'll be honest: They'll be safer if they leave."

"Let them stay in the temenos, and I'll make your arrows and spears and fight on your walls."

"I'll send a wagon for all of you and your supplies." One problem solved, another one created. If any of them told their friends or neighbors, we might end up with a crowd of people wanting to stay at the temple.

CHAPTER THIRTY-FOUR

"From now on," I told the temenos guards, "I want all gates to the temenos closed. No one should come in unless they belong here." I told them about the fletcher and all our workers sheltering here in the temenos. "If you aren't sleeping or at a gate, I want you to be drilling the priests and workers in the use of their weapons."

One of the guards spoke up. "High priestess, to use their bows, the men will need to be at the top of the walls."

"What do you suggest?"

"We need platforms along the walls near the gates. Wagons would work. Also tables. Chests. Piles of bricks. Anything the priests can stand on to see over the walls."

"You'll be charge of that. Choose another guard to help you." I dismissed them and visited the various workers to alert them to what was happening. I spent a long time with the cooks, discussing how to stretch our supplies to last longer.

Then I climbed the ziggurat to the very top. The dust cloud was much closer already. My legs shook, and I had to sit down. I wrapped a shawl tight around me to temper the cold wind. They should leave the temple alone, I told myself. I'll talk to Rimush himself if I need to. But it didn't stop my shivering. Victorious armies often burned and pillaged against their leaders' wishes. My barely trained priests would likely have to fight.

I sighed and went into Suen's sanctuary, where I prayed for a long time for the city and the temple. I climbed down, got a roll from the kitchen to eat, and went back out into the city to continue going door to door to persuade people to abandon their beloved city.

☙

The city gates of Ur were unguarded and open because of the lack of young men; Rimush's army spilled through and rushed in various directions like overturned wine. From my perch at the top of the House Sending Light to the Earth, I could see everything, including the thousands of naked captives, their hands tied in front of themselves, outside the city wall. I shivered and again monitored the soldiers within the city. Soon, the first fires flickered. People rushed out of their houses and businesses—Why did so many stay in the city after my warnings?—only for the boys and old men to be seized by soldiers and marched out to join the prisoners. Some of the women followed, wailing and lamenting.

At first I thought the soldiers wouldn't come to the temenos, that they would stay on the other side of the canal that ran through the city. The residential areas there burned a good part of the day, and I could hear broken screams in the distance. But then a soldier found the bridge over the canal, and soon many soldiers burst onto our side, only a few blocks from the temenos. I could hear them laughing.

I ran down the stairs, holding my hat tightly to my head. By the time I reached the bottom, the army had found the temenos. I ran to the main gate, shouting to the guards, "The soldiers are at our gate. I'll talk to them." I climbed into a wagon next to the gate full of priests. They made way for me, and I looked over the wall. The men below were pressed together tightly, yet they still managed to shove each other.

"Who is your captain?" I shouted.

No one admitted to leading the soldiers.

"I am the high priestess of Suen and the sister of King Rimush. Leave here immediately."

Some laughed. Others concentrated on ramming the gate with their shoulders. It shook with each thump. The temenos guards put their shoulders and bodies against the gate on our side to relieve some of the strain on the wood.

I tried again. "Leave at once, or you'll share the fate of the captives when my brother King Rimush finds out you threatened me."

This time some of the soldiers paid attention. The ones below me elbowed each other. "You go to the king!" "No, you go!"

A soldier shoved his way to the front. He whistled loudly and waved his arms in the air. "Didn't you muttonheads hear? The priestess here claims she's the king's sister." He pointed to two men. "You, and you—go to the king and find out his orders." He crossed his arms. The soldiers at the gate stopped trying to knock the gate down but stayed where they were. A jug was passed around.

A few soldiers left the mob to head into a residential area nearby. Soon I smelled smoke, and not long after black clouds billowed above the houses and joined the dark haze over the city. Those of us on the wall coughed and blew our noses, keeping an eye on the fire that could come our way.

I clutched my frog amulet. I remembered the times Rimush had been mean to me, the times he played tricks on me, the time he tried to frame me for stealing Mani's war booty. I could imagine him letting me die. But then he would not have a family member in the highest ritual office in Ur. That alone might save me. That, and the potential loss of respect for him if he didn't prevent a mob from killing his sister.

The midafternoon sun bore down on us. Sweat ran down my face from under my hat. Both guards in the temenos and soldiers outside took off their battered copper helmets to wipe sweat from their heads.

The temple cooks brought out jugs of beer and water that the priests and guards quickly emptied. My stomach grumbled. The temples' butchers joined us at the wall, gripping a cleaver in each hand.

The soldier below who had given the orders earlier shouted up to me. "Priestess, you come out here. We won't hurt you." Several men laughed.

If I wasn't in the temenos, they would have no reason not to burn it and kill the priests and priestesses. They might even take Suen's body to Akkad, leaving Ur without its paramount god. "I'll wait here."

Looking around at the destruction in the nearby blocks, I tried not to think of Ninsha, but it was impossible. There was no reason for Rimush to treat Lagash any more lightly than Ur. She was probably dead by now. My throat tightened.

At last I saw a wave of soldiers coming closer, a banner waving overhead. I stood on my tiptoes. Rimush was among them, and soldiers on the street saluted him as he passed. When he reached the gate, he stood below and looked up at me.

"Hello, sister." He looked tired. His helmet was dusty, and his skirt and skin were mottled with gore and worse.

"Hello, brother."

"Come out here so we can talk."

"Why don't you come in?"

He smirked. "I think I will."

I called instructions down to the guards and climbed down from the wagon. Rimush strutted in.

I led my brother to the privacy of a storeroom, where the air was cooler and the sun didn't beat down on our heads.

"Why are you king and not Mani?" I asked. The question had nothing to do with the current crisis, but it popped out.

"When Father died, I was home in Akkad, and Mani was off in Dilmun." He shrugged a shoulder. "The way was open, and I took it."

The flesh on my arms crept. "You should want send your soldiers away from the temple. It's good for Akkad that I'm the high priestess of Suen."

"I realize that. I'll spare you. But your temple personnel need to be taught a lesson along with the rest of the city."

My stomach clenched. "Why? None of them rebelled against you. Their lives are here at the temple."

"It sets a bad precedent to let them go free."

What a scorpion he was! "I've had the priests and workers trained in weapons. We'll resist."

Rimush grunted. "I don't want to argue with you. What can I give you to allow my soldiers in without resistance?"

This was my chance to become priestess of Inanna, perhaps at her House of Heaven in Uruk. My days would be spent in prayer and song, devoted to the goddess I loved above all others.

All I would have to do is give the order for the priests and guards to put down their weapons and open the gate.

But what a dreadful price. Everyone—priestesses, priests, workers—would be slaughtered, and I could not live with such memories. And Suen—what was a god without priests to feed Him and honor Him? "Nothing will convince me to give up the temple. Our duty

191

is to care for Suen for the good of not just Ur but all of Sumer and Akkad. I can't let your men into His compound."

"You're speaking reason. My men are beyond reason. They'll tear your gates down."

"Are you saying you can't control them?"

He jerked and clenched his jaw. "Of course I can."

"Why don't you prove it?"

He frowned. "You're still an annoying little pest. Order the gates opened. You can leave with me."

"Please, please, send your men away from here."

"You're begging." Vitality seemed to flow back into him, and he stood straighter. "You're actually begging." His face turned hard. "Beg some more."

I knew what I needed to do, but my pride resisted. I ground my teeth. Then I slowly forced my knees to the ground. "Please, Rimush, I beg you. Turn your men away from the temple. Let me serve you as high priestess of Suen."

He gestured. "More."

"Please, don't earn the ill will of the gods by destroying Suen's house and His priests. There are no traitors or rebels here. Please, lead your men elsewhere. Leave the house of Suen alone."

Rimush smirked. "Very nicely done. Get up. I'll take the men away. It's time to dispense with the captives anyway."

CHAPTER THIRTY-FIVE

I sat on the second terrace of the House Sending Light to the Earth, shivering with relief and residual fear and no little self-disgust at my begging. Fires still blazed in some parts of Ur, while other parts lay blackened. Women roamed the streets wailing and tearing their clothing. Already, people were rummaging through the ruins while buzzards soared in circles. The temenos was an island in a sea of destruction.

Adda crossed the platform and sat next to me. "Don't look so downhearted, Esh. You did the best you could."

"Did I? I feel as if I failed."

"You saved the temples and everyone in the temenos."

"Perhaps I could have crowded in more citizens." I had done my duty to Suen but perhaps not to the city of Ur.

"King Rimush would have heard children crying and dogs barking. He wouldn't have spared us."

A horn blasted. Outside the city gate, the army was pushing the prisoners forward while Rimush climbed into his chariot. The thousands of prisoners, who huddled in a tight group, now included women. As we watched, some of the women were separated from the rest. A rope was strung from one tied pair of hands to the next. Then the line of women were led away, stumbling and crying, presumably to be sold.

Another set of women were led away, then more, and more. Soldiers began picking out men and herding them to the side, where they too were tied into dozens of roped-together lines. Their heads hung down while they shuffled away, soldiers whacking their legs with spears.

The soldiers remaining outside the gate encircled the remaining prisoners. The horn blew again, and the soldiers cut their way through the prisoners, blades flashing and blood spurting. Prisoners collapsed.

Adda turned his head away from the carnage. "Some of the priests are saying the Akkadians are monsters."

I kept watching, a witness to my brother's actions. "The Akkadian army is an instrument of Suen's justice. He could have stopped the army and saved Ur, but He chose not to."

"Do you really believe that He's punishing us? The city did nothing wrong."

I hesitated in my response. I didn't know why Suen would choose to punish Ur. It was a city of good, hard-working people who honored Him. "The ways of gods are beyond my ken."

"Mine as well."

Meanwhile, the murders went on and on, accompanied by shouts and screams. Adda, looking greenish, went back to his duties, and still the killings continued. I wondered how many I knew of those going to be enslaved, and how many of those being executed.

It was true: We Akkadians were monsters.

One captive broke away from the others and raced away. Rimush unhurriedly took up his bow and shot an arrow. The escapee fell and didn't rise again.

When the sun was near setting, I left my spot to feed the god. The killings were still going on. The scent of charcoal and burned meat lay heavy over the city. The ground outside the city gate was drenched with gore, and the soldiers were dripping sweat and blood.

I felt guilty for being alive and angry at Suen for allowing the destruction of His city.

☙

In the aftermath of the invasion, I had to cut Suen's and Ningal's rations. Food was in short supply, and the line of hungry people at the temenos gate got longer each day. The temple cooks baked bread as fast as barley came in and was ground. Some of the temples' suppliers never showed up again, and I kept busy for weeks on trips to the neighboring cities of Uruk, Larsa, and Eridu, looking for new sources of meat for the gods and barley for the citizens.

Those who had left Ur before Rimush's attack slowly trickled back into the city and began flattening the rubble to build again. Some of my guards and Suen's priests went to help their families or former neighbors with construction, and they often didn't return: many were now a widow's only son. I lost a third of my priestesses to the needs of their families, too. Even though hammers rang throughout the city, the streets seemed eerily empty.

I admired the citizens for their eagerness to rebuild Ur and joined the priests and priestesses as they passed out bread to the hungry. I still flinched at unexpected noises and clung as tightly as I could to my daily routine of grinding groats for the gods' meals, feeding the gods, singing hymns, and conducting purification rites.

Meanwhile, Rimush sent a request that I accept a man named Dan-i-li to be the new ensi of Ur. I looked over his credentials and thought him suitable, and I wrote to Rimush to tell him so. The new ensi arrived a week later.

One day I walked for most of the day outside the city walls, visiting the temples' farms and stopping to talk with other farmers. After the gods had been fed that evening, I was blurry-eyed with fatigue and eager to retire to my rooms.

I entered the main room with a single lamp and immediately took a step backward. A large, hairy animal lay in my bed. Its smell was strong and unpleasant. Why hadn't anyone told me a sacrifice had escaped?

As my eyes adjusted to the dimness, I realized it was no animal but a person, his hair wild and his body filthy. How did a beggar slip past the guards at the entrance to the temenos? With several thousand of Ur's citizens dead or enslaved, uninhabited buildings, some still with a roof and four walls, were common. Any beggar could find a place to live. Why did this one come here?

"Hey there," I said, shaking the beggar's shoulder. "I'll get some food for you but then you have to leave." His arm was pink with recent scars.

The beggar rolled over and croaked, "Esh?"

In Ur, only Adda knew me as "Esh." I took a step back. "Who are you?"

"It's me, Ninsha."   195

"Ninsha?" Surely not. I was still coming to terms with her death.

The woman brushed her loose hair from her face.

I sucked in my breath.

It was Ninsha, but a Ninsha I'd never seen before, sunburnt and hollow-cheeked. She was alive!

I threw my arms around her. "I'm so glad to see you. I thought you were dead. I should have forced you to come with me back to Ur. What about your husband?" I babbled.

"Taken for a slave."

"I'm...sorry. What happened to you?"

She slowly propped herself up on an elbow. "Can I have something to eat?"

"Yes. Of course. I'll be back soon." I went to the Gipar kitchen, and the cook gave me some bread and cheese on a plate along with a mug of beer. I hurried back to my room. "Here."

Ninsha shoved the bread in her mouth, swallowing it in gulps, then ate the cheese the same way.

"Careful. You don't want to be sick." The tightness in my throat I had carried since Lagash eased.

Paying me no attention, she downed the beer.

"Did you walk all the way from Lagash by yourself?"

She stared at me with hollow eyes.

I didn't need to know the answer right then. "I'll get a pitcher of water and some linen. I'm sure you're eager to be clean again."

When I returned, she sat passively while I undid her robe and threw it into the corner for the washerwomen in hopes the linen could be salvaged. Her body underneath was covered with scabs and scratches.

I knelt beside her. Starting with her face, I gently washed her from the head down, squashing fleas as I saw them. When I got to her feet, I started to cry. She was barefoot, and the cuts, callouses, and deep cracks made it clear she had been that way for some time. No matter how I scrubbed, I couldn't get all the dirt off her feet. It was embedded in her skin, a permanent reminder of her ordeal.

She lay back down and stared at the wall. "I need to sleep now."

I sat back on my heels. "Tomorrow I'll wash your hair, and my hairdresser, Ilum-pal, will style it." I set the pitcher and clean linen on the table and sat on the floor with my back against the wall. Why hadn't

I forced her to leave Lagash? How could I have left her there? By letting her choose her own path, I ensured she would suffer.

៹

Late the next morning, after Ninsha had woken and eaten, I helped her to my bathing room. With a groan, she sat down by the drain and tilted her head back. I poured cool water over her head and combed out her hair.

"You'll be back to normal in no time," I said.

Ninsha stared, bleary eyed.

"What would you like to do next? Get dressed?" Two of her robes were still in my chest.

No answer.

I helped her to stand, and she leaned on my arm to shuffle to the other room. I opened the chest and took out one of the robes. I wrapped it around her and pinned it over the left shoulder. "There. Do you feel better now?"

She rubbed some of the linen between her fingers. "Yes."

"Let me find you some sandals." I looked in the chest again and found a rattan pair that belonged to her. I put them on the floor for her to step into, but she didn't. "Do you want to put on the sandals?"

She swayed back and forth. "Yes." She made no move to put them on.

"Should I wrap your feet first, or do you want to wear them on your bare feet?"

"Yes."

I rubbed my face. Ninsha must be injured in mind as well as body. I took her by the shoulders and gently pressed her down to sit on the bed. I examined the bottoms of her feet and then gently slid the sandals on.

I combed her hair and put it in a clumsy knot. "Ilum-pal will come by this afternoon and do your hair beautifully. Would you like to go sew with the priestesses this morning?"

She stared at her feet.

"That's where I'll take you. It will be good for you to be with friends." I urged her to her feet and put my arm around her. We walked slowly to the workroom. I announced, "Ninsha's back home."

"Come sit down next to me, Ninsha," Ningbanda, our youngest novitiate, said, patting the top of an empty stool.

Ninsha sat. Her sunburned skin stood out in the room full of pale faces. Ningbanda handed her a needle and thread.

I patted Ninsha's back. Sewing would provide a sense of normalcy, but I wondered whether she was too tired.

"We'll make sure she's all right," Buru said. "Don't worry."

In the days that followed, caring for Ninsha and taking her to sew with the priestesses became part of my routine. One morning a few days later, as I was getting her ready to go sew, I heard a noise in the courtyard. I went out and found Lugalanne bumbling about. He and Uruk had not rebelled, after all.

"You're not allowed in here."

"Don't tell me you've forgotten about the meeting with the new ensi of Ur, Dan-i-li."

I had forgotten. "You need to leave. I'll join you there."

A scream shattered the air. I turned around. Ninsha, clutching her robe, screamed again. Her eyes were wide and full of terror.

I turned again to Lugalanne, motioning with my hands. "Go, go!" I ran back to Ninsha and embraced her then led her back into our quarters. "Everything's all right. Shh, shh."

Her screams turned to tears.

"What's wrong?" I asked.

"The man. That man."

"Your brother Lugalanne."

"My brother?" Her forehead crinkled. "Are you sure?"

"Yes. He won't hurt you. I sent him away."

"He gave me to Lu-Ab-u." She started to smile then buried her face in her hands. "Lu-Ab-u's gone."

I put my arms around her and stroked her hair, and she leaned against me. We both cried then, I for my father, she for her husband, and both of us for each other.

CHAPTER THIRTY-SIX

I walked across the city to the ensi's house. A servant let me in and led me to the throne room, where Lugalanne and another man I assumed was Dan-i-li were discussing harbor fees. The atmosphere was tense. I saluted both of them, and Dan-i-li motioned to a stool.

"So you're the high priestess," Dan-i-li said. He was a young man, perhaps one of Rimush's friends, bearded and dressed in a linen robe.

"Yes. I'm Enheduanna, King Rimush's sister. And you must be Dan-i-li, the new ensi. I'm sorry I'm late."

Lugalanne turned to me. "How's my sister?"

"Calmer now. You frightened her terribly. Your face was in shadow. She didn't realize it was you."

Dan-i-li cleared his throat loudly. "I'll get right to the point. Lugalanne, you've been accused of stationing soldiers within Ur."

Lugalanne reared back. "You make it sound as if Uruk invaded Ur. But the soldiers were here for a personal matter. I was supporting my friend Sim-tur's in her desire to be zirru of Ur."

Dan-i-li drummed his fingers. "So you don't deny sending soldiers here and keeping the true zirru out of the temenos?"

"True zirru by what standard? Sim-tur was born in Ur and was sent to the temple as a small girl. She's the best qualified by far to be zirru."

Dan-i-li turned to me. "Do you have anything to add?"

"I should point out that Suen chose me, not Sim-tur, to be zirru. And I have been officially installed as zirru. Sim-tur stole the office illegitimately and broke tradition."

Dan-i-li asked me, "Why didn't you stop her?"

"I was out of town, trying to rescue a friend."

Dan-i-li's eyebrows rose. "So you, Lugalanne, interfered with Ur's temples for a personal matter, and you, zirru, shirked your temple duties for a personal matter?"

His accusation was true. I had put Ninsha above my temple duties, and I would do it again. I could only answer the truth: "Yes, I did."

"Lugalanne?"

Lugalanne sneered and folded his arms across his chest. "It's not your place to chastise me. I'm the ensi of Uruk."

"King Rimush appointed me not only to rule Ur but also to keep an eye on events here in the south. Keep your troops out of Ur." He turned to me. "Do your duties here in Ur, or I will ask the king to appoint a new zirru. The gods take precedence over your friends."

Like Lugalanne, I answered only to the king. But I said nothing. I needed to work with Dan-i-li on the twice-yearly Akitu festival and other matters.

"You may go now," Dan-i-li said.

Outside, Lugalanne turned to me. "What happened to your sharp tongue? You didn't even try to defend yourself."

"Unlike you, I live here in Ur and have to work with the ensi. Besides, he was right. I put my personal responsibilities above my temple ones. No defense for that." I thought of the danger I'd put myself and Adda in. "I'd do it again in the same circumstances."

꽃

"That's it. I've finished copying the hymns to temples," I told Ninsha that evening. Yawning, I set the last tablet on a reed mat. I had been tired after the meeting with Dan-i-li and Lugalanne and then had worked on hymns the rest of the day until now.

"What happens next with your hymns?" Ninsha asked.

"I'll send the tablets to Rimush. I assume he'll have copies made and sent to temples all around Sumer and Akkad."

"How many hymns did you end up with?" She walked over to look over my shoulder.

"About forty."

She read from the bottom of the last tablet. "'The compiler of these tablets was Enheduanna. My king, something never before created, I gave birth to it.' Why did you put your name on the hymns? Are the priests and priestesses supposed to sing that as well?"

"No. I put my name on the hymns because I want people to know who wrote them. They're supposed to bring north and south together. It's important that I, daughter of Sargon, wrote hymns for both the Sumerians and the Akkadians, showing we're one united country now with a shared set of gods."

"Do you expect ordinary people to understand the implications?"

"What's important is that the ensis and religious personnel grasp it. The hymns could make rebellions like Ur and Lagash's less likely." I put down my stylus and turned to look at her. "Lagash's rebellion...what happened to you?"

She turned away. "Nothing happened. I barely remember that time."

"If nothing happened, why were you so frightened to see someone you thought was a strange man in our courtyard this morning?"

"I wasn't frightened." When I started to object, she went on talking. "Remember how when we came here, you thought every day would be the same and you'd be bored?"

"That certainly hasn't happened," I said, giving up my probing for now. "May future years leave us with the boredom I once loathed."

Section IV

City of Ur

Age 26

CHAPTER THIRTY-SEVEN

The last day of the spring Akitu festival, which celebrated the barley harvest and the beginning of spring, dawned clear. Eagerly, I looked out of the doorway of the Akitu House, where I had spent the past three days with Suen. Across the river Buranun, drums were already beating in Ur, and crowds gathered around the main harbor. A temple boat festooned with garlands of red cloth launched and headed toward me.

I went back inside and took a last look at Suen. I had dressed Him that morning in new clothes embroidered in gold thread and ornamented Him with new gold earrings and many necklaces of gold and lapis lazuli beads. I could see no flaw in his adornment, no detail forgotten. Clasping my hands, I prayed to Suen that everything would go well during the festival. I wanted no bystanders crushed by enthusiastic crowds, no terrified pigs knocking over the paraders, no brisk wind spreading grit over the food and drink waiting at the temple. When I finished praying, I snuffed out the incense burner's fire.

The boat arrived, and the crew of priests beached it. Four naked priests climbed out. They reached back in to take hold of a wooden palanquin adorned with gold and gemstones. They climbed the small hill to the Akitu House, and I welcomed them with the traditional greeting. After nine years as zirru and two Akitu festivals per year, I no longer had trouble remembering the rituals.

Once I stepped aside, the priests set down the palanquin, went into the Akitu House, and came back out carrying the god, Whom they placed in His palanquin. The priests lifted the ends of the two poles and conveyed Suen to the boat. I walked behind, tapping a tambourine and singing. When we reached the boat, which was decorated with tied-together stalks of barley, the god's palanquin was lifted into it. Then the four priests and I climbed in.

I was as lavishly dressed as the god, so I chose a place to sit where barley seeds wouldn't drift into my hair or onto my robe.

A priest pushed us away from the island with a pole. Four priestesses in the boat played the harp and sang as we sailed to Ur's main harbor.

The arrival of the god in Ur sparked cheers and frenetic drumming from the waiting crowd. Citizens were dressed in their finest clothes and brightest jewelry to welcome Suen back to His city. As we docked, priests and priestesses sang a song of salutation to the god. Suen's palanquin was unloaded, and the god sparkled in the light. The four priests carrying Him took slow steps toward the temple, preceded by many drummers. Ensi Dan-i-li and I fell in line behind the platform, and the priests behind us. Then came the priestesses and harp players. As the parade passed the citizens standing alongside the road, they joined at the end.

For an hour, the parade snaked through the streets, getting louder and longer as more people joined. Spectators tossed flowers in our path, and the crushed blossoms gave off a sweet smell. We entered the main gate of the temenos into the god's courtyard, which instantly became full, with more people still squeezing themselves in. The god was carried up to the first terrace of the temple, where the statue of Ningal awaited, there to watch over the festivities together until the end.

Halfway through the festival, and no fights or tramplings so far. We were doing well.

Ensi Dan-i-li climbed the stairs to the first terrace, where a tall vase awaited him. Two priests followed, one carrying a mug of sweet light beer, representing the female principle, and the other a mug of strong dark beer, representing the male principle. The drummers stopped, and priests hushed the crowd. As the gods watched, the ensi took the two mugs and poured them into the vase at the same time. When the mugs were empty and the fertility of the land ensured, the people cheered.

I led everyone in a hymn, and then the priestesses danced, slapping tambourines, the bells around their ankles jingling. The spectators crowded the tables surrounding the edges of the courtyard. Some tables held mugs and crocks of beer provided by the ensi. Other tables held several kinds of small cakes and cheeses as well as dried dates and figs.

Meanwhile, jugglers juggled, and acrobats tumbled. The ensi's musicians and the temple musicians performed in different corners of the courtyard. I looked around with satisfaction—another Akitu festival nearly done, with no gaffes or mishaps. Suen would be pleased and would continue protecting the city and its fruitfulness.

My formal duties satisfied until sundown, when the gods would be fed, I slipped through the crowd toward the food tables.

A young priest stopped me. A dusty stranger was right behind him. The priest said, "My lady, this messenger brings you an important letter from Akkad."

The stranger saluted and handed me a tablet. "High priestess, I have other tablets to deliver, so I can't wait for your answer." He saluted again and headed toward the gate.

The jostling of the crowd made it impossible to read the tablet, so I moved toward the temple steps. There, I saw from the heading that the letter was from Kalki the scribe. I read the text, sat down on the steps, and then read it again.

To Enheduanna, zirru of Ur, from Kalki, scribe of Ubil-Eshtar. May the gods protect you and keep you in good health. Your brother Rimush is dead, strangled by his own counselors with the cords on which their cylinder seals were strung. Your brother Manishtushu is now king. Be wary. Some cities will likely revolt.

Tears ran from my eyes. Mani was at last in his proper place, and he'd be a better king. Still, I was surprised to find myself grieving for Rimush. He was my brother, even if he wasn't a very good one. Perhaps I grieved that we had never settled our differences and become friends.

I wiped my eyes and headed for the ensi to share with him the contents of the letter.

৺

"Lord Dan-i-li!" I tapped him on the shoulder, interrupting his stuffing a cake into his mouth. "I must speak to you."

"In the middle of the festival? Can't it wait?"

"It's urgent."

He looked around, as did I, but there were no open spaces in the crowded courtyard. He motioned for us to go up the steps of the temple. We climbed to the first terrace and sat at the top of the steps.

I handed him the tablet. "This message just arrived from Akkad."

He pretended to study it, but the tablet was upside down, and I realized he couldn't read. "Do you, uh, have a concern for Ur in this news?" he asked.

I took pity on his manly pride. "Now that Rimush is dead and Manishtushu is king, I worry that Sumerian cities will rebel again. I encourage you not to put Ur on a disastrous path."

Frowning, he handed back the tablet and rested his elbows on his knees. "My loyalty was to Rimush. Manishtushu is nothing to me."

"He's your king!" I said. "I expect him to be a better one than Rimush."

"I've never sworn loyalty to Manishtushu. Ur is a free city now."

"That's not how the king sees it. In his eyes, you are part of the Akkadian Empire."

Dan-i-li thought for several moments. "What if he intends to replace some of the ensis with his own men? I could lose my position unless I rebel."

"You're ill equipped to rebel. Ur lost two generations of men in the rebellion after Rimush took the throne, and the next generation of boys isn't old enough yet to replace them. I counsel you not to rebel."

He looked unconvinced. "High priestess, I need more than your advice. I need a divination."

Good. If I couldn't convince him not to rebel, maybe the goddess Ningal could. "I agree you need a divination. I'll do it tomorrow morning. What question would you like me to ask Ningal?"

He was silent for several moments, watching the crowd in the courtyard. "Ask Her, 'Will Manishtushu replace me as ensi of Ur?'"

"It will be done."

That evening, by the dim light of a lamp, I wrote a letter to Mani and placed the tablet on a reed mat to dry.

"Why are you writing to him so soon?" Ninsha asked. "Don't you think he'll be busy at first?"

"His being king changes everything, Ninsha. As zirru, I need to swear my loyalty just as if I were an ensi. Also, I asked to be made a priestess of Inanna. I'm recommending the priestess Buru to be zirru in my place."

"He'll think you a better choice as zirru than Buru. Whom else can Mani count on to be totally loyal? His own daughters are much too young to take up the post."

"Mani understands how I feel about being zirru. Father made decisions for both of us without our having a say in the matter. He'll remember how that felt."

"As your brother, he'll understand. But now he has to think like a king. He'll place people where they'll serve him best. I'm afraid you're getting your hopes up too high."

"Nonsense. He'll do this for me. I'm sure of it." I turned around to face her. "I didn't see you at the festival today."

She studied her hands. "Too many men, too many of them strangers. I preferred to stay here and sew."

"Ninsha, I wish I could help you go out among people again. What can I do?"

"You worry for nothing, Esh. I don't need your help or anyone else's. I like being alone. That's why I stayed here. Don't worry about me."

After all the years we had lived together, I knew better. She still avoided men, even men she knew. We had shifted roles since she came back from Lagash: Once she had taken care of me, but now I needed to take care of her. I hoped I did as good a job at it as she had done.

CHAPTER THIRTY-EIGHT

The next morning, after feeding the gods, I went back to my quarters and into my bathing room to prepare myself for the divination. There I washed my hair and my body thoroughly. With my hair dribbling water down my back, I put on a clean robe and, to make myself worthy of being seen by the goddess Ningal, adorned myself with my rolled-brim hat, gold canoe-shaped earrings, gold armbands, several necklaces of beads, and a belt of gold beads.

Through the Gipar House I walked to the temple side of the building and went into a storage room. I knew the shelf I needed, but the containers on it were unlabeled, so I opened jar after jar to smell the contents. After sniffing many containers of incense and perfume, I found the one I wanted: not sweet smelling like the others but with a dark scent with a slight tang of cat urine: opium.

I carried the jar to the kitchen and broke a corner off one of the dark lumps it contained, dropping the soft material into a mortar. With the pestle, I crushed and ground the opium until it was in small pieces. Then I poured a small mug of wine, jiggled the ground opium into it from the mortar, and stirred it in. The wine would reduce the bitterness and magnify the effects of the opium, making it easier to hear the goddess Ningal.

I took a sip. Although I knew it would still have a bitter edge, I grimaced and my eyes squeezed shut. I added some honey and stirred the mixture until the honey was blended in.

I carried the mug and a lamp to Ningal's inner sanctum. The lamplight flickered on the gold and beads that the goddess wore, and Her silver face and hands shone like Her husband, the moon. I sang praise songs to put Her in a generous mood. Then I drank the biting wine-opium mixture down.

"Lady Ningal, great goddess of the marshes and reeds, hear my petition. The man asks for it, the ensi of Your city asks for it, Dan-i-li asks for it. He asks for the answer to a question. A new king rules Sumer and Akkad, and Dan-i-li asks, 'Will Manishtushu replace me as ensi of Ur?'"

In the divinations I'd done so far, it took a while for the goddess to answer. I knew I'd get woozy from the opium, so I sat down in front of Ningal. I prayed for an answer to Dan-i-li's question. Soon, I was stumbling over the words. My prayers kept petering out midway through and needing to be restarted. Drifting off to sleep would have been so easy, but I fought the urge. I was now in the proper state to hear Ningal's answer.

I stared at Ningal. She swayed on Her daïs, her lips moving silently. The votive statues behind me chanted in a language I didn't understand. Although the lamp was still burning, the room darkened.

At last Ningal spoke. In a clear, sweet voice, She said, "Rise and feed the ravens; sit and starve the vultures."

I could see the two possible futures as clearly as if they were happening right then, side by side. But it was so hard to keep my eyes open.

When I awoke, the room was dark but for a grayness along the edge of the doorway. I felt around to find my lamp then rose and left the sanctuary.

Buru was leaning against the wall but stood straight when she saw me. "The ensi is waiting for you outside. I've already received his sacrifice."

"Thank you." Nauseated, I put my hand against the cool mudbrick wall to steady myself. Then I went outside to find Dan-i-li.

"There you are! What did the goddess say?" His eyes were bright and attentive, and he leaned toward me.

I put my hand above my eyes to shade them from the bright sunlight. "She said, 'Rise and feed the ravens; sit and starve the vultures.'"

He repeated it several times. The eagerness on his face disappeared, and his eyebrows squished together. "What does it mean?"

"It's for you to interpret. I am only the messenger of the goddess."

"What good's a prophecy that can't be understood? Are you sure you asked the right question?"

"I asked the question you gave me. Whether it was the 'right' question is another matter. Shouldn't the shepherd care more about the sheep than about the height of the rock he stands on?"

He blinked several times then flushed a dark red. He turned and stalked off.

ت

I wanted so badly to be a priestess of Inanna that although it would take at least half a month to get a response to my letter to Mani, I began preparing to leave the Gipar House. In the meantime, Dan-i-li remained loyal to Mani; the ravens did not feast on the men of Ur, and the buzzards had to look elsewhere for the dead.

I returned most of the zirru's jewelry to the House of Plenty—I still needed a rolled-brim hat and necklaces for the moon festivals—and began packing up my few personal items. I spent a day with Adda, making sure the accounts were in order and ready for the new zirru. As the days passed, it got harder and harder to maintain a dignified expression. The corners of my mouth stretched up in a grin anytime I wasn't consciously forcing them downward.

A month went by, and then I was requested outside the Gipar House. A man waited, dusty from the road. I summoned a mug of beer for him and let him refresh himself while I trembled with excitement.

"I come from Akkad from King Manishtushu with this message." He handed me a tablet.

"Thank you. I have no return message. Go to the kitchens of the Suen temple and tell them I ordered you fed and put up for the night." Clutching the tablet, I scurried to our rooms to read it in private.

Ninsha put down her sewing when she saw what I carried. "What does it say? Did he agree?"

Grinning, I started reading it out loud to her.

From Manishtushu, king of Akkad and Sumer, king of the world, to his sister, Enheduanna, zirru of Suen in Ur. May the gods Ilaba and Inanna keep you forever in good health! Your

loyalty was never in doubt. I know you will do what is necessary
for our family. I need you to remain zirru of Suen in Ur—

"Oh, no!" I took a sharp breath and put a hand to my forehead.
"How—what—how can this be? He can't mean it."

Ninsha reached out and put a comforting hand on my arm. "What
does the rest of it say?"

I need you to remain zirru of Suen in Ur, and you must also
become en-priestess of Anu in Uruk. I don't trust ensi
Lugalanne.

My heart pounded, and I felt faint. I slumped onto a stool and put
my face in my hands.

"How can you be high priestess in both Ur and Uruk at the same
time?" Ninsha asked.

"I'm afraid I may never be a priestess of Inanna."

"There are worse things in life than that."

I looked up. Ninsha's face was shadowed with sadness, as it had
been since she lost her husband to slavery. She had changed since her
time in Lagash. "You could ask Lugalanne to find you a new husband,"
I said.

"Who would want me? I'm too old."

"No, you're not. Are you afraid to marry again?"

"Certainly not!" Ninsha exclaimed. "Not at all. What makes you
think I'm afraid?"

She'd avoided men in the nine years since she came back from
Lagash, even the priests of Suen. Given the end of her previous
marriage and her presumed wartime ordeals, I didn't blame her.

"You'll always have a home with me," I said. "Maybe two homes
with me. I imagine the en-priestess of Anu has living quarters in Uruk
near the temple."

Her eyes widened. "You're going to take the position?"

"I don't have a choice. It's what's best for my family."

"Have you ever noticed that 'what's best for your family' always
ends up being best for whoever is king? Never for you?"

My jaw tightened. "Have I observed that the two men I have loved best in the world paid no attention to my wishes when they decided my future? Why, yes, I have."

Ninsha bowed her head. "I didn't mean to add to your pain. But it makes me angry for you."

I laughed. "I don't need your anger. I have enough of my own."

"But you're going to take the new position."

"Don't I always do my duty? Civilization would fall apart if people weren't loyal to their family, their city, and their patron god."

"I guess we should unpack, then."

It was almost painful to put my personal clothes and jewelry back in the chest at the foot of my bed. Each piece reminded me that I was not going to be a priestess of Inanna.

That evening, to soothe my sorry, I wrote a new hymn to Inanna. "The great-hearted mistress, the impetuous lady, proud among the children of Anu and preeminent in all lands, the great daughter of Suen," I wrote. I went on to compare her to things of power: a lioness, a mountain wildcat, a wild bull, a brush fire. I listed her powers and great deeds, greater than those of any other god. I prayed for her to stop her unkindness to me and to be merciful.

I emptied my heart, and it was calmed. With such a goddess as my patron god, I should trust her and not worry.

"What have you written?" Ninsha asked.

"A hymn praising Inanna and her powers. Tomorrow I'll go to Uruk and give the hymn to Her temple for the priestesses to sing."

CHAPTER THIRTY-NINE

When I came back from Uruk three days later, Ninsha was doing some mending in our rooms at the Gipar House. "Esh, you look drained and downhearted. I didn't expect you to stay so long."

I set some tablets on the table. "I encountered Lugalanne at Inanna's House of Heaven. He insisted that I go to the temple of Anu to begin learning the rituals."

"I have something to say."

"Yes?" I sat next to her and started taking my jewelry off.

"You so often seem sad and tired, even on festival days."

I crossed my arms. "Festivals are work days for me. I have to make sure everything runs well."

"The priests and priestesses are working too, but they enjoy the festivals. You're the only one who seems gloomy. You remind me of your mother."

My back stiffened. "I'm nothing like my mother."

"You're like her in that you devote yourself to your duty yet get no satisfaction from it."

"That's not true. I enjoy writing hymns to Inanna when I have a free moment."

"That's the only thing that gives you joy. Do you really want to spend the rest of your life yearning to do something other than what fate has given you?"

"I trust in Inanna to make me her priestess."

"Your poems praise the goddess' strengths and attributes. You say She's the greatest of the gods and the decider of destinies. She must have chosen you to be high priestess of Suen and Anu."

The heat of anger raced through my body. "That's blasphemy."

"Hardly. Don't you think you should be grateful to Inanna for elevating you so high, above all other women in the empire? And take joy in her gifts to you? Your only friend besides me is Adda. You haven't even made friends with any of the priestesses."

"As high priestess, I can't show favor to one over another."

"Face it. You serve the gods without joy. I wonder how that makes Inanna feel?"

I gritted my teeth, unable to answer her charge. "How do you expect me to like a fate I didn't want?"

"Your duties here are similar to what your duties would be as priestess of Inanna. If you think you would like serving Her, then it shouldn't be hard to like serving Suen."

I felt exposed, and it wasn't a good feeling. I changed the subject. "You don't enjoy festivals either."

Ninsha toyed with her necklaces and licked her lips. "That's different."

"I think you'd be happier if you didn't hide yourself away."

She looked me straight in the eye. "I'll work on becoming more comfortable around...people...if you work on finding pleasure in your duties."

I was silent for a long moment. "Let us do it."

~

My first challenge came the next day, when ensi Dan-i-li and I accompanied the cult statue of Suen on a barge trip upstream to the city of Nippur. There, the god would visit His father, Enlil, god of wind and air and chief of the gods, to give him gifts and ask for blessings. The yearly trip to the House of the Mountain took three days because we stopped at five cities, Enegir, Larsa, Uruk, Shuruppak, and Tummal, on the way to Nippur. At each city, Suen was greeted by a cult statue of a goddess of the city and Her high priest.

Mindful of my agreement with Ninsha, I resolved to enjoy the tedious barge trip this year. I couldn't deny it was a refreshing break from my ordinary activities. The day dawned clear, which seemed a good omen for the trip.

Leaving Ur, I bit my lip at seeing the plots of land still unoccupied since the rebellion seven years earlier. At least the temple's plots were under cultivation, thanks to Rimush sparing the priests and workers in Suen's temenos.

"We have little food to trade, and yet land sits empty," Dan-i-li complained. We both sat, dressed in our full official regalia, on the barge floor in the shade of a pile of baskets laden with gifts for Enlil.

"Ur went from a large city to a small one because of the rebellion against Rimush," I said. "We don't have enough men to take over the empty shops and garden plots."

"Yet the temple has money and men to build an extravagant barge each year for Suen's trip to Nippur."

"The god must have the best. Besides, since the revolt, Suen's temple has shared our harvest with the city instead of exporting it. We've done our part to make sure no one starves." Despite my defense of the expense of the barge, even I remained amazed at the god's desires for it: cedar from the mountains, fir from the hinterlands of Mari, pitch from Eridu, reeds from Tummal, timber from Ebla, and several other costly imports. When I returned home from this trip, it would be time to order the raw materials for next year's barge.

Dan-i-li harrumphed. "You should turn over some of the temple's profits from its weaving shop to the city."

I lifted my eyebrows. "Doing so won't help with the shortage of men. I suggest you write to other ensis about whether they can spare any laborers."

Dan-i-li got up and walked around the edge of the barge, and I stood to make sure he didn't knock over any of the first-fruits offerings to Enlil that took up most of the barge—ceramic jugs of goat and cow milk and reed baskets of butter and cheeses of various types.

"My lord, it would be better if you sat down," said the head bargemen.

The holy Buranun rushed with cold water, and the barge rocked. I spread my feet and held the edge of a large jar to stay upright. "Yes, Dan-i-li, please come back and sit with me."

He looked toward me. "Nothing's going to—" There was a splash, and Dan-i-li was in the water. The barge bucked from losing his weight at the edge.

"Stop the barge!" I dropped to my knees and crawled toward where Dan-i-li went over. He was struggling in the water and shouting.

"I didn't mean to hit him with my pole," a bargeman said he fought against the current to stop the barge. "He was too close."

"Never mind that now. Bring your poles over here!"

Motion caught my eye. Several crocodiles were sunning themselves on the right bank. As I watched, a crocodile slid into the water without a sound, and a second one and a third one followed.

"Crocodiles!" I said. "Hurry!"

The bargemen extended their poles across the water, but the poles didn't reach Dan-i-li.

The crocodiles were a quarter of the way to us.

"Can you attach the poles to each other end to end?" I asked.

The head bargemen said, "We could, but it wouldn't be strong enough to support the ensi's weight."

"Then move the barge closer to him."

The crocodiles had now covered half the distance.

The men poled the barge right up to Dan-i-li, who grabbed one of the poles and started to climb it.

The barge tipped. Baskets of offerings slid toward Dan-i-li.

'Stop, my lord." The head bargeman gestured to the other bargeman. "Go to the other side of the barge. You too, my lady."

The crocodiles were three-quarters of the way to Dan-i-li.

I crawled toward the sliding baskets and put my back and elbows against them, bracing my feet on the barge. I prayed to Suen that his statue not tip over.

The barge leveled out when the bargeman's weight on the other edge balanced the barge. I could no longer see Dan-i-li's head.

"Climb now, my lord," the head bargeman said.

"Hurry!" I shouted.

Dan-i-li clambered up the pole. Water poured off him. He threw himself onto the barge. That side tipped down again.

A crocodile lunged from the water and snapped its jaws. It missed Dan-i-li but caught the side of the barge. With a groan, the wood tore away, and the crocodile splashed back into the water with the edge of the barge in its mouth.

The bargeman scrambled away, but Dan-i-li lay there in a daze.

"Dan-i-li!" I held out my hand, and he grasped it. I pulled, and he was able to crawl toward me.

"Stay in the center of the barge!" the head bargeman ordered.

The water frothed with crocodiles. They were excited for meat and frustrated that their prey escaped. They bumped the barge, biting at the sides, and then one swam underneath. It rammed the bottom of the barge. Then the barge rose out of the water, lifted on the back of a crocodile.

Milk sloshed inside the jars, and baskets slid toward the water again. The statue of Suen wobbled on its base.

"What can we do?" I asked the head bargeman.

"Pray to the gods that the crocodiles don't tear the barge apart," he answered, white-faced.

Much as I believed in prayer, I believed more in action. I reached for a basket and started taking out cheeses, unwrapping them, and handing them to Dan-i-li. "Toss these to the crocodiles!"

The barge settled again on the water. The statue of Suen stopped wobbling. The crocodiles fought among themselves, gulping cheeses.

"Now throw them farther away!" I said to Dan-i-li. The crocodiles followed the cheeses.

The head bargeman shouted to the other one. They grabbed their poles and strained against the water. Gradually the barge started moving upstream again.

CHAPTER FORTY

When we pulled into the harbor of Enegir, Dan-i-li was still soaked and shivering. His jewelry was gone, and his clothes were brown with mud.

Dan-i-li straightened his clothes and stood erect. He climbed off the barge. "Don't leave without me."

The head priest stood on the dock next to a statue of the goddess Ningirida. The priest cried, "Welcome, welcome, welcome, o boat! Welcome o Boat of Suen!" He scattered first flour then bran on the dock in front of Suen and poured oil over it. He chanted a blessing: "May butter and wine be abundant. May the carp rejoice at the prow of your boat."

"I cannot give you my cargo!" I replied for Suen. "I am going to Nippur." The ritual continued. We were just finishing the final prayers when Dan-i-li returned in fresh clothes and borrowed gold armbands, salve on his wounds.

As we went from town to town, docking to visit the statues of goddesses and going through the same ritual at each place, Dan-i-li and I talked about the next moon festival and his plans to rebuild Ur. We stayed in the middle of the barge and both kept glancing at the shore, searching for crocodiles.

Dan-i-li got off the barge in Larsa, Uruk, and Shuruppak after we docked and disappeared into the city, which was not part of the ritual.

My curiosity grew with each city. "What are you doing?" I finally asked.

"I'm meeting with the ensis."

"About their sending men to Ur?"

"Yes, that too." He snorted. "Mostly about what to do now that there is a new king."

My stomach dropped. I never wanted to go through another rebellion in my life. "What did they counsel you?"

"They're rebelling, all except for Uruk. Lugalanne says there is more to be gained by being one of the few cities that remain loyal. He convinced me not to rebel." He paused then added snidely, "Are you going to write to your brother and tell him?"

"He and his army are probably already on their way to confront the rebels. I will tell him that you stayed loyal and commissioned a statue of him for the temple. That should please him."

"A statue? I never promised the temple a statue."

"I suggest you do so. What better way to demonstrate your loyalty?"

Dan-i-li's eyes flashed in anger. "I'll do it. I do want to keep my position."

"I'll arrange for the statue when we get home. You won't have to do anything but pay for it."

ṭ

When we arrived at Nippur the next morning, priests crowded the dock. The high priestess stood in front of them, adorned with necklaces, bracelets, and earrings of gold and lapis lazuli. "Welcome to Nippur and the House of the Mountain."

"We bring the god Suen to visit his father, Enlil," I said. "Open the house. I will give you what is in the barge as an offering."

Four priests came forward with a palanquin and placed the statue of Suen on it. Other priests came aboard to carry off the offerings. They headed toward the temple between rows of palm trees, and the priestess followed.

Dan-i-li and I got off the barge and followed the others to the temple.

Suen was carried into the dark sanctuary of Enlil. We could barely see as the priests offered bread, sweet cakes, and beer to Suen.

"Father Who begot me," I began Suen's part of the ancient ritual words, "I am satisfied with what you have given me to eat. O great mountain, I am satisfied with what you have given me to drink. Give to me, Enlil, give to me. In the river give me a flood of carp. In the fields give me speckled barley." I continued through the ancient list of requests until I got to the final one: "In the palace give me long life."

"I will give to you, Suen, I will give to you," said the priestess on behalf of Enlil.

Having concluded the ritual, I spent the night with the priestess, and Dan-i-li with the ensi of Nippur. We left on the barge the next day and arrived in Ur in the evening.

⁊

The morning after we got home, after feeding the gods and studying the tablets of ritual I had brought back from Uruk, I went to sew with the priestesses. Hesitating outside the door of the sewing room, I listened to the laughter inside. I took a deep breath and entered.

Conversation paused, and the ten priestesses looked up at me with frozen expressions.

"Is something wrong, my lady?" Buru asked.

"Not at all. I had some time, and I thought I would join you."

Ningbanda smiled. "You can sit next to me if you like." Although she was now grown, she still had a girlish innocence and an open face.

"Thank you." Relieved at her invitation, I sat and looked around for something to sew.

Buru leaned across the circle to hand me some fabric with a needle pinned in it and a hank of yellow yarn. "The embroidery on this daïs cover needs to be finished."

I took the fabric, studied the interrupted design, and began sewing.

Conversation restarted. The women first discussed safe topics such as the weather and songs for the next moon festival and then ventured into more personal matters: whether someone's young niece would make a good priestess, which of the new priests was the most attractive, whether someone's sister should marry a smith or a clerk.

Ba-u-ta-lu, a new novice who was Dan-i-li's youngest daughter, groaned like an actor on stage. "My nurse never taught me how to do this." She held up a robe that she was trying to hem.

Buru massaged her temples and then said gently, "I've shown you several times already."

"I can never remember." Ba-u crumpled the fabric in her fists.

"I can show you again," I said, surprising myself. "Come with me to my courtyard so we don't disturb everyone else." I stood and walked out of the room, Ba-u following.

"Do you like being a priestess, Ba-u?"

She dipped her head shyly. "Sometimes. I like the singing and dancing."

"Those are my favorite parts too." I would enjoy taking part in them more often, I realized. Both were within the dignity of the zirru. We reached my courtyard. "Here we are. Why don't you show me what you've done so far?"

She handed the bunched-up cloth to me as if she was glad to be rid of it, even for a brief time.

Opening out the cloth, I examined her hems. Counter to what she claimed, she did know what to do. I recognized her problem from my own childhood: She was rushing to get it done, and in the process she was folding the cloth unevenly and catching other sections of the robe in her stitches.

I remembered Ninsha's words from long ago. "You need to find a way to make sewing fun." Aloud, I said, "Enjoy listening and taking part in the priestesses' conversation. As for your sewing, slow down, first of all. Take pride in doing nice work. Can you try that?"

"Yes, high priestess."

I took my eating knife and severed her stitches. Then I rubbed a hem to flatten the fold. I handed the robe back to her. "Try again. It's all right if you don't keep up with the other priestesses. You'll get faster and better with experience."

Ba-u sighed and sewed the hem as I watched.

"Good job. Can you keep it up?"

"I think so."

"Then let's go join the others. And if you have trouble again with your sewing, come to me."

"Thank you, high priestess."

Warmth suffused me. Helping Ba-u gave me a surprising sense of satisfaction—and a feeling of shame that for years I had neglected the priestesses while I busied myself with rites and administration.

CHAPTER FORTY-ONE

My hairdresser Ilum-pal drew the comb through my hair under a glaring afternoon sun in the courtyard. "My lady, how would you like your hair done today?"

"Give me a tight knot in the back," I said. "I'm joining the other priestesses in their dance class."

"You seem uneasy. Is that why?" She pulled my hair back tightly and started to braid it.

"I've instructed the dancing teacher to be as demanding of me as of the other priestesses. I may have made a mistake."

"*Hmmm*. If she were easier on you, the other priestesses might lose their respect for you."

"Ninsha thinks I would enjoy my life more if I were friends with the priestesses. I worry that if we're friends, they'll be less respectful."

"Friend or not, you're still the zirru and the sister of the king. You have the right to insist on respect." She wound the braid around itself and pinned it with hairpins. "That should hold through whatever you do, my lady."

Not long afterward, I was at the door of the practice room. My apprehension didn't ease when I saw the other priestesses bending in improbable ways to warm up. I took off my sandals when I saw no one else wore any.

To my surprise, Ninsha was among the priestesses. She gestured me over.

"I didn't know you danced with the priestesses."

"Only for fun. That's why I'm here at the back, so no one gets in the habit of relying on me."

The teacher came in. She was tall and looked strong. "Ladies, come to attention! We'll practice turns again today. Remember: pivot on your left foot, turn halfway around, and place your right foot down. Then repeat. We'll start slowly."

I couldn't see the teacher's feet so I watched Ninsha's. She made the turn effortlessly. Heartened, I gave it a try and tripped myself. When I hit the floor, my breath left me in an *oof*. I jumped up to match Ninsha's position.

Several priestesses turned to look, and my face grew warm.

"Left foot *then* right foot," Ninsha whispered. "You'll get it with practice."

"No talking during class." The dance teacher motioned at me. "High priestess, come up here to the front."

My stomach dropped in dread. I made my way through the other priestesses until I stood before everyone else.

The teacher did the turn very slowly, and then she had me do it with her. As I improved, the teacher went faster, and I abandoned all attempts at grace, waving my arms to keep my balance. No one laughed, and for that I could have kissed every one of them.

My ankles weren't used to working so hard and at last started to wobble. On the next turn, I fell sideways. As I sat on the floor, rubbing my twisted ankle, the teacher pushed the others to go faster and faster, and their red robes whirled around them and me.

The teacher clapped her hands. "Get up, high priestess! No resting in dance class." Then she announced that we would work on a step pattern next. "Perhaps the zirru can keep up with us then." Again she demonstrated very slowly for me; it took me many tries to get it right. When she and the others sped up, I couldn't follow. And so the class went, with me trying each exercise and failing to get up to speed. I was so relieved when the class ended that I was the first one out the door.

"High priestess! High priestess! You forgot these."

I turned and saw Ba-u rushing after me, carrying my sandals.

My ears and face got hot. "Thank you for bringing these to me."

She smiled shyly. "If you like, I can help you practice the dance steps."

"That's kind of you. Thank you."

Ba-u shrugged. "I need the practice, and it's more fun to do it with someone else."

225

"Why don't you come to my courtyard this evening?"

"Thank you, high priestess."

After Ninsha and I ate, Ba'u showed up with another priestess to practice.

"You all looked so graceful today," I said. "It's hard to believe any of you need more practice."

Under the full moon, Ba'u smiled and tapped the shoulder of the other priestess. "This one has been only pretending to know the steps while hiding at the back of the room."

The other priestess grinned without embarrassment. "Please don't tell the dance teacher. I may be slow to learn, but I'm determined to practice until everything is second nature."

Ninsha joined us, and Ba'u repeated today's lesson at a slower speed. "My mother was a dancer," Ba'u said. "She always told me that the first step in dance was to get the moves in my bones. Only then increase the speed."

By the end of the evening, I was able to do everything from the day's lesson at a moderate speed without losing my balance more than a few times.

"Thank you, Ba'u," I said. "Your lesson made the difference."

She dipped her head shyly. "Different people learn different ways, at least that's what my mother said."

Ninsha fetched some linens, and we all patted ourselves dry. The two priestesses left.

"Ninsha, I've made my first steps to making friends. Now it's your turn. Come with me tomorrow morning when I meet with Adda."

She drew back. "Oh, I couldn't."

"You don't have to stay. Just greet him and leave. It would last only a few moments."

"But we might run into priests at any time."

"Wear your shawl over your head, then."

She looked stricken.

"Adda and several of the priests and workers helped me look for you," I added softly. "They have only the best of intentions toward you."

She swallowed. "I'll try."

I didn't give up on dance class. Ba'u came over many evenings, and more priestesses came along. My feet learned the patterns, and I found myself falling into turns and steps when I wasn't paying attention.

I also joined in when the priestesses practiced singing. There I could hold my own, thanks to the years of Bashtum's tutelage in Akkad, and sometimes the singing teacher taught hymns I had written. It was a thrill to sing my own work to Inanna, amid the other voices.

Ninsha fell into the habit of coming with me after class into the courtyard and conversing with the priests and workers—just greeting them at first and later exchanging pleasantries that we scripted out ahead of time for her to memorize. She became slowly but noticeably more comfortable at talking with men, and I rejoiced for her. Life was good.

CHAPTER FORTY-TWO

One day in late summer, Ninsha and I were standing in the shade of my office, talking to Adda about the upcoming fall Akitu festival. No matter how many years I had organized it, each time there seemed to be a new problem to solve. This year, a poor flax harvest had resulted in a shortage of linen cloth. The priestesses were expecting new robes for the festival, and Adda and I were discussing options while Ninsha embroidered a belt.

"Esh! Look there!" She threw down her embroidery, bolted out of the office, and rushed toward the temenos' main gate, where a man dusty from travel and pushing a cart had just walked in.

Although he was dressed as a merchant and his cart was piled with wool cloth, something about his posture said "military." My breath caught. "Did you know that a soldier in disguise was coming to the temple?" I asked Adda.

"I had no notice. Shall I arrange food and a sleeping room?"

"Yes. I'll find out his purpose." I followed Ninsha at a zirru-suitable pace. When I was face to face with the man, he gave me a salute and a smile that I recognized.

"Za-mu!" It was wonderful to see him again. "Welcome to Ur! If you'd let us know you were coming, I'd have had a feast prepared."

"I'm here on Mani's business." He looked around and then lowered his voice. "Since the revolution this spring, he has me going from city to city disguised as a merchant, learning the mood of each city. He doesn't want a rebellion to take him by surprise."

"So you're here in our city as a spy," I said, frowning.

"Esh! Don't be rude," Ninsha said. "I'm really glad you're here, Za-mu."

He smiled at Ninsha. "I'm keeping Mani and the empire safe."

"You won't find any rebels among my people," I said. "I forbid you to even talk to anyone here at the temple but Ninsha and me."

"I'm here only to listen to what rebellious thoughts are circulating, not to arrest or punish anyone."

"That had better be true, Za-mu." I paused and watched his face, which showed no signs of guilt. He served Mani wholeheartedly, it seemed. "My shaperum, Adda, is arranging food and lodgings for you. You may stay tonight."

"Thank you. I'm off to Eridu tomorrow."

"Good," I said. "I wish I could stay and talk now, but I have duties to take care of."

"Don't worry." Ninsha beamed. "I'll take care of Za-mu until you join us again."

I returned to Adda and our discussion of how to clothe the priestesses for the Akitu festival.

That evening, I found Ninsha and Za-mu sitting in the courtyard of the guest house. A flickering lamp behind them silhouetted them as they leaned slightly toward each other from opposite sides of a low table holding a jar of beer. Jealousy flared, although I wasn't sure of whom. I sat on an empty stool at their table, and Ninsha indicated which straw was mine.

"Za-mu has big news," Ninsha said, her face less happy than earlier. "Mani has found Za-mu a wife, the daughter of an Akkadian nobleman."

"I'm not sure what kind of husband I can be, when I'm on the road so often for the king." Za-mu took a drink from his straw. "But of course I can't refuse the king's matchmaking."

Do you carry a message from the palace?" I asked Za-mu.

He leaned closer. "Mani asks that you keep your ears open for antigovernment plotting in Ur."

"I'm supposed to spy on my own people and my own city? Mani shouldn't have asked that."

"He's the king. I'm just following orders." Za-mu turned his palms up. "Argue with him, not me."

Ninsha smoothed her hair. "He's right, Esh. Let's forget royal business. The three of us haven't been together in a long time. Let's enjoy it."

"Yes. Let's talk about our lives, not the empire." I was surprised I had been so prickly. Ur was "my city"? That was a shock to hear from my mouth. But it felt true. My memories of Akkad were faded. It was no longer home, and my loyalties now were split between my family and those here at the temple, who had become a second family.

Ninsha blushed. "He's already told me about his life, and I've told him about ours."

"Za-mu, yours must be so much more interesting than ours," I said.

"In truth, I'm a little envious. Routine and stability sound appealing after my weeks on the road."

"We've made friends here, even Esh," Ninsha said. "It's a good life."

She was right.

"To friends," I said.

"To friends," they echoed.

Section V

Cities of Ur and Uruk; the Marshes

Age 41

CHAPTER FORTY-THREE

Summer had come and gone, the farmers were planting barley, and I was fretting about the upcoming fall Akitu festival as I went into one of the storage rooms at Anu's house in Uruk.

Because it took half a day to go between Ur and Uruk by boat, I had appointed Ur-dumu-zi, the senior priest of Anu in Uruk, to handle my day-to-day duties there, and I spent most of my time in Ur. I traveled to Uruk regularly to solve any problems that might arise and make sure routines hadn't become slipshod.

This day, I had given Ur-dumu-zi time off and would tend to my temple duties in Uruk myself. Despite the sanctity of my tasks, my mind kept wandering. Both Ur and Uruk celebrated an Akitu festival in the fall, and I alternated years between Ur and Uruk. Now, I couldn't remember in which city I was due to celebrate this year.

I collected the ceremonial bread basket and went to the kitchen. Several loaves of not-quite-cool barley bread awaited me, and after exchanging greetings and gossip with the cooks, I piled the loaves in the basket. I headed outside and walked to Anu's ziggurat. I climbed the many stairs to the first and only level and, singing "Lord of the Great Above," walked toward the tall whitewashed temple that stood on top. I stepped inside the blindingly bright building into the cool darkness.

Someone grabbed my arm and jerked me toward them. My captor smelled of sweat and a heavy application of perfume.

My heartbeat pounded in my ears, and my breath rasped. I twisted and struggled. "Let go! Let go!" I shouted at the stranger. "You're not allowed in the god's sanctuary." Panting, I pounded on the hand that gripped me.

"There's no need to fight." The stranger grabbed my other arm and pulled me toward him. He kissed me full on the mouth. The basket tipped, and the bread loaves landed on the floor with thumps.

My stomach heaved, and I jerked my head back. "You profane Anu's temple and dishonor me, the highest priestess in all of Akkad and Sumer."

The man laughed and forced another kiss on me.

I tried again to pull away and got one hand free. I wiped the back of it across my lips, but they still felt dirty.

My eyes were adjusting to the dimness, and I now saw that my captor was no stranger but Lugalanne, ensi of Uruk.

He shoved me against the wall, and my head rang. "You think you're so special."

"You can't treat me like this. I'm the sister of the king."

He grinned. "Not anymore, you're not. Haven't you heard?"

My breath caught. "Heard what?"

"I just received news of your family. Your mother's dead. So is Manishtushu. Killed in a palace coup. His son Naram-Sin has taken the throne. All of Sumer is rebelling."

My favorite brother, dead? Or was Lugalanne lying to upset me? I swallowed a wail. "Don't you remember what happened the last time Sumerian cities rebelled against Akkad? You'll be crushed."

"Not with all the cities acting together. I want no authority over me. This is my chance to be free." Lugalanne ran at a life-size statue of Manishtushu, hit his shoulder against it, and toppled it. After it crashed against the floor, the head came off and rolled lopsidedly across the room.

I gasped in shock then sidled along the wall toward the door.

Lugalanne took two steps toward a libation jar and kicked it. It spun away and hit a wall, breaking into pieces and spilling oil all over the floor.

He looked around again and headed toward an offering table.

"Stop it!" I said. "These things are holy. You'll offend the god."

He turned and struck me hard.

I landed on my back and elbows on the brick floor. I groaned from the pain and struggled to a sitting position, rubbing my elbows.

Lugalanne threw a pitcher into the wall, and beer splattered. "We're throwing the Akkadians out at last. Get out of the temple, Akkadian! Get out of Uruk! You're not welcome here anymore."

I crawled to the doorway and used the wall to help me stand. I took a shaky step out and shaded my eyes against the glare. *Lugalanne has gone mad.*

Sim-tur stood before me, smirking. I hadn't seen her for years, since I had dismissed her from the priesesshood of Ningal. She looked me over, her gaze resting on my bleeding elbows and my smudged robe. "I've waited a long time for my revenge. The gods now favor me. I'll be en-priestess of Anu and zirru of Suen. You'll beg in the streets."

More crashes sounded behind me in the sanctuary. I needed to get away from Lugalanne before he killed me. I stumbled toward the stairs.

Sim-tur came after me. "Give me that!" She grabbed for my rolled-brim hat.

I pushed her away and ran. Down the stairs and to the nearby harbor I raced, ignoring stares from priests and citizens.

My boat was still moored at the dock, and the boatman still sat in it.

"We have to leave now," I cried.

The boatman held out his hand and helped me step in. "I thought we weren't leaving until tomorrow," he said as he untied the mooring rope.

"We need to leave for Ur right now. Uruk is rebelling against the king, and Lugalanne is deranged."

He tested the wind with his finger and then quickly put up the sail. "Is Ur rebelling?"

"I don't know."

Then we were off, sliding through the gate and into the holy Buranun. The wind caught the sails and sped us downstream.

The wind lifted my loose hair. I sat on a reed crosspiece, staring into the water while my heart beat a fast tattoo. The problem of where to be for the Akitu festival had been solved; I was no longer a priestess in Uruk. My stomach fluttered. I had no idea what to expect in Ur.

When we docked in Ur, it was afternoon, and I was eager to get out of the autumn sun. Still, in mind of my dignity, I walked regally toward the temple grounds. But when I reached the main gate, I found it blocked by strangers with spears and knives. Not a one saluted me, and their faces were grim.

Not again! "Who are you, and what are you doing here? Where are my guards?" I asked.

One of my temple guards peeked out from behind the strangers. "I'm sorry, high priestess. Dan-i-li's men overwhelmed us."

Dan-i-li betrayed me! My chest tightened, and my fingernails dug into my palms. We had worked together for twenty-two years, and I had thought we were friends. "Fetch Adda this instant!"

The temple guard looked embarrassed. "He's already been thrown out. I don't know where he went."

I couldn't retake the temenos by myself. I would have to seek help from Dan-i-li, the ensi, and hoped he had not turned against me. I turned.

"Stop right there, woman." Four of the strangers stepped forward and flanked me. "We're under orders to expel you from the city." One of them grabbed my arm.

"How dare you!" I slapped his face.

He tightened his grip. "We're just following orders."

"Whose orders? Lugalanne's? He has no authority here."

The guards didn't answer but marched me to the south city gate and outside and then kept going along a canal. In the farm plots on either side, men were planting barley and pruning fruit trees. Life went on as usual for them, and I wondered at how my life had changed so quickly in one day. Then the canal and farm plots ended. I thought the guards would free me. But the men continued to push me forward into the steppe. At last we came to a thicket.

"Through the bushes, now. Dan-i-li's orders."

When I didn't move, they shoved me forward. "Go. And don't come back. He won't be so easy on you next time."

I approached the thicket. The grayish-green branches were lined with glossy green leaves and yellow and green fruits. I reached out to push the branches aside.

"Ow!" My hand was bleeding, and I sucked on the cut for a moment. I gently reached out and pulled a leaf down to bend the branch. Hidden among the leaves and fruits were long spines.

"Keep going," a guard ordered.

I slid as carefully as I could into the tangled bushes. The spines caught my robe and my skin and tangled my hair. The pain was as sharp as the thorns, and as I pushed between the bushes, tears ran down my face. I was afraid of not being able to work my way free, but after what felt like a long time, I came out the other side.

Ahead of me were the marshes, smelling of fish and plants. Bright-green reeds in clumps swayed in the wind, and the waterways among them reflected the reeds and the afternoon sun. The dark heads of swimming water buffalo dotted the water, and shore birds squawked and called.

I was thirsty from spending so much time in the sun, so I headed for the marsh, startling dozens of egrets into flight. I squatted down and scooped up water in my cupped hands to drink. Then I looked at my reflection. Blood covered my face. My high priestess' hat was gone, and only half the necklaces remained around my neck. I rinsed my face and then my arms and legs. There were blood spots on my ripped gown, and I took it off to rinse it and the rest of my body. Some of the slashes continued to bleed sluggishly.

I dressed again in the wet robe and looked around. I had no idea what to do next. I knew nothing about which plants were edible, and I was exposed for any bandit to see. In the distance, a lion swaggered, and a frisson of fear rippled down my back. It would be dark soon, and I needed a safe place to sleep.

CHAPTER FORTY-FOUR

I struck out for the nearest reedbed, the water around my ankles making me stumble. When I got there, I saw between the soft-looking reeds that the stubble of previous years' reeds was sharp. They would cut me badly if I tried to sleep there.

I saw a cluster of small islands a ways out. I headed toward them, and soon I was wading through cold, knee-high water. The sun dropped to the horizon in a blaze of orange and red, and I started to worry that I wouldn't reach the islands before it was totally dark. The moon was rising, but it was only a quarter moon and the marsh was darkening quickly. I looked over my shoulder toward shore, but dry land was as far behind me as the islands were in front. Panic bubbled up in my chest. I forced my legs to move faster despite the heavy wet robe twisted around them. Soon I was panting from exertion, with the islands still far away and the sun lowering toward the horizon. Frogs croaked in increasing numbers.

"Great Inanna, queen of heaven and earth," I prayed, even though it was probably too dark for Her to see me. "Tell me what to do. Save me! I have always been your humble servant."

From behind one of the islands a boat appeared. I waved my arms above my head and shouted for help. The boat made a slow course correction and headed toward me. Fear gave me new vigor, and I shambled faster.

I glanced at the sun. It was halfway beneath the horizon. I waved frantically. "Help me! Please help!"

At last I could hear the soft swish the canoe made as it parted the water and rhythmic plops of the pole. A dark object curved high above me: the prow of the boat was close enough to touch. The reed boat turned in place until its side faced me. It was piled with reeds to the height of a person, and a naked boy sat in the stern.

"Climb in." The boy stretched out his hand, and I took it gladly. I swung a leg awkwardly over the side, which was only a couple fingers' width above the water, and the boy pulled on my arm. I tumbled into the boat and landed with a splat in a narrow space between the reeds and the boy.

"Where's your boat?" the boy asked.

"I don't have one. I'm looking for a place to sleep tonight."

The boy scratched his ear. "Come with me to our village."

"Thank you. I'm...I'm Esh." I was no longer Enheduanna or the daughter of the king.

"Silim." The boy poled away from the spot. In the moonlight, he looked no more than ten years old.

The air was cool, and I shivered in my wet robe. The moon had climbed only a small way in the sky before we arrived at a village. Reed huts sat on small islands big enough for only one or two houses each. Dogs barked and paced the tiny yards in front of the huts while groaning water buffalo heaved themselves up onto dry ground. Tall date palms stood in some of the yards.

Silim tied the boat to a thick reed stalk impaled in the bank and kept the craft steady with his pole while I clumsily climbed out. The boy leapt out and scrambled up the bank to the top. I attempted to follow his lead, but it was so slippery that I fell back three times before I gained purchase. Once on flat ground, I followed him to the door of the hut, which was lit inside only by a fire.

I stood in the doorway while the boy explained to his parents that he had found me standing in the water of the marsh. The three smaller children hid behind their mother or the young water buffalo by the fire, and the parents' gaze turned toward me.

"I need somewhere to sleep tonight," I said, staring at the fire the family sat around, unable to look at them straight on. "I have nowhere to go. Please, can you help me?" I shook with shame at having to beg.

"Come in and eat with us," the man said. As I entered the house, the woman stood up, and I saw that she was hugely pregnant. She waddled to a platform in the middle of the house and fetched a bowl and mug.

239

I sat where the man indicated, and the woman put the bowl and mug in front of me. Then she knelt by two pots on the fire. She took a bowl and scooped up something from a pot and poured it in my bowl. It smelled like fish stew. Next she poured warm milk into my mug and offered me a flat bread.

My mouth watered at the scent of hot food. I was suddenly ferociously hungry. "Thank you for your hospitality. My name is Esh."

"I'm Dingir-sukkal. My wife is Gan-Utu. Please, eat." Both appeared to be about my age. They were dressed in robes riddled with holes and thin from long use. The children were naked.

I forced myself to eat and drink slowly. When I finished, I was still hungry but no longer famished. I rubbed my hands in front of the fire.

"How did you come to be in the marsh at nightfall? It's a dangerous time to be out," Dingir-Sukkal asked.

"I am—I was—a priestess of Suen—that is, Nanna—in Ur and of An in Uruk. Sumer has a new king, and cities are rebelling against him. I was forced out because I am loyal to the king."

"What is a king?" Dingir-sukkal asked.

I blinked my eyes. "Do you have a village chief or big man? The king is like that, only for the entire land, sea to sea."

He shrugged a shoulder. "Do you have a place to go tomorrow?"

"No," I admitted, my head bowed.

"If you're willing to help my wife with her chores, you can stay for a short while with us."

My tight muscles turned soft and weak. "Yes, I'll work for you. You are very kind. Thank you."

Gan-Utu got to her feet again and hauled blankets from the platform. She laid them out on the reed floor matting, then pointed to a blanket at the side of the hut along the wall. She looked at me. "That one's yours."

"I need to pray before bedtime." I stood and went out the door. The three dogs immediately leapt up and started barking. I tried to hush them, but the dogs on the other islands joined in. I gave up trying to silence them and prayed instead.

"Light of the night, Lord Suen, ancient lord of wisdom, look upon your wife with pity. I have been removed from my position unjustly.

Aid me, and ask your grandfather Anu to help me get back my honors. Punish Lugalanne and Dan-i-li for their trespasses against the gods."

I quickly went back inside and lay on my blanket next to the wall. Gradually the dogs outside grew silent, and the sounds of frogs and crickets and the occasional groans of water buffalo took over the night. I couldn't sleep, though. How could I: in one day I'd been stripped of my positions, exiled from my home, forced into the wilderness without food, nearly was lost in the marsh, and became a servant to the lowest of the low?

At least I was safe and would have shelter and food to eat. The ensis Dan-i-li and Lugalanne may have thought they were sending me to my death, but I had no plans to die. I had to survive to once again be zirru of Suen in Ur.

I woke the next morning after everyone else was up and out the door. I hadn't slept so late since before I became zirru of Suen, because my temple duties started at sunrise. I must have been exhausted after the previous day of betrayals and physical activity.

I sat up and looked around. The hut was made of fourteen thick bundles of reeds, each set of two tied together at the top. Reed mats covered the entire outside surface of the house. Light came into the hut mainly through the door; the mats were woven tightly and little light pierced them. The air was stuffy with a somewhat unpleasant smell. I sniffed the wall; the smell did not come from the reeds. There was no furniture or decorations. The hut was nearly bare except for the fire, large jars that held water and milk, and a pile of belongings on the platform.

I rolled up my blanket and put it on the platform with the others. Then I went outside. The water buffalo had already left, and Gan-Utu was by the boat throwing the reeds Silim had collected the previous day up into the yard.

"Would you like me to do that for you?" I asked.

She wiped her forehead with her arm. "I'm almost done. Then I'll go out and cut more reeds. You should collect buffalo dung, cook lunch for the children, and refill the water jug in the house."

"Excuse me? Did you say collect buffalo dung?" I wrinkled my nose.

"I'll be gone all day, so you should do it."

"I never heard of collecting dung before," I admitted.

Her eyebrows rose in surprise. "You've never done it?"

"No."

"It's simple enough. Pick up each pat of dung, pat it into a flat circle, and slap it on the house so that it can dry in the sun."

I stared at her in astonishment. "Why?"

"We feed the fire with it."

No wonder the hut had an unpleasant smell. Now I was surprised that the smell wasn't worse. And I would have to touch the smelly dung.

For a moment, as my stomach heaved and my flesh crawled, I was sure that I couldn't do it. It was disgusting, and below a daughter and sister of kings.

But the truth was, I had little choice. Walking to Akkad by myself— the few necklaces I had left were not worth enough to pay for passage on a boat—would be dangerous, and I had no food. I had to collect dung and cook meals, or I would starve.

I decided I'd start by filling the water jars before I needed to wash dung off my hands. I went in the hut and found a copper pitcher on the platform. I took it to the water and filled it, then climbed the bank to go back to the house. I emptied the pitcher in the water jar and repeated the process three times. As I was scooping the pitcher in the water for the last time, some human feces drifted by. I gagged, and my eyes squinched closed.

I called to Gan-Utu, who was finishing up transferring fodder from the boat to the yard, "Where should I get the water for the house from?"

"Anywhere is fine. The water's all around us," she called back. Her face was dark red, and she puffed heavily.

I stood up and took in what she had said. I looked around and saw dozens of other islands holding similar huts and similar dogs. As a woman three islands down was filling a jar from the fouled water, her naked child jumped into the water and one of her buffalo submerged itself next to her.

Is this what it means to be a commoner? Drinking blighted water and living with almost no possessions? Using buffalo dung to cook food? Until I had a plan, I had to live this way too. I looked down at the pitcher. *I'll get water somewhere that at least looks clean and clear.* I edged along the bank until I was behind the house. I could see the bottom of the water there, and I filled the pitcher.

After I had emptied the pitcher into the water jar, I went back outside and looked at the buffalo dung scattered about the yard. Gan-Utu had already left in the boat, so I didn't restrain the sighs escaping my mouth. Trying not to gag, I picked up one dropping and gingerly patted it until it was flat and round. I carried it to the house, put it against the reed matting on the side, and pressed. It stuck.

One down; a yardful to go. I worked my way across the yard, until finally all the dung was on the house.

A groan came from the water, and a buffalo started up the bank. *Not more dung!* I waved my arms in front of it. "No, no, no. Get back in the water." But it came up anyway, groaning and nudging me aside, and began eating the green reed tops Gan-Utu had tossed up.

I went down the bank and scrubbed my hands in the water until they were red.

Now I had to prepare a meal for the children.

I went back up the bank and into the hut. I searched it for leftover food, but I saw none except a jar of bubbly brown liquid with a scent I didn't recognize. There was milk in a jar, so I poured some in a pot and put it next to the fire. It was a start, but I was almost certain children needed more than just milk. I would have to go to the water and catch some fish.

I would leave the problem of cooking them for later.

Back down the bank I went. I lay on my stomach in the mud and stuck my arm down into the cold water, hoping that it was shallow enough that I could stand on the bottom. But no matter how I stretched, I felt only water. *I'll have to lie here then.* I put both my arms in the water and waited for fish to come by.

It didn't take long for a school of fish to pass by, but each fish was only the size of a finger. I didn't try to grab them. Later, a group of larger fish swam by, and I snatched at them. I managed to catch one but it slipped out of my hand. Many large fish swam by after that but always out of arm range. I took my arms out of the water to rub them to warm myself up then plunged them again in the water.

High-pitched laughter rang out.

I looked up. The children had arrived by canoe, and I had been concentrating so hard on fish that I hadn't heard them.

"It's not funny. I'm trying to catch your lunch," I said crossly.

243

"You don't have a net!" said Silim, who was doubled over from laughter.

"Do you think you can do better?"

He reached down and picked up a reed with a net on the end and showed it to me. It held several fish.

I sat back on my heels. Water ran down my arms as I tried to brush mud from my robe. "You don't know how to cook those, do you?"

Silim looked at me oddly. "Men don't cook fish. Only women cook fish." He tied up the boat, got out, and unloaded the smallest child. The other ones climbed out on their own. He went up the bank, and the rest of us followed him.

"I guess we'll have only warm milk for lunch then," I said.

He shot me a panicked look. "I'll tell you what to do this one time."

In the hut, Silim set his net down near the fire. He pulled out his knife and gutted each fish. "Fetch the pot," he said, nodding toward the platform. "No, not that one, the wide, shallow one."

I found the correct pot.

"Now place the fish in it and add a dung cake to the fire."

I followed his instructions.

"Now place the pot on top."

I did so. "What next?"

"We wait for the fish to cook and then we eat them."

Mugs and bowls sat near the fire. I poured warm milk into five mugs and handed one to each child and myself.

"Watch out! The fish is burning!"

I grabbed at the pot. It was scorching, and I immediately let go and shook out my hands. "What do we do now?"

"Turn them over with a spoon!"

I did and kept a closer watch on the fish. It must not have been sufficient because, with a look of disdain, Silim picked up a reed, quickly speared a fish, and plunked it in a bowl. He filled four more bowls. He served me last; I received a fish that was burnt black on one side.

After eating, the children left again in a boat. I waved them off and went in the hut to think. To continue to take refuge with Dingir-sukkal and Gan-Utu, I would need to lower myself and learn how to cook. To

244

make myself indispensable, I'd best learn also how to cut reeds, bake bread, and care for the water buffalo.

I rubbed my forehead. How was I going to get out of the marsh? And where should I go? Would I ever see Ninsha again? Was she safe? Did she know what had happened to me?

I prayed to Inanna to intercede for me with Suen and Anu. Writing a hymn to the goddess would make me feel better about my situation, but I had no clay. I resorted to memorizing each line as I devised it.

CHAPTER FORTY-FIVE

Gan-Utu came home with a boatful of green reeds. I went down to the water and helped her toss the reeds up into the yard. Two water buffalo swam up and slowly, groaning, pulled themselves out of the water and began eating the reeds. The dogs rushed over to sniff them but didn't bark.

"Did you make some bread?" she asked as we climbed up the bank.

I froze. "I don't know how," I admitted.

"Watch me tonight. Then you do it from now on."

"Since your time is near, would you prefer that I gather the reeds?"

"Yes." She cast a scornful glance at my arms. "But you don't look strong enough."

"Perhaps I could go with Silim and help him?" I finished climbing and brushed mud off myself.

"Perhaps."

A little later, the children came home with another boatload of reeds, and their father, Dingir-sukkal, returned with fish.

I watched Gan-Utu make bread. She added flour to the bubbly slurry I had found earlier and mixed it together with her hands. When a dough formed, her hands moved quickly and powerfully to form balls and flatten them. She set one flattened ball aside in a bowl. She slapped the others on the inside of a wide copper tube set over the fire. She took the bowl with the set-aside dough and, after mixing flour and water in, set the bowl on the platform in the hut. She checked on the breads and then began cooking the fish.

Supper was a little easier than the night before. We chitchatted a little as we ate.

"How long have you been married?" I asked.

Gan-Utu smiled shyly. "Ten years, since I was about thirteen summers."

I was aghast. I had thought her my age or perhaps older. The leathery skin of her face was dotted with age spots. I put a hand to my own face and felt how soft it was. I hadn't realized commoners aged so quickly.

"Do you have a husband and children?" she asked.

"Neither one."

The faces of the adults looked surprised. "Where are your father and brothers, that they let you roam the marshes alone?" Dingir-sukkal asked.

"My father has gone to the Underworld." The hole I'd had in my chest in the many years since Father died opened wide. I put a hand on my chest and took a deep breath. "My brothers are dead or far away." I couldn't bear to talk more about my family, so I changed the subject. "I need to send a letter. Is there a scribe in the village? Someone who can read?"

Dingir-sukkal frowned. "The only one who might read is Gu-gu-la. He used to be a priest."

"Where might I find him?"

"Five islands down in that direction." He pointed toward the north. "There's sun enough left to visit him tonight."

I left as soon as the family had finished eating. Silim volunteered to take me in a boat, and I accepted. We glided across the water.

Gu-gu-la's island sat low in the water, with no bank to climb to get to the hut.

Silim leapt out and charged ahead. "Gu-gu-la! Gu-gu-la! Company!"

"Boy, you're not company. Come on in."

"I have a woman with me."

Gu-gu-la stuck his head out of the doorway. He was tall with graying hair. His bushy eyebrows rose as he eyed my torn red robe. "Priestess, come in. Be welcome."

Silim and I went in and we all sat down on the reed matting on the floor.

"My lady, what can I do for you? Would you like something to eat?"

"We've eaten, thank you. Please call me Esh. I need to write a letter. Do you have clay and a way to send the letter when I'm done?

Gu-gu-la scratched his arm, which was covered with flea bites. "I have clay, but I don't know if it's still soft. Let me check." He got up and started looking through baskets. "Here we go." He sat back down and worked with the clay until it was a rectangle somewhat flat on the top and bottom. Then he handed it to me with a reed.

"Thank you." I started writing, and Silim peeked over my shoulder.

To Naram-Sin, King of the Four Quarters, from his aunt Enheduanna, Zirru of Suen in Ur, En-priestess of Anu in Uruk. May the gods watch over you and keep you in good health. Ur and Uruk are rebelling against your rule. I have been expelled from both cities because I am your aunt and an Akkadian. I'm staying with a family in the marshes. Come, I beg you, to rescue me and restore prestige to our family.

I set the tablet down on the mat to dry.

"I'll take this to Ur the next time I get supplies," Gu-gu-la said.

"Be careful. Ur is rebelling against the king." I leaned forward. "For which god were you a priest?"

"For Nanna the moon god in Ur."

"Why did you leave?"

He grimaced. "I was young and foolish. The zirru kicked me out."

"Do you like living in the marsh? Do you wish you were still a priest?"

"Does it matter? I'm here with nowhere to go."

"When my nephew conquers Ur and rescues me, I can restore you to the priesthood, if you want."

His eyebrows rose. "Who are you?" He leaned over to look at my letter. He jerked back and put his hand to his nose. "My lady. Thank you. I'll think about it."

And I'll think about what to do if Naram-Sin doesn't come to my aid. I may end up like this poor priest-in-exile.

☙

During the night, I awoke. The air was chilly, and frogs and crickets made a racket. But I thought I heard other noises, ones I hadn't heard my first night in the swamp. I rolled over and lifted the mat next to my head and peered out.

"Someone's stealing the buffalo," I cried.

Instantly the whole family leapt up and ran to the door. I was only moments behind them. Dingir-sukkal grabbed his bow and quiver from where it hung on the wall. We all piled out of the door.

"Where is he?" Dingir-sukkal whispered.

"He was among the buffalo," I said softly.

"Go back in the house," Gan-Utu told the two smallest children. We then spread out and looked for the would-be thief. Everything grew still, and our breath was the loudest sound. The swaying palms gave the impression of movement around us.

"There he is!" Dingir-sukkal shouted.

"Where?" I asked.

A hand caught my arm, and I was pulled close to a man's body. A knife gleamed. I twisted but couldn't pull away.

"Don't shoot!" the man said. "I've got your wife." He backed toward the bank while Dingir-Sukkal followed his movements with the arrow nocked in his bow. The thief jumped off the bank, pulling me with him. A canoe that didn't belong to the family floated there, and the man climbed in, holding me between himself and Dingir-Sukkal's arrow. Then he pulled me in.

I screamed when I tumbled into the canoe, which rocked wildly.

The man jerked me back up to standing. He grabbed his pole and pushed the boat away from the island. Only then did I realize that a buffalo was tied to the back of the boat and was swimming behind us.

Dingir-Sukkal stood at the edge of the island, his arrow still nocked and aimed at the boat.

Silim looked toward the family canoes, but his mother held him tight.

If only I could swim! I could have jumped into the water and swam back to the island.

The thief maneuvered the canoe toward a reedbed, and from then on we kept to the waterways between reedbeds, the stalks arching tall on either side of us and blocking out the moon. After what seemed like a long time, he moored the boat by an island. The buffalo groaned.

"What am I going to do with you, hmm?"

I shivered. "You could take me back to the island where you got me and drop me off."

"Someone might see my face. Right now, you're the only one who can identify me." He wouldn't look at me but fiddled with his knife. "I can't let you go."

My heartbeat pounded in my ears. He was thinking of killing me. Every word I said now could tip the balance between life and death. "Do you have a wife or mother to take care of you?"

"What do you care?"

"I can cook," I lied. "Cut reeds. Mend your clothes." That last one I actually could do, but only if he had needle and thread. "Haul water."

"Your husband will look for you. If he finds you, he finds me."

"He's not my husband. I'm a stranger he allows to stay and work while his wife is with child."

"What about your brothers, your father?"

"Deceased or far away. So you see, no one will look for me. You can leave me alive."

He tossed his knife from hand to hand, muttering.

My breath caught in my throat, and my shoulders tightened. Should I say something more? Should I let him think?

At last he looked me in the eye. "Tie the buffalo to the palm so it won't swim home. You can stay."

CHAPTER FORTY-SIX

I awoke early the next morning to a bright light shining on my closed eyes. I rolled over and opened them. The sun was coming in through a hole in the reed matting overhead. I looked around and saw there were many holes in the mats. The hut was smaller than Dingir-sukkal and Gan-Utu's, with only five sets of reed ribs, and looked as if buffalo had rampaged inside. The reed mats on the floor were dirty and torn. I stood, folded my blanket, and put it on the platform. Then I went to the doorway and looked out.

The thief was milking the stolen buffalo into a ceramic bowl. Without stopping, he glanced over at me. "Make some bread for breakfast." Although his hair was black, his beard had red streaks in it, and his face was thin and pinched.

I went back into the hut and looked around. I found a bread oven like Gan-Utu's. Then I searched for a bowl of leavening. I found it on a rickety platform along with a crock of flour. Trying to copy the manner in which Gan-Utu had made bread the night before, I beat flour, salt, and water with the leftover dough and pulled off small balls. Setting two balls aside for later, I flattened the others between my hands into circles. I pressed them against the inside of the bread oven and put it over the fire. I waited until they became a little puffy and brown and pulled them out onto a ceramic plate. I waved one in the air to cool it and took a bite. It tasted like bread. Better than that, it tasted good.

The thief carried in the milk. We had breakfast.

"Now that I have a buffalo, you'll be able to make butter," he said.

My heart sped up, and my face grew hot. *Butter is made?*

251

He continued, "The jar to shake the cream and a jar of day-old milk is on the platform."

I let out my breath. Making butter had something to do with old milk and shaken cream. Maybe I could do it. "I'm Esh."

"Tila."

"Do you live here alone, Tila?"

"My wife has gone to the Underworld, and my daughters live with their husbands' families in other villages. It's just me in the house now. Until today."

An awkward silence followed. We finished our bread, and then Tila spoke. "Don't untie the buffalo or she'll swim away." He grunted, got up, and left in the boat, presumably to gather reeds for the buffalo to eat.

I rinsed out our bowls and mugs in the water of the marsh then filled the water jug. I took a large bowl, filled it with water, and took it out to the buffalo. It drank quite a bit, and I watched it, thinking that buffalo must be quite clever if they can find their way back home when taken away. With their lazy movements and frequent groans, they didn't seem like bright beasts. This one showed no sign of realizing it was in the wrong place. I rubbed the top of its head.

I went back inside and looked around. Spoons and bowls were scattered here and there, and the things on top of the platform were in disarray. I spent the beginning of the morning straightening up. Then I skimmed cream from the top of yesterday's milk and put it into the butter-making jar. I shook it until my arms were trembling with pain and a lump of butter sat in a pool of liquid inside the jar. I went outside again to collect buffalo dung and pressed it over the holes in the hut's walls that I could reach. I was refilling the buffalo's water bowl when an idea struck.

The buffalo needed to be tied to a tree to keep it from swimming back to its previous home. If I were on its back, then we both could return.

A wave of dizziness struck me, and I sat down. Could it be that simple to go back to Dingir-sukkal and Gan-Utu's house? I couldn't escape the thief's island now; I didn't know when he'd return. But tonight...tonight I could leave and he wouldn't know until morning.

I climbed to my feet and went over to the buffalo. I made several attempts to get on its broad back. I slid off several times before I learned how to balance myself. I leaned forward and held onto the backward-curving horns. I could do it. But could I keep hold of the horns for the time it took to get back to Dingir-sukkal and Gan-Utu's house?

I slid off the buffalo's side and went in the house to get a knife. I carried it outside and hid it on the other side of the palm tree. Now I just needed to be patient.

☙

Tila was snoring, and the moon was up. Slowly I stood, and slowly and softly I walked toward the doorway. I slipped out of the house; Tila snored on. I hurried to the other side of the palm tree and got down on my knees to feel for the knife. Frogs and crickets put up such a racket that I could no longer hear Tila's snoring. I found the knife and sawed at the rope, but it was slow going, and my breathing was getting harsh. I stopped to catch my breath.

In that moment I suddenly realized I had no reason to risk my life going back to Dingir-sukkal and Gan-Utu's house. I knew them no better than I knew Tila, and I was only welcome there until Gan-Utu had her baby and was back on her feet. Meanwhile, Tila needed me. I could probably stay with him until my nephew Naram-Sin came for me.

If he came for me.

No, he would come, and he would take me out of the marsh and restore me to my offices.

But I now had a new problem: how would I explain the buffalo's partially cut-through rope to Tila?

A few moments of thought gave me the answer. I crept back into the house. "Wake up! Wake up! Someone's stealing the buffalo." I shouted loud enough that someone outside would hear it, if there'd been someone outside.

Tila rolled over. "What?"

"Someone's stealing the buffalo," I yelled again.

Tila leapt to his feet and ran out. I followed.

"Where's' the thief?" Tila looked out over the moonlit water. "I don't see anyone."

Pretending to look around, I made my way to the palm tree. "Look here. The buffalo's rope is partly cut."

"Stupid thief," the thief said. "He should have just untied it. Thank the gods that you heard him."

My face heated because I hadn't thought of untying the rope. "Thank the gods."

"I need to get another rope." Tila said and headed back into the house. I did too but turned around in the doorway.

The buffalo was at the edge of the platform, trying to reach the water, and its rope was stretched out taut. The buffalo pulled steadily. The rope gave, and the buffalo walked into the water.

"The buffalo broke her rope," I shouted.

The creature leisurely swam away.

Cursing his luck, Tila ran out the door with a rope and jumped into his canoe.

I looked up at my husband in the sky. He was shining brightly now and could see me well. I clasped my hands and prayed again for Him to intercede with Anu to punish Lugalanne and reinstall me as priestess.

I fell asleep quickly and didn't hear Tila come back. But the next morning, there was no buffalo on the island. The day after, however, there were two buffalo cows. I didn't ask where they came from.

As the fall got colder and winter came on, I came to learn Tila was more than a thief. He was also a liar and a gambler and a reckless man to boot. He sometimes came home drunk at suppertime, with the bottom of his canoe barely covered with reeds. Because the buffalo were kept tied up, they went hungry on those days. It seemed a poor way to win the buffalo's loyalty, but Tila preferred to toss dice and drink date wine with his friends than to work.

Even so, we got along surprisingly well. Feeling lucky to have a place to stay, I didn't meddle in his goings-on, and he didn't criticize my poor housekeeping skills.

One day after I'd been there for a couple months, Tila came home in the middle of the afternoon with a friend. They moored their canoes and stumbled into the house, both reeking of wine.

"Hab-ba, this is the woman." Tila's voice was slurred. "What do you think?"

Hab-ba crossed his arms and looked me over. "She's too skinny."

"That's none of your business," I said. I wrapped my blanket tighter around me against the winter cold and started for the door.

Hab-ba grabbed my arm.

"Let go!" I snarled, pulling away. "Who do you think you are?"

Tila wore a hangdog look. "Uh, Esh, we were gambling."

"That's none of my concern," I said.

"I ran out of things to bet."

"Why are you telling me this? I have chores to do."

Tila stared at the mats on the floor. "I lost you playing dice. Hab-ba is your new master."

Furious, I glared at Tila. "I'm not yours to give away. I'm a free woman and better born than either of you drunken fools."

Hab-ba slapped me across the face. "Be quiet, woman. You're mine now."

I reeled backward. When I regained my balance, I looked around me for something I could use as a weapon, but there were no knives or sharp objects nearby. I grabbed a large, heavy pot and lifted it above my head. "Stay away from me. I'm not leaving. Tila, you'll have to come up with something else to give him."

The men exchanged a glance then rushed me, each grabbing one of my arms. The pot fell and cracked on the floor. I dug in my heels, but they dragged me stumbling across the hut and out the door.

"King Naram-Sin will kill you for this," I shouted, but they didn't answer.

They dragged me to Hab-ba's canoe and forced me into the bottom. "She can't swim," Tila said, "so once you launch, she can't get away."

I squirmed and fought as hard as I could. "How dare you manhandle a royal princess? Let me go."

"I can't," Tila said. "I have nothing else to give Hab-ba."

"Give him a buffalo," I shouted.

Hab-ba untied the mooring rope. Tila gave the canoe a push with his foot. We were in the marsh.

Hab-ba frowned at me. "Tila didn't tell me how mouthy you were. I won't tolerate it in my house. You work hard and keep your mouth shut, and maybe I'll feed you."

255

"Or what? You'll hit me again?"

He grabbed a handful of my hair and pulled hard. "I'd hit you now but I don't want to tip over the canoe."

I glared at him. "Treat me with respect, or I won't do anything for you."

He let go of my hair. "You're a slave now. You have only two choices: work or starve."

CHAPTER FORTY-SEVEN

Hab-ba shoved me into his house, and I fell down in front of two women who looked as worn as Gan-Utu had. "Put her to work," he said.

They looked at me haughtily. One of them tipped her head toward the door. "Get out there and pick up dung to dry."

I pushed myself up to sitting and returned the look. "I'm a free woman, not a slave. Hab-ba kidnapped me."

Hab-ba kicked me in the stomach. "Do as they say, or I'll drown you in the marsh. Now get outside."

Groaning like a buffalo, I dragged myself to the doorway and outside. I lay curled up for some time getting my breath back while the two dogs barked at me ferociously and three small children kicked dirt at me. At last I stood and began collecting buffalo dung and shaping it into cakes. I got angrier and angrier, but I didn't stop. I didn't want Hab-ba to drown me before I could escape. I would have to play along.

The women, who I learned were the wives of Hab-ba's sons, kept me busy with chores the rest of day. Although my hands were occupied, my brain was free to scheme.

Hab-ba's house stood on a long island shared with several families' houses. At first I thought I would ask one of the other families to help me escape, but I decided it was too risky. They knew Hab-ba and would probably return me to him.

Hab-ba's family did have several boats, and they seemed my best option for escape.

For supper, they gave me the scraps left over after everyone else had eaten. I was exhausted by bedtime, and my stomach growled

257

loudly. I lay down and closed my eyes, waiting for everyone else to go to sleep.

The children tossed and giggled for a long time, and after they dropped off to sleep, the husbands and wives murmured. At last the house quieted. It was time to escape.

Then someone got up and came over to me. "Stick out your hands!" Hab-ba ordered.

I cowered against the wall and put my hands behind me.

Hab-ba pushed me onto my stomach, grabbed my hands, and tied them together. Then he tied the ends of the rope to the nearest upright reed bundle. "That should hold you in case you get any ideas."

The days that followed were monotonously dreadful. Hab-ba's daughters turned over all the chores to me. They beat me when I didn't know how to do something or didn't move fast enough. I was still tied to the reed bundle at bedtimes, but it hardly mattered because I fell asleep from exhaustion immediately every night.

Then one night, Hab-ba didn't come home in the evening, and his sons didn't remember to tie me up. I was dizzy with exhaustion, but I knew this was my chance. I pinched myself to keep myself awake while the others fell asleep. At last, all sighs and murmurs ceased. I rose slowly and tiptoed to the door. Opening it as little as possible, I slipped out.

Outside the frogs were calling, and the dogs were moving their paws in their sleep and barking softly. The moon had gone to the Underworld to judge the souls.

With only starlight to see by, I made my way to the canoes and climbed into one. But its knot was looped so tightly that I couldn't free it. I climbed out and moved to the next canoe, aware that any moment someone might come outside to relieve themselves or Hab-ba might come home. Again I gingerly climbed in and began working on the knot. It loosened and then fell free. I grabbed the pole and used it to push away from the bank.

Now I needed to get away quickly. I thrust the pole downward into the muddy bottom and pushed. The canoe turned in a circle around the pole. I was still only a person's length from the bank. I tried again and nearly lost the pole. How in the world did one pole a canoe in a direction one wanted to go?

The night wore on, and the canoe turned in circles. At last, I pushed the pole with the correct direction and force to move in a straight line...but it slid back toward the bank.

Someone came out of the house.

I lay down in the canoe and held my breath. Water still sloshed against the bank from my poling efforts. The footsteps came closer and stopped. Had they seen me? One of the dogs growled, and a man's voice spoke to it. I heard splashing nearby. It seemed to go on and on, but at last it ended, and the man went back inside without seeing me.

I waited until I thought he was probably asleep again then sat up. I pushed away again with the pole and this time the boat moved away from the island.

My hands were burning from the pole, but I couldn't wait for them to recover. I was still close enough to the island to hear the dogs' sleep noises. I poled and poled until I came to reedbeds. Once surrounded on all sides by reeds, I set the pole down in the canoe and rested.

A snort came from my left.

A dozing hog lay an arm's length away. I froze. I had heard stories from Dingir-sukkal and Tila both about how dangerous the boars' sharp tusks were and how even the sows could kill a person by biting them. I picked up the pole again and pushed away.

I was lost and had no destination, but I knew I had to get as far from Hab-ba and his family as possible. As soon as I caught my breath, I poled the canoe through and out of the reed bed. If not for the constellations crossing the sky, time would have seemed to stop: the croaks, squeaks, and chirps of wildlife were an unchanging cacophony; pushing the pole against the bottom of the marsh seemed as relentless as a heartbeat. Water rippled from the boat in a ceaseless susurration.

When the sky lightened and an edge of pink appeared on the horizon, I knew which way was north, and I poled in that direction. Nighttime sounds gave way to those of the day. As the sky brightened, gulls and terns flew overhead. Dragonflies alighted on the water. By midmorning, I could see the pink of a flock of flamingoes, and I knew I was close to the edge of the marsh. Soon after, a small town of mudbrick buildings rose above the horizon, and I headed in that direction, praying to Inanna.

"Great Inanna, my husband, who is your father, Suen, and the great god Anu have not restored me to my offices or helped me survive in the marshes. You are all-powerful and the greatest of the gods. Please, queen of Heaven, help your servant. Feed me. Bring my nephew to me. Put me back in my accustomed place."

When I reached the shore, many canoes lay on the sand, and I beached mine beside them. I walked to the village. I had always looked on beggars with a mix of disdain and pity. Now I would have to beg myself. I dreaded receiving the same reaction...although at least I wouldn't see it because my head would be bent in shame.

I went to the closest building and called inside, "Hello."

"Come in, come in," a voice yelled.

I went into the vestibule and from there into a large courtyard. It was set up as a trading post, and several men of the marsh were looking at the goods or seeking to sell reed mats, butter, or cheese. I got in line behind the marsh dwellers and stared at the floor, my face getting hot. When my turn came, I said, "Please. I need food and a job."

Loudly, the man said, "If you want work, there's a brothel behind this building. They'll feed you if you agree to work there." Some of the other men laughed. "Now get out."

I turned around. The floor blurred from tears. I stepped out of line and headed away.

A hand touched my elbow. "High priestess," a familiar voice said gently. "We were worried you were dead."

I looked up at the man. I didn't recognize him at first without his beard. "Gu-gu-la?"

The former priest of Suen led me outside. "I've been looking for you for weeks, but the marsh is a big place."

"Do you have any food?"

He reached into a satchel and pulled out some flatbread. "Have as much as you want."

Hands trembling, I took it and started eating. It was the most delicious bread I'd ever eaten. I had to battle to keep from stuffing it into my mouth.

"What happened to you?" he asked.

"I stayed with the buffalo thief. I did chores in exchange for food and a place to sleep. Then he decided I was his property, and he gambled me away. I escaped by stealing a boat. Now here I am."

"Come back and stay with me," Gu-gu-la said. "I've decided to take your offer to make me a priest again, so you can be sure I'll keep you well fed and safe."

Tears welled up in my eyes. "Thank you. I will."

ṭ

While waiting for Naram-Sin, Gu-gu-la and I settled into a routine similar to the one I had with the thief Tila. He spent part of each day cutting reeds for his eight water buffalo and the rest of his time making cheese to sell. I cooked and did other household chores.

One day, about a week after I had returned to stay with Gu-gu-la, he came home with news. Refugees from Ur and other nearby cities were pouring into the marshes. "Your nephew Naram-Sin must have taken the fight to the rebelling cities."

"If so, we should be rescued soon," I said. "If he can find us."

"We should go look for him," Gu-gu-la said.

"He will look for me in the marshes."

"What do you suggest?"

"I must pray first." I went outside into the cold breeze and clasped my hands. "Great Inanna, queen of heaven, look down on me in pity. My nephew Naram-Sin is near. How will he find me?"

The day became even brighter, and a shape took form in front of me. The goddess wore battle dress and held a gory battle axe in each hand. Her mouth was smeared with blood. Yet she still smelled of sweet incense.

I shaded my eyes. It had been so long since she last visited me, I felt a distance between us. "Great goddess, I am your servant." I knelt in front of her and put my forehead to the ground.

"I have heard your prayers, little one. I will guide Naram-Sin to you. Afterward, you will write a praise hymn to me that will last through the ages."

Something wet and warm dribbled on my face. I put my hand to my forehead, and it came away bloody. I looked up.

261

The goddess was gone.

I rinsed off my face in the water and went back in the hut. "We should stay. Naram-Sin will come for us here."

CHAPTER FORTY-EIGHT

People shouted, and dogs barked. Gu-gu-la and I left our breakfast and went outside. Dozens of boats approached the village, and in the first boat stood a tall, handsome young man. He wore several gold armbands, and necklaces of gold, carnelian, and lapis lazuli were draped over his bare chest.

Gu-gu-la and I walked to the edge of the island and waited.

The first boat bumped gently against the island. I put my hand to my nose. "Hail, King Naram-Sin!"

"Aunt?" The king looked from my bare feet to my torn, dirty robe to my tangled hair. "Aunt, is it you?"

"Yes, nephew. I am so glad to see you." I felt as if a weight had been removed from my shoulders.

"Get in. Let us proceed to Ur and right the wrong that was done to you."

I stepped into the boat. "May this priest of Suen ride with us?"

"Yes."

Gu-gu-la climbed into the boat. We settled ourselves on the bottom. Gu-gu-la had given away his buffalo and possessions, and we needed nothing from the house before we left.

Naram-Sin shouted an order, and the canoes turned around. Naram-Sin's boatman poled us through the canoes to lead the rest to Ur.

"You look so much like King Sargon," I told my nephew. "Your father was very dear to me."

"My father talked about you often. You're not how I pictured you."

I laughed and motioned to myself. "This is not how the earthly embodiment of the goddess Ningal usually looks."

As the boats passed through the marsh, birds rose before us from their hiding places among the reeds as if they were heralds of the king. The trip to dry land was quick, and then we left the boats and marched the rest of the way to Ur. A large army was camped outside, and a pen held captives. I led the way through the wrecked and empty city, so reminiscent of the last time Ur rebelled, to the main gate of the temenos.

"Get Sim-tur," Naram-Sin told the startled guards at the gate. One ran off and returned soon with Sim-tur following.

Sim-tur ignored the king, his guards, and Gu-gu-la and stared at me. Then she laughed. "Not so high and mighty now, are you?"

"You're no longer a priestess here or in Uruk, Sim-tur," I said. "Leave, and this time stay away. I don't want to ever see you again."

She frowned at me and didn't move. "You can't tell me what to do."

"I can," Naram-Sin growled.

Sim-tur turned toward him, and her face went white as she brought her hand to her nose.

"Enheduanna is too kind," Naram-Sin said. "Exile is not sufficient for you. You defied the gods' will and harmed the royal family. You must be made an example of. Take off the temple's jewelry."

Her hand went to her throat, clutching the necklaces. "No."

"Give them to Enheduanna," Naram-Sin said. "Take off your priestess robe and give that to the zirru too." He motioned to one of his guards, who moved toward Sim-tur.

"I'll do it. I'll do it." Sim-tur pulled off the high priestess' rolled-brim hat and threw it at my feet. Rings and necklaces followed. She pulled off her robe and shoved it at me.

"You can have my robe," I said. It was dirty and full of holes, but it was better than no robe.

"No, aunt. She must be punished." Naram-Sin turned toward his guards. "Whip her. Ten strokes."

I gasped and felt as if I would faint.

The king's guards grabbed Sim-tur and forced her against one of the wall posts. They tied her hands in front of her and then to the post. I turned my head away. I heard the first lash strike her skin, and her

264

scream split the air. I flinched as if I were the one under the lash. Ten strokes, and then it ended. I dared to look at Sim-tur.

Her back was torn and bloody, and she dangled loose-limbed from the rope. When the guard cut her free, she collapsed.

"Set her upright," Naram-Sin ordered and turned to Sim-tur. "Go, and do not return."

Naked and bleeding, Sim-tur staggered away.

I quietly gathered up the jewelry and bundled it in the robe. "Will you stay the night, nephew, and allow me to offer you hospitality?"

"I can't. There are other cities that need to learn a lesson."

"At least stay long enough that I can ask Inanna to bless you."

"Inanna? Not your husband Suen?"

"She's the one who watches over Sargon and his family. Come. It won't take long." We went inside the temenos, and I handed off the bundle of robe and jewelry to Buru, who walked by. "For my room."

Buru stared at me, and a smile broke across her face. Then she saw the king and knelt.

The courtyard was a welcome sight. I couldn't keep from smiling, and my shoulders released tightness I hadn't realized I had. But my mouth drew down when I saw the temple of Suen. The god had betrayed me.

I led Naram-Sin toward the ziggurat, and we climbed to the top. The wind whipped around us and made our robes flap. I lifted my arms to the sky. "Great Inanna, mistress of chaos, who conquers mountains and makes the impossible possible, you are the queen of Heaven. I called on you, and you sent Naram-Sin to me. Please look on Sargon's grandson and protect him from evil. Help him keep his grandfather's empire intact."

The wind picked up speed and howled around us. Our robes whipped around our legs. I clutched my hat to my head to keep from losing it. A blinding light made me cover my eyes with my hands. My skin tingled. Impossibly, I could smell incense despite the wind. "Inanna!" I cried out.

"What is going on?" Naram-Sin asked. "Is it a dust storm?"

"The goddess is here. Can you see Her?" I squinted at him.

Shading his eyes with his hand, the king opened his eyes slightly. "Yes, I see Her," he said. He fell on his knees in front of Her. "Truly you are the greatest of the gods." 265

Inanna set her shield down and lay Her hand on his head. "You have my blessing, grandson of Sargon, and my promise that your legend will be as great as his."

Naram-Sin bent over and kissed her foot.

The goddess disappeared. The wind immediately died down, but the scent of incense lingered.

Naram-Sin turned to me with wonder on his face. "You can call the gods?"

"Rather, Inanna sometimes deigns to visit me."

"Your prayers are powerful," he said. "Please continued to pray to Her for me."

"I will do so."

We silently walked down the staircases and toward the main gate. Gu-gu-la still stood there; I had forgotten all about him.

Naram-Sin bent down to kiss my cheek. "Take care, aunt."

"Thank you for rescuing me." I squeezed his hand. He marched off with his escort, and I turned to Gu-gu-la. "Let's go in."

I led Gu-gu-la to Me-zi-da's office. We found the priest reading a tablet.

"Hello, Me-zi-da," I said.

Eyes wide, Me-zi-da jumped to his feet and saluted, a big smile forming. "Praise Suen! Welcome home."

"Inanna has brought me home. Sim-tur's gone," I said. "I'm back for good."

"We all worried you were dead."

"I was in the marshes. This is Gu-gu-la, who used to be a priest of Suen."

"I think I remember you," Me-zi-da said.

Gu-gu-la winced. "I will be a better priest this time around, I promise."

"Me-zi-da, will you take care of getting him settled? I must see Ninsha."

"Yes, of course," Me-zi-da said.

"It's so good you see you, Me-zi-da."

"It's a big relief to see you too. When you have time, I have matters to go over with you."

"I'll return this afternoon." I turned to leave.

"You were greatly missed," Me-zi-da said as I departed.

I hurried toward the Gipar House. Priests, priestesses, and workers hailed me or came up to me as I walked. I acknowledged their greetings but did not stop to chat with any of my friends. When I reached the Gipar, I ran to my suite.

Ninsha wasn't there.

I began searching all the public areas, starting with the needle room. The room was empty today. The dance class was meeting in its usual place, but Ninsha was not among the priestesses. I glanced in all the rooms in the dormitory half of the building then went to the temple half. In front of the altar, I found her in a red priestess robe, looking up to the sky and praying.

"Ninsha."

Her head jerked up, and she turned. "Esh? Esh!" She stood and ran to me. "It's really you." We embraced for several moments and then pulled apart, still holding each other's forearms.

"So you're a priestess now?" I asked. "You never wanted to be one."

"I didn't want to live with my brother Lugalanne. Sim-tur would only let me stay here if I became a priestess."

"Sim-tur is gone for good. I'm zirru of Suen and en-priestess of Anu again."

"I'm so glad. Where were you?"

"Living in the marshes. I have so much to tell you, Ninsha. I know how to cook now!"

"I can't imagine you cooking, let alone surviving all this time in the wilderness." She put her hand on my cheek. "Your skin feels as dry as it looks. It needs oiling. But first a bath."

I laughed. "Can you imagine? I managed to survive these months without you to take care of me."

She looked at my ruined robe and tangled hair. "Barely. You lost your sandals, your robe is no better than rags, and you're sunburnt."

"Do you know where my shaperum, Adda, is?"

"He's living in town. I'll take you to him later."

We walked back to our suite arm in arm.

CHAPTER FORTY-NINE

"Queen of all given powers, unveiled clear light, righteous woman wearing radiance, beloved in heaven and earth." At last I had words worthy of Inanna, and I wrote them down on a fresh tablet. Now that I had caught up on the tasks Sim-tur had neglected, I was starting my hymn of praise, the one Inanna said would last through the ages. I wished she hadn't told me the last part; the thought made words clog in my throat. It had taken me days to come up with the hymn's first line.

I knew what I would include in the hymn. I would praise her attributes and tell my own story as an example of Her power: how Lugalanne betrayed the god Anu and me, how I went to the wilderness, how the gods Suen and Anu failed to help, and how Inanna rescued me and restored me to my rightful positions. I just needed to find words that deserved lasting fame.

"Esh! I have a surprise." Ninsha's sudden entrance startled me, and I dropped my stylus.

"What is it?"

"You have to come with me to find out." Her face beamed.

Now that I had a first line, I wanted to keep writing. "I'm finally making progress on the hymn. Can the surprise wait?"

"I'll tell you one part of the surprise: You received a letter from King Naram-Sin."

"May I have it?"

"You're spoiling things. Take a break and come with me. Please."

I got up, and we walked across the city to the ensi's house. "Do we have a new ensi at last? And why does he have my letter?"

Her eyes twinkled. "Come and see."

A servant let us in and led us to the familiar audience room. A beardless man whose hair was graying sat in the one chair in the room. "Please take a seat, Ninsha, high priestess."

His deep voice was familiar and so were his eyes, but I couldn't place where I knew him from. I sat down on a stool, waiting for him to speak.

"Esh, what's wrong with you? It's Za-mu," Ninsha said.

I couldn't contain my grin. "Za-mu! You're the new ensi?"

Za-mu matched my smile. "Yes. King Naram-Sin asked what reward I wanted for my service during the rebellion, and I said I wanted to be ensi of Ur. My days of spying are over, and we're all together again."

"Is this what the king sent me a letter about?" I asked.

"Why don't you read it and see." Za-mu handed me the tablet. Both he and Ninsha were grinning.

I read out loud:

From King Naram-Sin, king of the four quarters, to his aunt Enheduanna, zirru of Suen in Ur and en-priestess of Anu in Uruk. May the gods Ilaba and Inanna keep you forever in good health! I've established order in the country, and I expect that you have restored order at the temples of Suen and Anu. Your relationship with Inanna seems stronger than with Suen. If you want to be a priestess of Inanna, I will appoint you to Inanna's House of Heaven in Uruk.

"At last. I can barely believe it." I stared at the tablet as if the characters might change at any moment. Expecting to be elated, I found my emotions instead a mix of relief and disappointment. Relief, because I had wanted to be Inanna's priestess for so long, so singlemindedly, and it had finally happened. Disappointment, because the Giparu House had become home and its priestesses my friends. Disappointment, also, because so much of my life had gone by before receiving the offer. I was forty-two now, my best years behind me, rather old to be a novitiate.

269

I closed my eyes. My father had lived to an old age. I might live a long while yet, serving the goddess at Her temple for decades, and look back at this moment of choice as happening when I was young.

"At last," I repeated. "So many years I've wanted to serve the queen of heaven as her priestess. Ninsha, will you come with me to the House of Heaven?"

"Should we tell her the other news now?" Ninsha asked Za-mu.

His eyes sparkling, Za-mu grinned, looking more like the boy he had once been. "Go ahead."

"Esh, Za-mu's wife died last year, leaving him with five children. I'm going to marry him and raise them." Ninsha's face was radiant. "You know I've always wanted a husband and children."

She is going to leave me. I cringed at my selfishness. Yet her news left me feeling bereft, and I couldn't swallow. With a strained voice, I said, "We both have good news today. I'm so glad you finally will have the family you wanted. You deserve to be happy."

Ninsha stepped toward me and threw her arms around me. "Please, don't look so troubled. Za-mu and I will be only a boat ride away from Uruk. We can visit each other sometimes." She patted my arm and then moved back to Za-mu's side.

Chest tight, I looked down at the tablet and said nothing. What should I do? What was more important to me, becoming a priestess of Inanna or being near Ninsha?

❦

The stonemason showed me the piece of calcite he had transformed into a plaque to my specifications. He had chiseled it round, as I had requested, with a flat front and back.

I sneezed. The room was choked with stone dust. The mason looked as if he had been dipped in flour.

"What do you want on it?" he asked.

"On the front I want a carving showing me at Inanna's House of Heaven in my regalia with my hand to my nose. The priest in front of me pours a libation onto a plinth shaped like a tall vase. Two priestesses stand behind me. On the back, I want the inscription on this tablet." I handed the tablet to him.

He read it and grunted. "I'll deliver it to the Gipar House in ten days."

"Good. In the meantime, if you have a question, I'll be in Uruk."

I left the stonemason's shop and walked to the harbor under the hot summer sun. I got in my boat, told the boatman to go, and spent the trip to Uruk thinking about my future. Once the boat docked at the House of Heaven, I went to the office of the high priest of Inanna. He was freshly shaved and wore bracelets on both arms.

"Good afternoon, en-priest. Has the plinth arrived?"

"Yes, yesterday. Your gift's in the courtyard, waiting to be dedicated. Everything's ready. Shall we go?"

"First, I wanted to give you a copy of a new hymn to Inanna that I wrote."

He took the tablets and set them on a rattan bench. "This is a long hymn."

"I included how Lugalanne wrecked the temple of Anu and cast me out of Uruk and how Inanna rescued me when Suen and Anu ignored my prayers."

"You certainly have good reason to dedicate the plinth to Inanna." The priest called for two priestesses to bring milk and beer, and we walked into the courtyard of Inanna's temple. The priest led the way to the new plinth, I behind him and the two priestesses, singing, behind me, just as I'd told the stone mason to carve. At the plinth, the priest lit incense and performed a ritual of cleansing. Then he took the pitchers from the priestesses and anointed the plinth with the liquids of life. The priestesses sang another song, and the en-priest said a long prayer.

The others went back to their duties, but I went to the altar and prayed. Inanna now had the poem she had prophesized I would write, as well as the plinth I commissioned to hold a statue of her. Soon the disk commemorating today's dedication would be ready, with its inscription: "Enheduanna, zirru priestess, wife of the god Nanna, daughter of Sargon, king of the world, in the temple of the goddess Inanna, made a plinth and named it 'Daïs, Table of Heaven.'" It would hang in the Gipar House as a reminder of today's ceremony, where I would see it every day.

Yes, every day. The Gipar House was my home; its priestesses were my kin. It felt strange to give up something I had wanted for nearly forty years, yet it also felt right. I would continue to sing Inanna's praises and bring sacrifices and gifts to Her House of Heaven, but I realized now that I could honor Her no matter where I was or who I was. And the place I needed to be was near Ninsha and the gods I had served for so long.

Section VI

City of Ur

Age 72

EPILOGUE

I hobbled into my office in the courtyard, propped my cane against the wall, and plunked myself onto a stool in front of Adda's worktable. "Old friend, it's time for me to let someone else be zirru."

He set down his stylus. "Where did you get that idea?"

"I've been feeling it in my bones for a while now. Today I received a letter from my nephew Naram-Sin. He wants to install one of his daughters as high priestess of Suen. I think I'll say 'yes.'" It was hard to tell him, but once the words were out I felt as if a weight on my shoulders had been lifted.

"Being priestess has been your life for so long. What would you do if you weren't zirru?"

"Visit Ninsha and play with her grandchildren. Train my grandniece to be zirru. Sing the rituals with the priestesses. Pray to Inanna and perhaps write more hymns to Her."

"No matter what the king says, I don't think you're too old for your post."

I smiled. "You've always been so loyal, you and Ninsha. You're both my family, now that all my brothers have gone to the Underworld."

"Your brothers may have been ensis and kings, but your name will live on longer than theirs. Your hymns to the temples of the empire showed the Sumerian cities that the Akkadians honored their traditions and patron gods. When I go to other cities, I still hear those hymns sung. In the tablet houses, boys copy them as exercises."

"Inanna put me on a strange and wondrous path. I always knew I would write hymns for Her, but I thought I would be Her priestess. Instead, She put me here in Ur to serve Her father. It took me a long time to realize I could serve Her just as well here."

275

"You served the people of Ur well. You saved many of them when Rimush attacked the city."

I shrugged it off. "What about you, Adda? You're older than me."

"Your great-niece will need me. I'll stay to serve her."

"I've had an interesting life. For all that I fought my fate, I find in the end I am satisfied."

HISTORICAL NOTES

We know little of Enheduanna before she was zirru of Suen other than that she was the daughter of Sargon the Great, who created the world's first empire. We can conjecture Enheduanna received scribal training and training in the Sumerian language, but otherwise her childhood, including her birth name, is hidden from us.

Her adult years are a little more open. We have the calcite disk known as the Disk of Enheduanna with its image and inscription. We also have cylinder seals or seal impressions for four of her employees: the scribe SAG-A-DU, the scribe X-kitus-du, the hairdresser Ilum-pal, and her estate supervisor Adda.

Enheduanna is credited with writing forty-two short hymns to temples (although a few of these hymns praise temples that were built after her lifetime, so some, at least, are not her work) as well as three long hymns to Inanna, all in Sumerian, the literary language of the time. The third hymn, known today as "The Exaltation of Inanna," tells the story of Lugalanne expelling Enheduanna from the temple of Anu.

Her hymns give some insight into her personality. She was the first writer in history to sign her name to her work, which argues for a healthy ego, as do her rather demanding pleas to the gods in her hymns. The hymns' figurative language suggests a poetic and perhaps mystical turn of mind. Here's a short example from "The Exaltation of Inanna": "Like a dragon you have deposited venom on the foreign lands. When like Ishkur [god of rain and thunderstorms] you roar at the earth, no vegetation can stand up to you. As a flood descending upon those foreign lands, powerful one of heaven and earth, you are their Inanna."

Here is another example, the beginning of the temple hymn praising the temple of Nanna/Suen in Ur: "Oh Ur, bull standing in the wet reeds, House Sending Light to Earth, calf of a great cow...."

Although some of the people in this novel actually lived, we know little more than their name, city, and occupation for those who weren't royal.

Rimush was indeed killed by his councilors using their cylinder seals.

ACKNOWLEDGMENTS

My deepest thanks to my critique group of twenty years, Laurie L. Bolaños, Rosalind M. Green-Holmes, Margaret Hauck, and Farrah Rochon (http://www.farrahrochon.com). They helped brainstorm this book when it was only an idea, and they commented on the written draft. Five brains are better than one!

I'm very grateful to Nicholas Bede Stenner for a thorough reading and comments.

Many thanks to editor Jennifer Young (https://www.the-efa.org/memberinfo/jennifer-young-25719/) for a wonderful content edit.

My husband, David Malueg, was a source of support throughout the writing of this book.

Any mistakes in grammar, spelling, or history are mine alone.

AUTHOR'S BIO

Shauna Roberts grew up in Beavercreek, Ohio, and started writing stories in elementary school. Her love of reading was fostered by her father, Edward Arthur Roberts, who took her to the library weekly, and by her aunt Janet Louise Roberts, who was a librarian and author of one hundred twenty romance novels.

After a career as an award-winning science and medical writer and editor, Shauna Roberts retired to write fiction: science fiction, fantasy, romance, and historical fiction. Her publications number more than a thousand and include magazine articles, journal articles, newsletters, essays, flash fiction, short stories, novellas, and novels.

Shauna Roberts is a 2009 graduate of the Clarion Science Fiction and Fantasy Writers' Workshop.

She won a 2014 National Readers Choice Award, a 2015 Romancing the Novel Published Author Award, and the 2011 Speculative Literature Foundation's Older Writers Grant.

After living all over the country, Dr. Roberts now calls the Blue Ridge Mountains home, and she lives there with two ragdoll cats and her husband of thirty-nine years.

You can find her website at http://www.ShaunaRoberts.com. Signed bookplates are available on request. You can contact her at ShaunaRoberts@ShaunaRoberts.com.

ALSO BY SHAUNA ROBERTS

Like Mayflies in a Stream (historical fiction set in ancient Mesopotamia)

Claimed by the Enemy (historical fiction set in ancient Mesopotamia)

Ice Magic, Fire Magic (fantasy)

Log Cabin: Erikka (historical romance set in 1890s Montana)

The Hunt (novelette; science fiction)

The Measure of a Man (novelette; historical fantasy set in Indonesia in 1598)